ISLAND
RED

MATT SERAFINI

**SIGN UP FOR MATT SERAFINI'S
THESE DARK WOODS MAILING LIST
AT MATTSERAFINI.COM AND
RECEIVE AN EXCLUSIVE EBOOK**

FROM THE SKY TO THE SEA

"Follow me, okay?"

It was less of a question and more of a command.

Kurt's brain was slush, though he'd follow Kelly anywhere if it meant getting a piece of that.

It was last call, and she had just returned from the ladies' room, though *room* was a generous description since the Shifting Tides' "beachfront accommodations" included a row of porta potties just off the sand, hidden in the nearby tree line, looking like holdovers from the resort's construction phase.

Hygienic patrons such as Kelly were expected to wash their hands in the communal fountain between the beach and bar. It was disgusting to watch a lion's share of patrons, men and women equally, rush past it on their way back to their drinks. But Kelly kept clean and that was a good thing because he wanted tonight to be special.

He really, really wanted it.

"Where are we going?" Kurt tried for a wry smile, a dash of hard-to-get, but his reluctance seemed only to insult her. After three years of college and every last effort spent on winning her over, why roll the dice? Guys like Kurt never got girls like Kelly. He'd already beaten the odds.

Kelly walked off doing that thing girls did when they knew they had eyes on their asses. Her hips swayed and accented her jiggle. The off-pink bathing suit bottom had deliberately ridden up a few inches to give a glimpse of her tanned cheeks. The sight prompted horny catcalls as she sauntered from the restaurant's artificial light toward the beach's natural shadows.

The approval of strangers turned Kurt on just a little more. Nobody needed to tell him that Kelly was a stunner, but where was the harm in other dudes checking out his girl? Was it better if no one wanted to look?

He shot from his seat and took the Malibu bottle by its neck, dancing around the other tables with coconut rum grace. The kind of coordination to be expected after a night of drinking, one near-pratfall after another until his luck ran out and he tripped over the last chair in his way, stuttering toward the sand. The bottle flew from his fist.

Kelly's giggles carried over the rhythm of the Jamaican reggae band. The smell of her body, a mixture of coconut suntan lotion and salty ocean residue, sent him scurrying to his feet. His eyes widened with awe as those toned legs, perfectly sculpted, threatened to slip beyond the last band of torchlight.

Kurt was charged, powered by an afternoon of booze that

had been funneled straight into his sex drive. He kicked up sand as he scrambled to his feet and toward his girlfriend of two months.

She heard him coming but didn't turn. Instead, she scrunched her shoulders and braced for his impact. "Kurt, no, no, *noooooo...* you're all sandy."

Too late to stop, he wrapped his arms around her hips and lifted her off her feet. Her neck tasted exactly like she smelled—acrid coconut that somehow made her skin more exotic and lickable.

Her laughter became a song of soft moans, a sudden shift in trajectory that got Kurt excited. Her protesting limbs settled into complacency. Fingers reached back, the tips gliding the length of his chest, a measured touch that was teasingly deliberate. His heart jolted like ten thousand volts was being pumped straight into it. He wanted more and lowered her to the sand as she turned to face him.

They were beyond the rabble of the bar. The reggae band had just completed their last number and the lead singer was slurring his appreciation into the mic, wishing everyone a wonderful night.

I'm well on my way, Kurt thought, his body pressed against hers. Her rising breasts mashed against him, delivering a sensation that busted from his heart and zoomed through his veins. He pushed forward for her lips, and a sadistic grin grew from the corners of her mouth. She loved to tease. Loved it. And Kurt loved it more. The eventual conquest would be sweeter because of it.

"I want you right here," Kurt said and threw his lips against hers. She returned the gesture with a soft peck before breaking away.

"No way," she said. "There's a bunch of people over there."

"They're going back to their rooms so they can keep drinking." It happened like clockwork after last call. For the past two nights, he and Kelly had been a part of that migration. But Kelly was making it seem as if the tease was finally over, and he'd always wanted to do it in public. What better place than on the beach?

"Don't tell me you're going to be shy," he said.

"Shy?" Kelly reached behind her back to loosen the wrap bikini top. It slid off her shoulders and her breasts spilled from it.

Kurt stared slack-jawed. He'd spent all that time imagining them, studying their shape, obsessing over Kelly's revealing bathing suits. And after everything, she just decided to unleash them in the dark.

If he cared for the sport of it, it'd be anticlimactic.

He rushed forward, but Kelly spun as his hands closed on her hips and she ambled toward the breaking ocean waves, pulling at the sides of her bikini bottom until he was staring at her moon in the moonlight.

My God...

He geared up for another bull's charge, tunnel vision on the tanned heart of Kelly's ass.

"That your girl?" A dark figure moved toward them from the shallows. "Not tellin' you what to do, boss, but y'all may not wanna swim out too far tonight."

"Uh, thanks…" Kurt said.

The figure crossed the beach beneath the moonlight, close enough for Kurt to see the deep scar carved into his cheek. It ran straight up to his left eye which held an empty milk-white orb. The black man glanced in Kelly's direction, but only for a second. He tapped Kurt's chest with the back of his hand and flashed a knowing smile.

"You gotta keep a girl like that happy, I get it. But wade in up to your knees, all right? Then take her back to your bed. You'll be happier there."

Kurt was about to ask why, but the man continued walking toward the bar. Probably for the best since Kelly was out there without any clothes on, and he didn't need anybody getting in the way of making his fantasy into reality.

He heard the sound of splashing footsteps but couldn't see Kelly through the darkness. "Hey, Kell, wait!"

His feet transitioned from dry sand to beach mud as he took off running, catching a glimpse of Kelly wading in the water up to her calves.

She turned around with brazen confidence, and her body looked even better once he had the chance to admire all her curves as drawn by the moonlight. Her flat belly was slick with water, and her large breasts lifted and fell with excited huffs.

"I swear you're not that interested in me, Kurt."

It was high tide in his pants. He begged to differ.

She held out her hand with a single finger raised in command. *Stay where you are.*

He did. His toes sunk into the mud and he stared at the gorgeous sight the way his dog watched him eat a burger.

"If you want to join me, get naked."

Kurt looked over his shoulder to make sure One Eye wasn't peeping. In the distance, the bar had gone dark. To the left, the pier was awash with bright light and loud music. Like clockwork, the party had moved to the cabana block. There didn't appear to be anyone around them.

He only needed one more glance at Kelly before he slid out of his shorts and began marching toward inevitability. Kelly stared at his manhood as he approached, taking it in the palm of her hand as soon as their mouths touched.

They tumbled into the water, breaking waves crashing over them. Her legs wrapped around his lower back while her hands glided across his strong shoulders. She wanted him close.

Her mouth tasted like fresh plucked mint, and his tongue divided its attention evenly between her lips and neck while he cupped her breasts with gentle squeezes. His thumbs brushed her hardening nipples, aroused by the way her face reacted to his gestures.

The Atlantic brought a constant swell down on them. The intensity matched his rising passions. Each time he tried entering Kelly, she wiggled her hips to keep him at bay.

It was fine because this was all new, seeing her like this, feeling every part of her, all of this happening in public. The notion that someone could be watching excited him, and he suspected it maybe stoked her fires, too.

She shifted her body weight in search of enough power to roll on top and leaned in for a deep kiss as her hair, mud-caked and mottled into primal strands, raked against his pecks. Then she stood, leaving Kurt to glimpse between her legs. She caught his eyes going there and smiled.

"You want that, dirty boy?"

Kurt tried lunging up like an animal but she retreated out of reach.

"I take it that's a *yes*," she said. "So catch me." She headed for deeper water, up to her hips first, and then quickly to where she was able to dive beneath the waves.

Kurt didn't allow her any distance this time. He followed her under, reaching for her body. Catching it. In the onyx water, dark, amorphous shadows embraced and floated together like painted silhouettes.

They broke the surface in unison, colliding in a kiss that might've gone on forever. They couldn't stop, and their tongues continued to touch even as their mouths searched for pockets of air. He whispered in her ear how much he loved her. She responded by locking her legs around him.

An invitation to enter her.

"Make me feel it." Her tone was forceful and nasty, and it was almost enough to make him finish on the spot as he brushed against her thigh.

Her body tasted like salt, but it was Kelly, so it was the best thing his taste buds had ever enjoyed.

Then he slipped inside and Kelly's body tensed. Her moans cut the night as her nails pinched down into his back with enough force to draw blood.

He didn't care about that.

Screwing in the water was harder than it looked. The way his legs pedaled, it was like riding a bike forever uphill, and each time Kelly rocked her hips to catch his thrusts, they slipped beneath the waves. Wiggling back up toward the surface stalled their momentum. He wished they had just done it in the mud bed, but he wasn't ever going to say that. He loved the way Kelly's skin felt as she clung to him, and he could listen to her breathy moans all night long.

Struggling back up into the Florida air, Kelly's body was suddenly bathed in orange-red glow. Kurt's must've been, too, if the look on her face was any indication.

Suddenly, something other than the moon lit them. The surrounding water looked like the ocean at sunrise, but they hadn't been out here that long. Had they?

Kelly's eyes met his in confusion, and they turned toward the sky for answers. The starry darkness had been ripped wide to reveal a fireball hurtling through the night's curtain.

Only then did Kurt realize how far out they were. The pier lights looked like an airport runway from twenty thousand feet. Before he could recommend they swim back, Kelly screamed out, "That's headed for us!"

And it was. It grew in size until it seemed to fill the entire sky. Heat from the falling rock kissed their faces as Kurt realized the meteor was on their trajectory. It descended toward them with certainty, and there wasn't time enough to deflect. A watery shockwave rose as it touched down with a massive splash.

They were lifted on skyscraper waves and thrown against the searing boulder like ragdolls, their bodies sizzling like bacon.

Kelly screamed first, but the painful protest was short-lived. Her head knocked back and her eyes pulled wide in abject pain. The meteor was sinking, but Kelly had already slipped back into the water, her once golden flesh now resembling a piece of charred meat.

Kurt's own body touched back down in the water. It hurt to even paddle. He reached for Kelly in time to see her disbelieving stare. In the moonlight, his arm might have been in worse shape. It was as charred as Kelly, the skin melting from his bones, unsheathing a layer of runny tissue beneath.

The meteor had gone under too, and Kurt's consciousness was eager to follow.

Kelly sprung back up over rocking waves and reached for him.

She tried to cry out, but her throat had already burst open. Blood poured down her blackened cheeks like an explosion of red tears.

Then she slipped forever beneath the dark water and was gone.

It was the last thing Kurt saw before his mind caught up to his damaged body. His vision faded as the water ushered him into the cold grave below.

The frilled shark slithered up from the depths, moving through water that was brighter than he was used to. He had no concept of color, but his large brown body glided across a warm tint of blue that was more welcoming than the ebony darkness he had spent much of his life prowling.

A chance encounter had lured him to the surface for the first time a few days ago. He spent time circling the island, acclimating to the sounds that tingled his senses beyond the surface.

Rhythmic vibrations provoked him the most. Bass-heavy drumbeats reached out across the Atlantic with rippling tremors. The shark had believed them to be a tease, and he swam up to locate the source, annoyed to discover they were on land.

The whirring and chopping of boat motors were equally antagonistic, and it frustrated him that he could not easily breach the offending hulls.

This was also a reminder of why he preferred life at further depths. That world made sense to him. Prey he could easily claim. He went after squids most often because they were helpless and often found injured. Other times, he only had to wait until their energy was spent and they were simply floating.

Unlike most sharks, he had the ability to creep through the darkness, floating between depths of one-hundred-and-fifty to six-hundred feet. Marine life was at ease when he prowled, and ignorant of his presence until it was too late.

He was able to distend his flexible mouth in order to swallow his prey whole. Victims were raked along rows of tricuspid teeth, shredding their flesh and often ensnaring them so that escape was impossible. This was advantageous because his bite was not as severe as other species, even though he was the largest of his kind, an anomaly at twenty feet in length and weighing nearly twenty-five-hundred pounds.

He had been on the trail of a larger specimen of squid when he suddenly lost interest in that would-be prey, enticed instead by quakes that reached down through the darkness to tingle his recessed ear canals.

This was not the first time he had seen a human being, but it was the first time he had tasted one. He was naturally wary of them and avoided their type when he ventured up on rare occasion. This time, though, something urged him toward the pair of legs scissoring through the water to stay afloat.

Instinct suggested that he should retreat back into deeper waters, but he had no desire to listen.

A large band of ripples came thundering out of the dark and he swam toward them. A rush of water drizzled through his nostrils, alerting him to the presence of human blood.

He leaned to his side and tilted his head toward the surface, sensing continued splashing in the distance while that blood spread through the water. He moved toward the irregular commotion while, around him, other predators sensed the same. Maybe they were, for a moment, contemplating their own investigation but stopped when they felt him gliding up toward it.

Warm water was one thing, but this patch was something else. It grew hotter the closer he got, almost boiling. Rather than swim headfirst into the uncomfortable heat, he glided around it, hovering on the line where the Atlantic was seasonal against the anomalous hot spot.

A boulder plummeted toward the darkness before him. Overhead, two pair of kicking feet. Loud screams taunted him. He lowered his mouth and sliced through the watery heat.

Just as he headed up, the ground below quaked in

competition for his attention. The fallen rock had gone to rest on an ocean cliff, cracking and splitting down the center. A series of smaller vibrations set his detection system on edge.

The shark glanced at the bodies. Both were floating through the gloom. Two blackened and unmoving corpses. His only thought was which to eat first.

He noticed the split in the rock. A spindly pink head lurched out of the opening and leapt for him as he headed past. A smooth but unwanted attachment coiled around the length of his body, slipping inside one of his gills.

The shark turned toward the burnt and drifting bodies while the invading organism latched onto his innards. He felt it stretch out inside, wigging and adjusting until it felt like it had always been there. The shark was alarmed but accepted the changing circumstance, as his functions were not impaired. Then something cool spread across his basilhyal, the closest thing a shark has to a tongue, sinking little pincers into the meaty flesh.

The shark struggled with this, but his instinct fell away amidst the outrage. As he reached the two dead bodies, his urge to eat them was quelled. The gnarled and twisted corpses were as appetizing to him as a pyre of rubber tires, and he knifed between them, choosing to keep his jaws locked tight.

The bodies started their ascent back toward the surface and he was fine with letting the dinner escape. The urge had passed.

He glided back down into the mire. His thoughts were swapped out almost at once for those belonging to the passenger presence inside of him.

It was driving this body now.

WELCOME TO SPRING BREAK

Manuel caught a glimpse of his reflection in the mirror and thought, *Fuck!* just before they smashed his face straight into it.

Hungry glass sliced his cheeks, each shard stinging like he'd been driven headfirst into a hornet's nest. He crashed down into the sink, jagged debris crunching as it cradled his head.

The two goons that used him as a battering ram took the opportunity to launch a flurry of fists into his ribs, beating him breathless. Manuel tried for air but his body protested the gesture. Pain was everywhere. He managed one shallow breath and felt an odd stitch of relief. These guys had been waiting to do this since grabbing him off the sidewalk last night.

In a way, he was glad the wait was over.

"Enough," Garcia said in between Cohiba puffs. "Drop this *cabrón*."

One of the goons, either Tavo or Quino, pulled Manuel by a clump of his hair, lifting him so that he could see the puddle of bloody glass that had become his pillow. The hand continued to yank Manuel's head back further until the skin of his neck stretched tight against his throat. He sputtered, tried to speak. That was the signal to smash him back down. His skull shattered the porcelain like plywood, gliding through ceramic haze, crashing to the floor.

Manuel landed face-down in piss, prompting the puddle to splash up and pock Tavo's striped cigarette pants. From somewhere above, Garcia let loose a deep belly laugh.

Tiny drips of water fell from the now-busted faucet. The room otherwise silent. For a second, Manuel believed the worst was over. Then Tavo and Quino began stomping his back.

"Okay, okay," Garcia said, shooing his boys off with a wave of his cigar. Neither of these goons—leather cuts, tattoos up and down their sculpted torsos—looked too happy about being leashed. "You'll break his fuckin' spine. Then what? Pay his hospital bills?"

Manuel swallowed the blood that bubbled at the back of his throat. He reached for his face using only the tips of his fingers. Even the slightest touch brought snakebite agony, and he began to wonder if maybe he couldn't ask Garcia to cover those inevitable bills.

He decided not to ask.

Garcia knelt beside him. His knees cracked with arthritis and he chomped down on his cigar with a grimace. A puff of smoke rushed Manuel's face. "There are two different philosophies when it comes to a wounded animal." He reached into his white linen suit and took a second Cohiba from the pocket. An offering.

Manuel nodded and moved with caution as he rearranged himself into a sitting position. His back pressed against the slab wall, blood continuing to dribble down off his mangled face.

Garcia nodded too and then extended the courtesy of clipping the cigar tip and placing it in Manuel's mouth.

Didn't light it, though.

"If I listen to Tavo and Quino, I put the injured mutt out of its misery. Makes sense, *sí?* I mean, the dog ain't ever going back to the way it was, limping along when it should be running. So it makes sense. But that's the thing about Tavo and Quino. I pay them to be cruel so I don't gotta be. You understand this because you used to be like them. You understand I don't like that feeling so much. Here…"

Manuel's teeth came down hard on the tip of the cigar, filling his mouth with tobacco grains and wrapper shreds. Garcia narrowed his eyes and continued to milk the dramatic pause. He wanted to see the fear on Manuel's face. Savor it.

"The animal lover in me remembers the good times," he continued. "All those years my mutt was obedient. Part of me doesn't believe I need to kill him 'cause he no longer fetches." Garcia slapped Manuel's cheek. A jolt of lighting coursed through his whole body. "You follow?"

Manuel nodded with his eyes because his head was in too much pain to move.

"Good," Garcia said, "'cause here's what I'm thinking… you… you ain't been right in a long time. A long fuckin' time. But who can blame you? See, that's what Tavo and Quino don't get."

Garcia looked back at his goons to make sure they were listening.

"Maybe they'll limp home one day, too," he said. "And if that happens, they'll hope the dog lover in me remembers all the sticks they fetched." He took a butane lighter from his pocket and pushed down on it with a heavy thumb.

The sizzling flame brought Manuel's cigar to crackling life, and Garcia kept it there until grey ash appeared.

Manuel took a few puffs. They helped steady his breathing. Once he felt comfortable, he pushed away from the wall and sat upright, continuing to look his boss in the eye. Couldn't get to his feet and risk Garcia interpreting that as a threat. Best to stay where he was obviously subservient.

This hadn't been the expected outcome. Last night, when Manuel made the decision to run, he was sure it was over. That's what he wanted.

The headache that thundered behind his eyes matched his busted ribs and shredded face. The cigar tasted slightly stale, or maybe he never could stand these fucking things. Either way, the puffs restored clarity.

Looking back on it, Manuel's decision had been stupid. He hadn't cared then, and only cared now because Garcia was here in the flesh, calling him out on his betrayal. Forcing Manuel to reconcile the disappointment in his eyes.

Last night, he'd been at Velocity, Garcia's nightclub on 23rd Street. Everyone there was high on their fifth consecutive win as "Miami's Premier Nightclub" as deigned by some magazine that paying customers were influenced by.

Cristal flowed through the VIP lounges like piss while girls jiggled their asses on neon stages and guys perfected new ways of staring at them from the corners of their eyes.

Manuel mostly dealt with the club's talent, currying favors once they were on site. Sometimes that meant accommodating weird requests, like finding a pair of snake moccasins in size fourteen or ensuring their hotel suite was stocked with all the bitches and XTC Garcia was willing to provide.

Most people at Velocity looked at Manuel like he was in the wrong place. Didn't exactly seem like a man who'd make a career in hospitality. That's because, in another life, Manuel had been Garcia's problem solver, especially good at finding those who didn't want to be found. The ones with gambling debts the size of California, or low level *maricons* who hit Garcia's supply lines thinking they could hide in the glades like shit would just blow over after a long weekend.

Last night, something in Manuel snapped. He couldn't explain it.

The local talent had been a millennial DJ. *Muto*, or *Buto*, or whatever the fuck. Some twenty-two-year-old with skinny jeans and a patch goatee dyed into a rainbow. He leaned into Manuel's ear and asked for a couple of thirteen-year-olds, ordering them like it was McDonald's drive thru.

Thinking about it now, it wasn't that Manuel no longer cared, but perhaps that he finally did. What snapped had been his patience, civility folding beneath an avalanche of rage. Normally, whatever. You want black tar? Six whores? Fine. Cost of doing business.

But kids was a line no man should ever cross.

Muto, or *Buto*, or whatever the fuck hadn't understood Manuel's outrage, wrinkling his brow like the word *no* didn't exist. A brat who lived out of hotel rooms three hundred days a year, only accustomed to people waiting on him. Kid got warped into believing he was royalty.

"Willing pussy's willing pussy, bro. Ain't no girl at thirteen confused as to what she wants, either." As an olive branch, *Muto*, or *Buto*, or whatever the fuck had even suggested they share her because he was so certain Manuel only needed to taste that forbidden fruit on

his tongue to become a fan of it for life.

So Manuel reached for the fire extinguisher tucked away behind the bar and split the DJ's face open with the bottom ring of solid metal. Child raping teeth shot across the VIP lounge like confetti, and his bottom jaw bled blacker than chocolate syrup. In that moment, Manuel had resolved to kill the motherfucker, descending on him with the tank raised high, imagining his brains looking like mashed potatoes on the floor as he beat them out of the DJ's skull.

Only security had intervened. Everyone at Velocity knew Manuel, the forty-year-old loner who kept to himself. *"He's Garcia's boy from way back,"* they said, and that was why they only tackled him out of commission as opposed to turning him into a grease spot. *"Step outside,"* they told him. *"Get some air."* They had bigger problems, like trying to get the pedo's teeth back inside his runny mouth.

Manuel did exactly that, breathing in a half pack of Marlboros while the gravity of his decision and actions seeped in, like the aftermath of jacking it to something really depraved.

The thing of it was, he knew the story's ending. At least he thought he did. The years spent at Garcia's side serving as his own personal Ghost of Christmas Future.

Maybe he was the injured dog after all, begging to be put out of his misery.

But he hadn't known that last night when he was on his way down the street thinking about the ways in which he might disappear. That's when Tavo and Quino came calling.

"Manuel, let's take a ride."

"Look," Garcia said, back in the present. For the slightest of seconds, the gangster's smile was warm. But just for the slightest of seconds. "I'm cutting you loose, *cabrón*. I got no choice. You cost me a lot of money and a whole lot more in reputation. I gotta do some things to you that you ain't gonna like."

He took the ring of the cigar cutter and glided Manuel's middle finger through it. With a quick clip, the blade sliced through the bone and severed his finger with the slightest crunch.

Manuel bit the Cohiba so hard it split.

"This goes to the DJ so he knows I dealt with you," Garcia said. "Got it?"

Manuel did. His eyes watered and the tears stung every time they reached one of his facial cuts. It was nothing compared to the spurting wound on his left hand where his finger used to be. He wanted to cry out, but remembered he owed Garcia an answer to his question and was quick to nod.

"Good," Garcia said. "Now this is where you get a choice. Either we leave you here, at some shitty rest stop near the glades, and you find your way out of Florida. Forever. Or you do one last job for me and make a little money. You still leave Florida forever, but you leave with enough money so that you'll never have to be a greeter at Home Depot in order to pay rent."

Manuel spit cigar tobacco across the floor and put the Cohiba back in his mouth to rescue the rest of it. The tip glowed orange, and his constant puffs slowed his thoughts, helped everything fall into perspective. Garcia was crafty like that. Didn't want his boy making any rash decisions.

Their history, mutually respected.

"What's the job?" Manuel asked after some time.

"Really?" Garcia asked with a laugh. "That's good, Manuel. That makes me happy. Because it's *El Rastreador* that I need."

Manuel didn't care about living. He just never cared for the idea of suicide. His mother's voice echoed even now, reminding him that it was a sin to even consider such things. *"You'll go straight to hell just like your father did, Manny."*

How was that for Catholic guilt? Manuel wasn't worried for himself, but for the off chance he might one day be reunited with Marie and Sanson. He couldn't risk mortal sin.

He looked at Garcia and, through the haze of smoke that languished between them, gave a confident nod that showed he was ready to become *El Rastreador* again.

"You're going to find someone for me," Garcia told him. "Let's get you cleaned up and I'll tell you all about it."

❦

"Reginald, I asked you to clean the kitchen while I was gone."

Reggie hit the dashboard button on his Xbox so he could see the time. It was nearly noon. A whole morning spent on *Fallout 4*. Understandable to anyone who played, but Mom wasn't going to be on board with that excuse. She was more likely to put the whole system on eBay.

He gusted from his room so fast the pictures that decorated the hallway rattled. "Lost track of time, Ma. I'm on it."

"Last time we try making authentic Mexican tacos in the house," she said. "Even my damn bedroom smells like greasy pork." She was in the middle of the kitchen slipping off her coat and folding it over the chair. She reached for the Tide pen on the table, uncapped it, and began to scribble the coffee stain out of her suit collar.

"You all done court for the day?"

"Yes, thank God, but I need to be back at the office at two for a meeting with a new client. Only came home to say hi."

"You don't have to keep checking in on me, Ma, I'm thirteen."

"I also placed a bet with myself to see if the kitchen would be clean."

Reggie pulled the tin foil off the baking sheet and crumpled it, careful not to spill the hardened but still oily pork grease. "Did you win?" He tossed the foil in the trash and started washing the tortilla pan.

"Nah, I lost twenty on you. But how about I let you make it up to me tonight? Early supper at Fire & Ice, followed by *Big Trouble in Little China* at the Brattle?"

Reggie wasn't in the position of passing up Mongolian BBQ or John Carpenter, but both were undeserved in this instance. He recognized Mom's game. Dad had raised him on those movies. Mom always found an excuse to get up off the couch before they popped in *Assault on Precinct 13* or *Escape From New York*, but he supposed real effort was being made here. It was hard not to appreciate it.

Mom went into her bedroom while Reggie finished cleaning. By the time the counters had been cleared off and washed down, the trashcan stunk from a week's worth of rotted food scraps. He wrestled the bag from the stainless steel container and tied it off as the phone rang.

Mom cracked her door and appeared in the jamb. "Ugh, get rid of that trash!" She picked up the phone.

Taking out the garbage was awful because it meant carrying it down two flights of stairs in order to deliver it to the communal barrels in the alley. Mom must've been anxious to pass the duty along because she'd pawned it off as soon as Reggie turned ten. Over the last three years, Reggie tried to find the most painless way of doing it but was beginning to suspect one didn't exist. If you waited too long, the bag was a bulging mess, a real pain to lug down two flights. If it broke on the way down, as had happened before, your night was finished—scraping up banana peels and chicken bones while your neighbors stepped over you and glared like you just spilled nuclear waste.

And when he took the proactive approach and carried the bag down at half capacity, Mom yelled at him for being wasteful. It was an unwinnable game.

Reggie deposited the bag and wiped his hands on his jeans to clear the oily residue that had somehow gotten on his fingers. He headed back inside and decided to take the elevator up, pressing '2' and stepping inside.

The doors were about to slide shut when beyond them, Becky St. George came in off the sidewalk. She moved past the mailboxes in slow motion, the gemstone in her navel piercing making every effort to pry his eyes down. He wasn't falling into that trap, though, not when she was looking at him for the first time. Only a year older, but already a goddess. The Catholic schoolgirl outfit seemed like an accessory to her beauty, more Britney Spears than Sister Janet. And she was smiling as she approached.

In the six months she'd lived here, she had never even given him the time of day.

Reggie jammed his hand out to prevent the elevator doors from touching.

Becky slid in and threw him a tight-lipped smile. "Four, please."

The temptation to say *"I know"* was real, but he resisted it. Her simple acknowledgement set his heart racing, but he wouldn't give in to the lure of small chat. He planned his attack instead as he pressed the button.

The little number 4 glowed yellow and the elevator

bucked, then started climbing. The doors slid open on the second floor after the blink of an eye.

Becky looked at him questioningly. "Isn't this you?"

"It is," Reggie said. "But, ima go up to the roof and check for squirrels."

"Huh?"

What the hell are you saying? "Um, I thought I heard them in the walls last night, just wanna see if there's any sign of them up there. Droppings, acorns. Whatever."

"Ew, really? In the walls? Just call Mr. Albert. It's his job to take care of that stuff. Shouldn't be our problem."

"I just want to be sure before I tell him that it *is* a problem."

Another ding and they reached floor four. Becky stepped out but turned back as she sauntered beyond the threshold. "My skin's itching just thinking about those things in the walls... let me know if I need to set some rat traps."

"I don't think you can just kill squirrels like that."

"Whatever, I'm not about to risk rabies."

"I'm Reggie, by the w—" The door closed but the elevator wasn't moving because he hadn't told it where to go. With a defeated sigh, he hit number 2 and rode back toward his apartment.

Squirrels? That's your first conversation with Becky St. George? Squirrels. Now she thinks I spend my free time checking the roof for rodent poop.

Reggie came back to his apartment to the sound of Mom going off.

"Luther, *please*," she shouted into the phone.

He froze, hoping he hadn't interrupted by making too much noise opening the door.

"I don't know what to tell you," Mom continued, "you

said you were more than happy to take Reginald. How many times am I supposed to check in with you after you've said 'yes' before I can safely plan a vacation? I haven't told him yet. I was going to do that at dinner… I think he'll be fine with it, honestly."

Her footsteps paced back and forth like she was waiting for a doctor's prognosis and there was a long bout of silence as Dad responded.

"No," she said at last. "You're making too much of a big deal out of it… He loves his father. You know I don't say anything to make him feel otherwise. Come through for me, Luther. I'm not going to leave him home for a whole week… I know he's growing up, but no mother is going to leave her baby home alone for the week of spring break."

Seething, Reggie stomped into the kitchen and tore a bottle of Mexican Coke from the fridge. He popped the cap with the bottle opener magnet stuck to the front and threw it across the room.

Mom paused mid-sentence at the sound of his protest, then continued on.

"Look, I need to go. He's here and probably heard the whole thing. You can't do this to me now, Luther. You can't."

Reggie downed half the contents of the frosty glass bottle before Mom returned to the kitchen. She put the phone back on the wall cradle but didn't look him in the eye. Her gaze drifted to the dark tile pattern beneath their feet, mumbling something about having to re-grout it.

"I ain't going to Florida," he said.

"Reginald, please…"

"Mom, it's my week off. Why can't I just hang out? I'll be in my room. You won't even know I'm here."

Mom winced at the thought. She couldn't come to terms

with the fact that he was growing up, and that was Reggie's problem for some damn reason.

She took a seat across the way and reached for the soda bottle. He slid it over and watched her take a long pull. "I don't know why you think this Mexican stuff tastes that much better," she said.

"It's the cane sugar," Reggie mumbled in a way that sounded like *duh, stupid*.

Mom's eyes hardened and her mouth tightened like she was about to give a sermon. "It's not about you, Reggie. You act like I'm sending you to camp, but this isn't about getting you away from me. Not even a little."

"What then? When were you going to tell me?"

Mom sighed. It wasn't like her to ever want Reggie to leave the house, so he believed that. And it was even less like her to try and keep secrets. He just wasn't used to seeing her this way.

When they talked, Dad always reminded Reggie that he was Man of the House and with that came the responsibility of looking after Mom. He did it despite wondering why any adult needed to be looked after.

Shouldn't they have that part down by now?

"Okay, Reginald, I'm going to be straight. As straight with you as I expect you'll be with me. I've been seeing somebody for the last few months… I haven't told you because I know you're… sensitive about that…"

"What's wrong with Dad, though?"

"Nothing." She twisted the empty Coke bottle by its neck. Anything to avoid eye contact. "We just realized it wasn't working."

"And it's working with the new guy?"

"Anthony. Yes. He's taking me to Italy next week, and I thought you'd enjoy spending some time with your father."

Visiting that island was the last thing Reggie wanted. A boring place with terrible food. Seafood that made him shit on the best days, where Wi-Fi was slow AF because everyone had ten devices tethered to it. No Xbox. Or TikTok. Or Instagram.

Mom might as well be sending him to military school.

"You have a funny way of rewarding me," he said. "That's a damn punishment."

This was supposed to be a lazy vacation, but not without purpose. This was going to be the week of Becky St. George, and he was planning to find the nerve to ask her out for burgers and a movie. Timing had to be perfect, and that was easier said than done because the last sixteen times they'd crossed paths hadn't been right.

Today wasn't good either, but at least Reggie had a chance to look her in the eye and say something.

I talked about squirrels…

Maybe I'll jump into the ocean once I'm on the ferry.

If Mom was putting him on a plane to Florida, then it was game over. Becky St. George would continue to be elusive, except in his imagination, and would definitely have a boyfriend by the time he got back.

This was a disaster.

He wanted to protest, but the tired look in Mom's eyes caught him just right. She was wrong to keep this a secret, but what choice had Reggie given her? Last time she brought a dude home, Reggie snuck outside and put a whole package of bologna on the hood of his car. He was younger then, but she didn't think he'd grown up all that much since.

Mom's weakness read as *Please, Reginald, just let me have this.* He knew there was no leg to stand on. The island Dad called home, Crystal Key, sucked, but it would be good to see him again.

He thought about Becky St. George's golden-baked midriff and clenched his jaw.

"I guess seeing Dad won't be so bad," he said, failing to understand why he had moved so far away in the first place. The divorce had murdered his pride, and Reggie got that. But when Dad tried selling a line about seeing his son as much as possible, the distance made it a hard buy. If you wanted that, why move halfway across the country and onto an island the size of Concord?

"You're the best, baby." Mom's eyes lifted and a smile followed when she saw that Reggie had accepted the idea.

"Can we still do early dinner and a movie tonight?"

She slid the bottle toward the center of the table and took a deep breath. "You bet."

"I guess I should get packed. Do I get to know when I'm leaving, or is that a surprise?"

"Early tomorrow. I really shouldn't have kept it from you."

"No you shouldn't have," Reggie said. "My bologna throwin' days are over, Mom."

"Go on and get packed," she told him. "And tell your father I said hello."

Luther Bradshaw stood on the dock and watched the fishing trawler, *his* fishing trawler, return to port. He should've been on it, but today wasn't about catching fish. It was about hunting shark.

His ship, *Eve*, puttered through calm island waters that swelled up from 2600 fathoms to about eleven feet on this side of Crystal Key. Some forty-seven miles behind the boat was the

Miami coastline. You couldn't see it from here, but lately he'd been missing the safety of the mainland.

To his right, the Bahamas were another forty miles away, across water that was even deeper at 3800 fathoms.

Crystal Key was a convenient weigh station for those traveling between the two. People might stop for a night before realizing how little their slice of paradise had to offer. Others maybe stayed longer because the cay's southern side was home to a small resort called Shifting Tides that had been strategically positioned there by an enterprising mind in order to capture some of that critical Bahamian overflow.

It was much cheaper than those premium resorts, and that was by design. Not quite a tourist trap, but maybe Florida's answer to a spider web.

When people took impromptu vacations to the Commonwealth of the Bahamas, and that happened a lot, they'd come to realize the island hotels and resorts were booked solid, at which point "locals" were kind enough to tell the tourists about Shifting Tides.

"Only forty miles back the way you came!"

The place was owned by retired three-star army general Rand Hamilton, who ran his business like a military operation. He strategically placed his people in those lobbies during peak seasons to scoop potential clientele as they struck out at the front desks.

It worked more often than not, and right now Crystal Key was sitting on approximately thirteen couples too dumb to have booked destination rooms in advance.

Normally, this didn't bother Luther. Tourism was good for the island economy because guests at Shifting Tides got tired of its accommodations—the pool's lazy bar, sweaty beachfront conga lines, third-rate concerts, and hiking trails through razor thin foliage. Distractions that could only eat up so much time before going into town seemed like the better idea.

Thing was, town wasn't much better. Tourists came with grand vacation designs. They wanted beach bonfires and underwater cave tours. Five-star restaurants. What they got was a watering hole called Lashonda's, a few places to get authentic knick-knacks like conch shell jewelry, and a couple of family run seafood shacks.

They'd tire of Crystal Key's rustic island ways before long and would either head back to Miami or book the next available room anywhere in the Bahamas and simply bide their time until check in.

The other problem Crystal Key had was fish. Everything here stunk of it because that's what Crystal Key lived to do. Catch fish. That's what Luther did. And when he considered all the other occupations he'd held down over the years, fisherman wasn't so bad.

He wished today had been like any other, out on the Atlantic with his men: Parker, Breyer, Zane, and Taffy. Together they formed the five-man crew of the *Eve*. It would appall any lifelong seaman to hear that Luther had opted for land duty, but captains made tough decisions every day.

One of them had to stay behind. Since he had the least amount of experience hunting marine life, it made sense. He trusted Parker at the helm more than himself anyway. Wouldn't admit that to his face, of course, but Luther always felt Parker would've made a more capable captain.

He put the binoculars to his face and squinted his one functional eye. The falling sun turned the ocean's gentle swell into orange ripples. He scanned one way and then the other, keeping his eye trained on the water around the trawler's hull. There was nothing.

It has to be here.

"Good to see you're taking this seriously." Rand Hamilton's gruffness was like broken glass.

Luther hadn't yet turned when two pairs of boots stomped down the dock toward him. "Afternoon, general," he said.

"Got enough trouble calming my guests after last night's goddamn sky fire... they don't need to worry about your imaginary shark, too."

Luther bit his tongue. No sense in making things worse. The *Eve* would be here in five minutes, and once his boys were on shore, he'd relax.

"See anything?" That voice belonged to Frank Westbay, and Luther hadn't been expecting him.

Frank's custom G31 rifle was banded across his chest in a non-threatening manner. He wore a vest with its sleeves torn off, leaving jagged little fabric tendrils around the seams. A knife sheath hung off his belt and he stepped loud in Army surplus boots.

The closest thing Crystal Key had to actual law enforcement. The island, like the real Florida Keys, was somehow part of Monroe County, and the police didn't get out here too often. To most, Frank made better company than the blue boys anyway. He wasn't elected to any position but had been the arbiter in so many local disputes over the years that the mantle simply attached itself.

"Quiet all day," Luther said.

"Beautiful." Frank gave him a *hello* tap on the back. "Hopefully she's gone back down to whatever depths usually hold her."

"Tasted human flesh and, what? Didn't like it?" Luther asked.

"Bullshit, Bradshaw," Rand said. "If there is a shark, you don't know it tasted anyone."

"I know that Anne Munro's missing, and she didn't swim off the island."

"How do you know she's missing?" Rand asked. "You go door-to-door?"

Luther wasn't about to tell them how he knew. The girl was an adult, but at nineteen, barely that, especially when he was north of fifty and once divorced. Crystal Key didn't have to know they'd been a thing. People here pretended at open minds until it came time for them to prove their close-mindedness. They'd accuse him of preying on the vulnerabilities of a runaway college dropout.

Luther asked himself if he'd been doing that on more than one occasion.

He kept his jaw locked and went back to watching the water.

"She is missing," Frank said. "She goes to the mainland with Mrs. Blankenship every couple of weeks. The old woman knocked on her door yesterday morning and kept knocking 'cause she didn't answer."

"Doesn't mean a thing," Rand said.

"Possible Anne's just laying low," Frank said, shrugging. "I dated an artist once. The whole world revolved around her. I couldn't call her past six because she might be in the middle of an *artistic breakthrough*. She's an afternoon dancer at the Lamplighter now."

"She's got exactly one place on this island to lay low," Luther said.

"And she's paid up 'til June," Frank agreed.

"Well, if she ain't there, where is she?" Luther asked.

"Lots of single men on this island," Frank said. "Women, too."

"She don't shack up."

"Oh please," Rand sighed.

"Nobody knows jack about her," Frank said. "I've checked... she stays in her room most days... hammering away on that laptop in pursuit of the new American Novel. A book future generations will buy Cliff's Notes for. Beyond that, she goes to the bar on occasion. Sits on the beach at night and scribbles her thoughts in a journal."

"Gone doesn't mean dead," Rand said. "Maybe her parents are sick..."

Her parents are dead.

"...or maybe she missed her boyfriend..."

He used to beat the shit out of her.

"...for all we know, she wanted the comfort of her own bed and took off home."

"And maybe a shark got her," Luther said without irony.

"There's no shark," Rand said, thinking if he repeated it enough times it would be true. "You can't expect any of us to take Breyer at his word."

Luther did, though, because Kirby Breyer had *seen* the fish. And while Kirby Breyer was a man who courted an honest bottle of whiskey at the end of every honest day's work, he preferred the honest day's work too much to risk mixing the two.

Luther had known Breyer for as long as he'd been in Crystal Key. Didn't know what the poor bastard was hiding from, or what had happened in his life that made him talk the way he did, but he was always on time for work and had a sixth sense for finding fish.

He believed Breyer's tall tale because it was the only

one he'd ever told. Rest of the guys went hard at braggadocio, sitting in the pub talking about that one time something incredible happened while they were alone and how everyone should've been there to witness it in all its non-verifiable glory.

Miller, for instance, fucked supermodels each time he went to Miami alone, but couldn't so much as smile at a waitress here.

But Breyer usually just nested in the bar's darkest corner, quiet like. The only man in the crew with diving certification, which meant he could go under and look for salvage when word hit the scanner that there might be something out there worth recovering.

Last week's word was that two tourists had been on a boat to the Bahamas when a drunken brawl erupted between them. The guy hadn't liked his girl wearing a string bikini and hated all the eyes that went along with her wearing it.

The misses wound up tossing the mister's luggage overboard. Mister wouldn't say what was in it but offered a five-thousand-dollar reward for its return. He booked a flight home as soon as the boat reached Harbor Island, leaving her and her string bikini alone in their honeymoon suite.

Luther figured it couldn't hurt to look for that luggage. They were crushing the season, fish-wise. The job didn't pay each man more than $30k a year, and the boss never discouraged a little salvage expedition as long as it didn't get in the way of catching fish.

So they took a looksee by following the passenger boat's coordinates from Miami to Crystal Key, reviewing the weather patterns of that day along with the ship's speed in order to estimate the location.

And Breyer had been 160 feet beneath the surface looking for that luggage when he'd seen it. "*A sea monster,*" he later cried. A gigantic snake that was also somehow a shark. Even Luther had to question whether he'd been drinking.

But his description was downright poetic, and wasn't something Breyer could fake. He said the creature floated toward him without motion, gliding straight out of a nightmare while the ocean around him stood petrified.

To hear Breyer tell it, he panicked at the sight and pushed toward open air. Luther was there to pull him back on board without ever seeing what had spooked him.

Took most of the morning to calm him down, and it was the only time Luther had ever seen the man drink whiskey while on the job—and only because it was Captain's Orders. He sat with a blanket draped around his shoulders staring out at the ocean for most of the afternoon until he found enough liquid courage to tell his story.

Breyer's *nightmare* turned out to be a frilled shark, easily identified after a little research. But if they really had one in these waters, at a depth of nearly two-hundred feet, then it was a problem. Those sharks were so reclusive the world didn't have a photo of one until 2004. A long time for something to stay hidden.

"I take Breyer at his word," Luther told them. "And Breyer's word is shark. Fishing's in his blood and he ain't never steered us wrong. Never done a thing out there to make me doubt his abilities."

"Nobody's saying he can't work," Rand said, "but you never know what's going on in a man's head. He could be cracking."

"Could be, I suppose. Or maybe there's a simpler explanation. Maybe there's a fuckin' shark in the ocean."

Luther's walkie-talkie crackled. "I see you guys on the

docks… you the welcoming committee for our heroic return?" It was Parker from the water.

They were bringing the *Eve* in for the night, and their day had been anything but eventful. They'd gone up and down the Atlantic corridor from the Miami shore all the way back around the Bahamas. The only thing they'd found was a porno shoot on a yacht off Key Largo.

"Shit!" Luther laughed. "I hope you got video of that."

"Hamilton could've offered them a place to stay," Parker said. "That's the kind of party Shifting Tides needs. Once he realizes it, half the rooms will be sublet by *Girls Gone Wild*."

"Funny guys you've got there," Rand sighed. "Why are they wasting their time fishing with that kind of wit?"

"I'm too old to see that anyway," Luther said. "And my kid's coming out tomorrow, so this place better not go all Porn Hub this weekend."

"Your boy's how old now?" Rand asked.

"Thirteen."

He snorted. "He comes out and sees something like that, he'll never want to go home again."

"Yeah, and then his mother stops custody. I think your racket's got enough going on without all that added skin."

"Right now we do," Rand agreed. "I'll table that idea for the off season."

Frank pointed his rifle to the ocean and squinted through the scope, gliding the gun side to side as he scanned. "Shark ain't there. I think we can say that if it was here at all, it was just passing through."

"Humor me," Luther said. "What if that fish decides he likes the taste of human?"

"I'm not fighting you," Frank said. "If there's reason to

believe that a shark got one of our own, I'm on the next boat out. But I need more than the testimony of some island drunk."

It was Rand's walkie-talkie that crackled this time.

"Rand here."

The response was a snowy voice that Luther recognized as one of the night managers at Shifting Tides.

"You'd better get back here, boss. Now, if possible."

"What've you got?"

"Two bodies washed up on the shore. Both of 'em burned pretty bad."

"I'm on my way, over and out." Rand hurried off for his jeep.

Frank followed but stopped when he was almost off the dock. He turned back. "I guess the silver lining is that we can't blame your shark for that, huh?"

"Yeah," Luther said. "Guess we just have to worry about why the sky's spitting hellfire at us." He paused for a second and looked at the trawler to make sure it was safe. Once his mind was at ease, he said, "Mind if I come along?"

The motorboat's engine sputtered and kicked, jerking Colleen forward and then backwards with enough ferocity to knock her out of the driver's seat. She spilled to the floor, legs splayed in the air.

"Ow."

In the passenger chair, Beth tugged the seatbelt away from her chest and wiggled it back and forth, taunting her friend while giggling with the kind of hysteria that suggested she'd never seen anybody fall before. "Too cool for safety, that's what you get."

Colleen picked herself up, scooping her cell phone off the boat's floor. Of course there was no signal. Crystal Key was Florida, but they must still be in international waters and therefore had no service.

She wasn't working over spring break to pay off roaming charges.

The sun was nearly asleep for the day. The relaxing crystalline ocean became an ominous body of ebbs and flows. They were halfway between Crystal Key and the Bahamas, but it might as well be the middle of nowhere because the surrounding silence was deafening. Small waves licked the boat while tiny stresses on the hull created minor haunted house creaks.

"What the hell are we going to do, Beth?"

"I guess we're rowing."

"Rowing. I'm serious."

"Jesus, Colleen, how many times have you done this?" Beth snatched the radio transceiver in her fist and tried to make contact with Shifting Tides. The reception desk manned a radio for these types of emergencies because they were sort of expected. Mr. Hamilton had people shuttling back and forth to the Bahamas to try and siphon some of that business, and today Colleen and Beth had drawn that straw.

It hadn't been bad, sitting around in various foyers, allowing single men to buy them drinks, their ears tuned to the front desks, waiting to pounce on the unsuspecting while getting their buzzes on.

Mr. Hamilton liked to send his *"two best girls,"* as he called them. They knew this had little to do with their aptitudes and everything to do with their bodies. Both girls were smart enough to realize they could get better work on the mainland, but hustling for an old pervert had its perks. He paid them more because he liked having them around. So what if their uniforms made Hooters look modest? Shorts that put their butt cheeks on display and t-shirts tight enough to stop their blood from flowing.

The plus side was that they made their own hours, got all the free booze they could drink, and spent the entirety of their workday crafting their tans.

Up until this moment, adrift in the middle of nowhere, it had been the life.

"Why is no one answering?" Beth tossed the marine radio against the console in tantrum.

Colleen turned the dial over to the U.S. VHF channel that allowed them to raise the Coast Guard. "Mayday," she cried into the receiver, realizing they were sitting ducks and could get clipped by a bigger ship that didn't see them, or get taken by pirates like in that Tom Hanks movie.

Something collided against their hull, pushing the boat into a tilt. The girls toppled against each other and smashed the rail with conjoined grunts. The boat dropped back down with a splash as a large shadow darted just beneath the surface.

"This is the U.S. Coast Guard, what's your emergency?" the radio asked.

Colleen grabbed the CB as Beth's gaze fixated on the water, her friend mumbling beneath her breath.

Colleen read the coordinates off the boat's electric compass, stressing their need to hurry. "Please help——" she started to say as Beth's scream cut her off.

"What the hell is that?"

Colleen saw it, too. A serpentine face knifed through the water, somehow smiling wide as if delighted to make their acquaintance. At twenty feet away, rows of teeth glinted like brand new steak knives. Her body went cold in pre-shock, the ocean breeze suddenly freezing as the terrible head bladed forward with eyes that seemed locked onto her in anticipation.

Beth sidled against Colleen, her friend's body offering familiar warmth. Colleen slid an arm around Beth's bikini-bare torso and pulled her tight, searching for comfort.

The swelling ocean seemed to break around the monstrous head, the creature's green eyes blinking with mechanical coldness. It glided toward the hull again, coming this time from the other side.

Both women realized this and screamed. The thing was fast, and it smashed the keel with enough force to nearly capsize the boat. Gravity turned against Colleen and sent her flying once more, this time toward the opposite guardrail. Beth stumbled, too, and her elbow smacked Colleen's mouth on the way overboard. A splash of water doused the back of Colleen's Shifting Tides shirt as the boat dropped back into the ocean with a craterous plop.

"Oh my God," Colleen gasped. She leaned over the rail before she knew she was doing it, her arm stretching toward her friend, fingertips dipping in and out of the water while the boat rocked. Beth was just out of reach, thrashing wildly and calling for help.

"Colleen, please!"

"Swim to me!" Colleen shouted. Her voice drowned by Beth's screams, while the Coast Guard's radio static compounded the commotion.

Colleen turned back toward the boat and took stock of everything they had on board, which wasn't much. She took the orange life preserver and hurled it overboard like a Frisbee. It skipped to a stop just beside one of Beth's flapping arms. Thankfully, she wasn't so far gone to ignore it. Her hand closing around the floater, pulling it close and then pushing toward the boat.

"Swim," Colleen cried, so terrified she could no longer focus on her friend. Her eyes bounced everywhere else, searching the water for the monster's terrible grin. It could be anywhere, and it had to be close.

Beth seemed to paddle forward in slow motion. Colleen gripped the metal rail with such force her plastic manicured nails splintered down the middle.

Swim, she thought. *Fucking swim!*

That's what Beth was doing. Close enough now for Colleen to hear her pathetic whimper in the water below. Colleen's hand lunged back over the side, begging for Beth to take it. Their fingers locked in a grip without leverage. Colleen couldn't pull her up from that angle. She reached down with her other hand to grab Beth's forearm.

Beth's free hand reached for the top of the hull, fingers slipping off the boat's slick wall. Panicking, she grabbed the only other thing she could: Colleen. Beth's fist closed around her shirt, pulling up in hysteric desperation.

In the second before Colleen lost her balance, she saw the monster lift out of the water right behind Beth. Then she felt herself slipping over the rail and screamed, first at the sight of that awful, endless smile, and then because she realized she was on her way to greet it.

She splashed into the water headfirst and darted straight down. From above, Beth's legs kicked her repeatedly, though not on purpose. Each time Beth's feet collided with Colleen's body, Colleen got tamped down further as her friend made every effort to get back aboard the boat.

One heel struck Colleen's face, and the other crashed against her mouth so hard, Colleen's teeth clamped down on her tongue and severed the muscle clean off. Blood drizzled through the surrounding blue mire, wafting past her lips like red strands of cigarette smoke.

Colleen reached up. One final push for her friend's heel. Her hands were kicked aside and that heel stomped down again with sledgehammer force.

Colleen's head fell back. Her eyes rolled. Her detached tongue floated up toward Beth, blood trails following in gory pursuit.

Beth's legs shimmied from the water as the bottom of the hull rocked back and forth to accommodate her weight.

Colleen's body heaved, and the ingested water closed her throat as she saw the monster again, blood from her mouth leading it straight to her like GPS. It slithered through the gloom, jaws distending, widening as if swallowing the entire ocean on its way to devour her.

Her scream was a mess of red bubbles. The monstrous smile was only feet away, and its neck pushed back on itself before lunging forward as if spring-loaded. Her feet disappeared into its mouth as those cold, unblinking eyes wormed even closer. It had her legs next, and its teeth frayed her flesh in thick strips as they raked her shins, knees, and thighs. Its jaws snapped closed and clipped her lower torso in a single bite.

Somehow, Colleen still had consciousness. The water turned from dark to impenetrable. Her outstretched arms drifted overhead as she sunk so far down the boat's hull vanished in the mire. The last thing she saw through stinging seawater was her entrails drifting like puppet strings.

Then her head lazed back to embrace sleep.

And the shark's face was there. Its mouth opened and flashed a dozen fleshy strips caught in its teeth, waving back and forth like decorative paper.

Colleen barely felt her remaining body dock inside its mouth and was already dead by the time it bit down on her skull, crushing every remaining bone at once.

ONE LAST JOB

It didn't take them long to reach the other side of Crystal Key. The island was ten miles in length and four miles wide on average. They buzzed along the narrow, two-lane perimeter road which wasn't for residents because hardly anyone on the island drove. The pavement provided infrastructure to the most cloistered parts of the island. It allowed delivery trucks to keep the downtown shops and restaurants stocked which, in turn, made residents feel like they weren't forty miles off the mainland.

Rand Hamilton was on the phone for the entirety of their drive, demanding his employees get out on the beach and make a human wall around the guests. Prevent them from seeing whatever ghastly sight had washed up. "Keep them back," he continued to shout. "Just keep them back."

Frank's foot was a cement shoe on the pedal, and Luther wasn't much company because he kept thinking about Anne. The last time he saw her. The last thing she'd said. *"You never cared about me at all."*

The jeep broke from the road, rolling onto sand. A branch of wavy green stalks bent beneath its grill as it eased to a stop where the beach receded into tall grass and ocean mush. A Shifting Tides employee was there to greet them, wiping wet splashes of mud off his uniform shorts.

"Down there," he said and jerked a thumb toward the water, pointing to a small cluster of reeds at the water's edge.

There were two charred bodies, all right. Luther wasn't normally queasy—you couldn't afford to be when part of your paycheck was cashed for gutting fish—but the sight of these gnarled corpses tied him in knots. It was impossible to tell which of these crusted husks was the boy and which was the girl, but he knew right away that he'd seen them both alive last night. Her, bare-assed and tugging on him with an invisible leash. Almost looked like too much woman for a limp noodle to handle, but Luther had liked that about him. Everyone loved an underdog.

Shit, man, why didn't you take my advice and go back to your room?

"I know them," Luther said.

"You don't," Rand snapped. "Luther, you don't know them."

"You're going to find you've got two missing guests," he said. "And once you pull your head out of your ass, you'll realize they're right here."

The bodies reminded Luther of barbecue chicken left on the grill for too long. The longer he looked at their fire-molded poses, the more his stomach seemed to constrict. Black char wrapped around exposed bones. One arm slightly raised toward them, a gesture of eerie recognition, skeletal fingers poking through crispy fingertips. The other body lay face down in shallow water, too burnt for even the fish the nibble.

Frank knelt beside them. His hand hovered over the carbonized flesh, too afraid to touch.

"Probably trying to buy drugs," Rand offered. "Crossed the wrong people..."

"Cuba ain't far," Frank said, happy to humor that absurd conclusion. "And the cartels do move in these waters. But they ain't gonna waste their time with a couple of kids. Naw, we gotta get Monroe County out here."

"The sky," Luther said. "We all saw the fireball, man."

"Right. Halley's Comet did this." Rand had all the warmth and compassion of an asshole. He whispered something into his employee's ear and then sent him down beach with a shove, the poor boy tripping in the sand as he hurried back to the resort.

"The county medical examiner will tell us everything when he gets here," Frank said. "Until then, I assume you want to get these bodies off your beach."

"Yes. Right now."

"Luther, will you get the jeep? We've got to bag these things and get them out of public view."

"Should you be moving them?"

"They weren't toasted alive in the water," Frank said. "This isn't a crime scene."

"Yeah, but—"

"But if any of the guests see this," Frank continued, "it'll cause a panic. If it causes a panic, they'll up and leave faster than shit off a shovel." He motioned to the village with the round of his chin. "And they'll lose what little money they stand to make from our spring breakers. I'm not doing that to them unless there's a good goddamn reason."

Luther took the keys in a gesture of agreement and jogged to the jeep. He drove it down into the mud and helped Frank fill up two body bags. By the time they were finished, the front of his clothes had scuffs of black char, and it somehow felt disrespectful to brush any of it off.

Rand wasn't concerned with any such disrespect, lording over the corpses as Frank and Luther wrapped them, muttering something about a legal defense, then storming off once he, in the tiki light down shore, caught sight of two staff members playing volleyball with some of the guests, carefree laughter daring to haunt the air in the rushes of the Atlantic breeze.

"Goddammit," he muttered and marched into the night, becoming a silhouette walking along the tide.

"Nice guy," Luther said.

"He micromanages his kids to the point they can't take a piss without logging it," Frank said. "Makes our life easier, though." They loaded the bodies into the back of the jeep and covered it with an all-weather tarp.

"You're not stashing those at your place, are you?"

"I don't get paid enough for that," Frank said. "I'll bring 'em just over the hill to Rand's."

"They're going to start smelling any day now. Ain't tryin' to be uncompassionate about this but..." Luther didn't want to have to explain the dead body smell to his son as soon as he stepped off the boat tomorrow.

"Rand's got storage at his place. Catches some of the resort's overflow. That's where these suckers will live until the county can get out here."

"With the hurricane coming, how long you think that'll take?"

"Hard to say. We're outside the season, but they're still projecting a real bitch of a storm, huh?"

Luther hadn't checked. He wasn't in the habit of feeding the news cycle's constant fearmongering. The storm wasn't due to pass through Crystal Key for a few more days. Plenty of time for it to shift.

"Whatever happens," Frank said, "at least they'll be out of sight. Hidden well enough away to avoid panic."

"Unless someone else wanders in and finds them," Luther said.

"Won't be his family, that's for sure." Frank cast a look down beach to ensure Rand was out of earshot.

His paranoia made Luther chuckle. "I forgot he was even married. Never seem 'em visit."

"He takes his ring off every time he boats over here. You don't think he's such a hands-on manager 'cause he's in love with the service industry, do you?"

"Hey, it ain't my business." Luther hands raised defensively.

"Shouldn't be mine, either, 'cept his wife likes to check up on him when he don't come home for days on end. Guess who she calls when he don't pick up?"

"You don't get paid enough, man."

"Amen. You want a ride back into town?"

Luther declined. He didn't want to mess with those bodies again, figuring that's what Frank *did* get paid for. Actually, he didn't know if Frank collected a wage from the state at all for his service to the island. And the agreement between Frank and Rand was separate and shady, but Luther didn't look down on that.

"Luther... one question before I go..."

"Shoot."

"You *really* don't know where Anne is?"

"Wish I did."

"I guess a girl like that ain't ever gonna settle down."

Luther waved goodnight and opted to enjoy a nice breezy walk into town that would do his nerves some good.

He pushed his hands into his pockets and started away from Rand Hamilton's house of stilts—half the rooms at the resort extended out over the ocean. And the pier never felt secure enough for Luther to want to go out on it.

Shifting Tides was in trouble if that shark was sticking around, but it wasn't his place to play island protector.

Someone else could worry for a change.

Who was he kidding, though? He'd make the rounds again later tonight, walking the shore, wondering if that was a shrieking voice calling out from beyond the breaking waves, or just the wind riling his imagination. It was that or lay awake all night in fear for Anne. At least while he was moving, it was easier to get her off the brain for a bit.

Luther crossed the sand dunes and left the beachfront behind. The evening music and drunken laughter turned to ambient noise and was soon swept aside by a heavy island breeze. He passed into the patch of almacigo trees known locally as the "Crystal Forest." It wasn't much of one, though, and could be walked in under fifteen minutes.

The crashing ocean could be heard up and down the business strip of Crystal Key, what they thought of as their "Main Street." The waves carried a sense of isolation that a dozen fully stocked stores couldn't hide. The façade of civilization. They *were* out in the middle of nowhere.

For Luther, that was by design. Up until Breyer's shark

sighting, he'd loved it here for that very reason.

Now, he was beginning to have second thoughts.

Lashonda's Bar was down on the left. The allegedly soothing sounds of Conway Twitty carried out onto the street. The bar always was a little jealous that it *wasn't* a redneck joint. And that wasn't for the lack of trying. They boasted homemade BBQ smoked out back on homemade cinder blocks and spigots, and the interior floors were lined with sawdust so that spilled beer and flying vomit could be swept up easily.

Parker, Breyer, Zane, and Taffy were in their usual spot, sitting around a Jack Daniels bottle that was near-drained on the table. They cheered their captain on with an exaggerated clap as soon as he walked in.

"Nothing?" Luther said, taking a seat. Parker had already poured a shot and pushed it over. "Tell me you at least got a damn iPhone picture. Some kind of proof."

Parker shook his head but that didn't stop him from smiling.

"S-sorry, Luther," Breyer frowned. "We're gonna need a plaster man to find it again."

"A master plan," Parker corrected. He poured another shot and slid it Breyer's way.

Breyer shrugged. People adjusted his every mispronunciation. It happened so often that it no longer fazed him. He simply downed the shot and poured another.

"Listen guys," Luther said. "I'm not gonna be around this weekend. The kid's staying with me this week and I want to at least take a few days to show him the sights. Maybe even take him to Miami, although I figure that'll be my trump card for when he realizes there ain't shit to do out here."

"That's too bad," Parker said. "Nothing against Reggie, but I was going to tell you—"

"No," Luther said. "Don't say it, man."

"Damn right I'm gonna say it."

"It's a bad idea," Luther growled. He glanced sideways at Breyer. "Definitely not a *plaster man*."

"You haven't heard me yet," Parker said.

"You wanna take the weekend to hunt the shark. That about sum it up?"

Parker grinned. The reckless twinkle in his eye kicked off a game of nervous glances that circled the table. Once looks were exchanged, the rest of the crew watched Parker, waiting for him to make his sales pitch to the captain.

"That thing ain't endangered yet," Parker said. "But it's getting there. Fast. So right now's the time to do it. I found a guy in Miami looking to add one to his personal aquarium, and he's willing to pay us. Willing to pay a *lot*."

Luther liked the sound of *a lot*. Parker waved them into a huddle, and their dialogue disappeared beneath the block of Conway Twitty that was still rolling off the juke.

"These things ain't easy to get, right, 'cause they're usually at 100 fathoms. That's why it took from the beginning of fuckin' time 'til one decade ago for someone to snap a glimpse of one. We know we've got Mr. Frilled in our backyard, and my buyer wants it. He's not talking about giving us gas money, either. A hundred grand. No questions… as long as it's alive."

With cash like that, the whole crew could get out in front of the ball for once. Pay bills, bank a college fund, and plan for retirement. Relief. This life rarely afforded it. Guys like them were never supposed to be ahead of the game. That was okay in Luther's mind because it was the life he chose. It still beat climbing a corporate ladder loaded with broken rungs.

"What's the catch?" Luther asked.

"No catch, Cap," Parker said. "We need your permission to use the boat. And you don't even have to be on it. We catch this sucker, we're still divvying up the shares five equal ways. The people at this table take all."

Parker went on to explain that he and Zane were boating over to Miami in the morning for a supply run. Breyer and Taffy planned to stay behind to give the ship some loving. A top-to-bottom cleaning, an engine tune up, and a jerry rigging below deck to keep the bastard contained, should they catch it.

They had thought this through.

Part of Luther felt he should let them do it. They were willing, and his cut stayed the same no matter what. Money for nothing.

How hard could it be to capture a frilled shark? If it wasn't supposed to be this close to the surface, then its instincts could be compromised. It might be vulnerable, easy to catch. And a hundred grand made it worth the risk. Luther hated to be so mercenary about things, but these boys would never forgive him if he passed this up.

Not that he wanted to let go of the money, either. Twenty grand was a lot of bread.

Reggie's mom would be impressed if he handed over even half that amount toward his college fund.

"Of course you can use the boat," Luther said.

The crew breathed a sigh of relief and laughed as thoughts of their great big bonus assembled in their minds. Luther saw the fantasies fill their faces, greedy little daydreams that manifested in their glimmering eyes. Most of them had already spent their share.

Only Parker would go through the trouble of setting up a rainy-day fund. Maybe. But what the hell? It was a free country, and while he had to take care of these guys at sea, on land was a different story. They were big boys and if they wanted to drink and smoke their share away, at least they'd have fun.

Life was meant to be enjoyed.

"That's what I like about you," Parker said. "You're a man who knows a good deal when he sees it."

"I'm coming with you," Luther said, his turn to flash a shark's grin. It probably wasn't the best idea, but Reggie hated it here, and Luther suspected at least part of that was because he didn't think very much of his old man's decision to leave his family behind. Luther wasn't crazy enough to bring the kid on an actual shark hunt, but he wanted him to be here when they brought the killer back.

Dad needed a win.

Parker didn't seem to like that idea at all. He refused to hide the disdain on his face, but would not voice an objection. The captain did as he pleased when it was his boat to barter with.

"Glad to have you aboard, cap," Parker said, and then ordered a round of shots for the table.

Manuel sat inside the rusted out Civic, puffing an unfiltered Camel and staring at the manila envelope on the empty cushion beside him.

In the rearview reflection, his face wore bee sting kisses. The cuts and scrapes had been doused in hydrogen peroxide to prevent infection. His finger, gone above the knuckle, was hastily stitched and mummified, with Garcia telling him to "get it checked when you get to wherever you're going, *cabrón*, but don't even think about doing it on my time."

My old friend.

At least Garcia had cared enough to stuff a package of gauze inside Manuel's pocket before handing over the keys to this shitbox and sending him on his way.

Little gestures were sometimes all you could hope for in this business. Often, they carried more meaning and spoke louder than a *"good job"* or an extra stack of hundreds.

Manuel cracked the window to allow the swirling smoke to escape into the harbor air. Island Hoppers wasn't open for another hour. It was a little past five and the parking lot was his alone.

The morning DJ couldn't stop talking about the majesty of this soon-to-be gorgeous Saturday in Miami, encouraging everyone to enjoy the weather because Hurricane Margot was coming to kill us all. Bad moods were forbidden, the DJ added in that morning zookeeper voice, because how could anyone be down when the sun was about to be shining so, so bright? If you were sour today, it had to be a *you* problem. You simply weren't looking at the good things in life.

Manuel considered riding into Miami proper to wait by this guy's car. Thought about catching him walking out at the end of his shift and jamming a gun down his throat to ask, *"Are you in a good mood now, pendejo?"* Maybe breaking his nose was the key to enjoying the bright, sunshiny day.

There was already one DJ in the market for reconstructive surgery, though.

The temptation passed.

Manuel reached instead for the soft pack of Camels and reminded himself that this had to go off without a hitch. One last job for Garcia, who had asked for *El Rastreador* by name. A name that no longer existed.

Manuel took a final puff off the Camel and flicked it to the gravel lot. He went for another while he popped the cap off the vodka and swallowed an early breakfast.

This and a steady flow of nicotine were going to get him through it. His eyes caught the mysterious envelope beside him, and his coursing blood became ice water. Whatever was in there, whatever Garcia needed... it couldn't be good.

Another couple of swigs for this unquenchable thirst. Manuel imagined the exaggerated lumps in his throat while swallowing each gulp. A blunt force way to dissolve the stress eating his stomach like cancer.

Fuck it! he thought and scooped the folder up.

A single photograph slid into his lap, and a decade of bottled memories spilled with it. The girl in the picture looked up at him and his soul lurched at the sight. She was young. Eighteen or nineteen. That made her the right age. Aviators that were too big for her face rested on her forehead, and she wore a piece of pink floss for a bikini. She was on her knees in the sand, her arms reaching back, palms buried, her thighs splayed. The smile on her face, wide but forced.

Seeing Anne sexualized like this made Manuel want to shiv the man who'd taken the snap.

"Don't do this," Manuel whispered. He didn't know what those words meant, exactly, and they were so far beneath his breath that his throat had rendered them as a couple of airy pops.

He remembered the day Anne had been born. On the way back from Orlando with her father, Ray, both glad to be alive after Garcia sent them north in a car filled with shotguns, Kevlar, and rubber lizard masks. The job was to discourage some competition from expanding their operation all the way to the coast.

On the way home, they pulled into Rite Aid for sodas and smokes when Ray called to check on his wife. She'd been in labor for two hours, and they raced back with minutes to spare.

"It changes things," Manuel remembered telling Ray, thinking of his own newborn that was less than three months old at the time. "Every minute away from them feels like a waste. And how do you make sense of our world, of the job we do, while pretending you're making a better one for them?"

"We only need to make their lives better, I think," Ray answered. "The world's a lost cause."

He was dead less than six months later, and Garcia had made a gangster's promise to take care of his widow. Except every dime deposited into her pocket got invested in nose candy she hoped could bury the grief. Before long, she was shaking her tits on Garcia's stage for whatever greenbacks her G-string could carry. But that wasn't enough either, and so she went to turning tricks in the parking lot until she caught a screwdriver to the throat because one of her johns simply didn't feel like paying.

Garcia had no choice but to send *El Rastreador* out after the killer. It took Manuel a week, but he caught up to him on the shit-smeared streets of Philly and returned the favor with the very same screwdriver. He'd done that for Anne, who as a toddler had been made into an orphan.

Marie told Manuel *they* were going to look after Anne, but that edict only lasted as long as Marie.

Everything fell apart after Marie. Manuel lost track of Anne, lost track of everything. And now she'd run away to Crystal Key.

That shithole.

"Crystal Key ain't even part of the Florida Keys," Garcia had said as they dressed Manuel's severed finger. "Only got that name 'cause it's floating out there past the real keys and they need people to visit that jerkwater place."

Manuel reached into the glove box and took the semi-automatic in his hand. With half his finger missing, the gun felt strange. Lopsided, like he was going to have to learn to shoot it all over again. His thumb slid around the backstrap, but with only two fingers curled around the grip, his hold was loose. Unconfident.

Fucking Garcia had to cut his left hand.

He climbed out of the Civic, shaking at the thought of seeing Anne again as he walked to the water. It was past six now, and the sky was lighter, a crack of orange banding across it. He drank the rest of his vodka while watching the sun rise, head growing heavier, knowing there'd be time to sleep it off on the ferry.

By seven, the sun was beating down, making him sweat while the Island Hoppers staff reported to work. A few passengers had arrived, sitting in their cars, and Manuel made sure the pistol was secure in his pants, buried beneath his untucked Hawaiian shirt.

It was almost time.

Garcia requested that Anne be returned unharmed. He could do that. But what if she resisted? Would he force her leave the island if she was out there trying to make a new life for herself?

After all the pain Garcia had caused her, wasn't she allowed some peace?

Manuel decided that he needed a black coffee to get his head straight, but as he considered the looming reunion waiting for him on that island, he wished he had more vodka.

The taxi brought Reggie to Island Hoppers just in time to make the 8:30 boat. He'd flown out of Logan the night before and hung around Miami International long enough to beat his *Lara Croft Relic Run* high score twice. Next, it was a ninety-minute cab ride where the driver battled Miami traffic and hurled Cuban expletives at every swerve.

Reggie picked up a few choice swears, *me cago en el coño de tu madre* being his favorite. He tipped the guy a twenty for that and the close shave.

The ferry was smaller than expected. Nothing like the Hi Line he and Mom had taken to Nantucket last summer. But it buzzed with surprising speed and turned the waves into fizz as it shredded the water, Crystal Key-bound. He sat on the top deck, hoodie pulled over his head to keep the wind away while he crept Becky's Instagram feed.

Squirrels. The embarrassment dawned on him every couple of hours. Each time the thought was resurrected, Reggie wished to crawl inside himself and die. There was a good chance Becky had long since forgotten about it. Or, she hadn't stopped laughing to her friends.

That vicious emotional circle started up in his guts again. Making things worse was Becky's Insta feed. Last night's pic made his stomach lurch. Her face mashed against some Bieber-looking white dude. Her eyes were glossed, as were his, and their mouths were twisted to the sides so their lips could touch in that cutesy social media way.

"Damn," he mumbled and closed out of the app. Why'd Mom have to go and do this to him? Because she was smart enough to know what he'd have been up to. She wouldn't have been out the door a minute before Reggie was upstairs asking Becky St. George if she wanted to Netflix and chill at his pad, which was empty for the week, by the way…

Mom kept forcing her way into his thoughts, and he realized it was because he was supposed to call her once he was on the boat. He scrolled to her contact and pressed it.

She must've been waiting by the phone. "I'm looking at a schedule that says the ferry departs at nine sharp, Reginald."

"Sorry, Ma, forgot. They said we should hit Crystal Key a little after ten."

"How was the flight?"

"Sat next to some fat dude who kept farting in his sleep."

"Oh, honey," she laughed. "I'm sorry."

"I'm out of your hair. Congratulations."

"Thanks. I'll bring you back something from Italy. Call you mid-week to check in?"

"Can't wait."

"I already talked to your father. He's headed to the ferry landing to meet you."

"Yeah, you guys don't want me getting lost on Crystal Key. Might take a few minutes to check everywhere."

"I love you, baby."

"Love you too, Ma."

He reopened Instagram with absentmindedness. In a second, he was looking at the offending picture again. Becky and Bieber. The deck was so far stacked against him, Reggie knew that he shouldn't bother. He was just a freshman in high school, at a private academy, no less. If he could just get through to Becky, though, he knew he could win her over.

Unless she only liked Bieber-lite dorks. Always a possibility, though Reggie was confident he could overcome that obstacle.

He scrolled past the offensive picture, over a few generic dinner snaps and bathroom mirror selfies. Damn, she looked fine in a few of those, especially the one where she teased her bum in blue booty shorts, flashing those golden legs. He wanted to give that one a heart. *Nah*, he thought. *Too creep-ish.*

There was more etiquette than that. The pic couldn't be too old, because then he was stalking. Definitely couldn't be the bikini pics from last summer, because then he was admitting that he was on the prowl for jackin' material.

His thumb paused on a pic that was nearly perfect. #NoFilter. Green eyes the color of rainforest stared through him. Her mouth curled into a mischief grin and a cocked eyebrow to complete the portrait. Sexy without being sexy.

Reggie's finger hovered over the heart. It hung there, dropping close to the screen but refusing to land. His chest pounded, cheeks numbing. Pins and needles shifted beneath his skin.

If he didn't do this, she'd forget all about him while he was away. His inroads would be gone. He was shoveling six feet of snow in a blizzard.

Fuck it, he thought, and pressed down on the heart.

It felt... good. It said, *'Hey, I'm thinking about you'* without laying it on too thick. Then he remembered he wasn't actually following her. He'd been too timid for that, manually searching for her feed each time he opened Insta.

He never swiped so fast. The page blurred back to the top. Had to click "follow" before she noticed the errant like, because then his strategic search was all for not. You couldn't like someone's picture that you knew IRL without following them, because then you were the creeper to end all creepers.

Boom. Followed. Reggie inhaled one great big sigh of relief. Once he got to Crystal Key, all the way on the fringes of his provider's network, he wouldn't have a chance to see the 'gram for a few days. Dad promised better Wi-Fi than on his last visit, but Dad didn't even own a smartphone. What did he know about download speeds?

Reggie tabbed out of Insta and opened his music, Flo Rida between the ears as he tipped his head back. As soon as he was comfortable, his phone buzzed with a notification. On the unlock screen, he saw it, and his heart nearly exploded.

BeckyTheSaintG is now following you.

He stared at the words and it was probably the best he'd ever felt. Indescribable triumph. He went back into Insta to make sure she hadn't accidentally followed and then unfollowed. Nope. His follower count was sitting pretty at one hundred and ninety-nine.

Another notification bubble called out from the bottom of the screen. Becky hadn't *just* followed but commented on a shot of his luggage from last night. His last post right before leaving for Logan. His caption said *By Air, By Sea, I'm Spring Breakin'.*

It wasn't his best content.

Becky wrote: OMG, have fun! The squirrels will still be here when you get back.

He closed out again, grinning like a dope. Victory was short-lived, though, because his insides suddenly stirred and bubbled. It had been this way since the cruise started, his queasiness originally disguised beneath embarrassment brought on by those damn squirrels. Now, the early morning Dunkin' breakfast sandwich was threatening to come oozing back up.

No time to find the bathroom. Reggie booked it for the railing, throwing himself against it as creamed coffee vomit flung into the sea breeze.

He turned around and saw the small handful of passengers glaring, heads shaking.

A weird looking guy on the bench behind Reggie leaned in as he returned to his seat. "Got any ginger?" he asked, eighty proof breath roaring hot against the side of Reggie's face.

"Nah, man, all out of ginger." Reggie tried to look anywhere but at this guy's busted face. He might've lost the fight with his Gillette this morning, if the forty nicks told any kind of story, and his cheeks puffed like his fillers had gone terribly wrong.

"Not for me," he said with a prevalent Spanish accent.

"You eat a little bit, stops the puke in its tracks."

Reggie put his earbuds back in. The guy kept talking anyway.

"If you feel like you have to do it again, look out on the horizon and keep your head still. Focus on whatever's out there. Bird, lighthouse, boat..."

Reggie thought his stomach was on the rebound but felt the back of his throat bubbling again and realized he wasn't done.

The stranger stood and came around to Reggie's side of the bench. He sat down beside him, locating the panic in his eyes. He pointed to the rail, excusing their conversation with a *take care of business* nod.

"I used to take a ferry to work," the stranger told him. "When I first started, I was the same way. Puked all over my shoes. Took about a year to get used to the rocking. You can beat it."

Reggie hobbled over to rail and tunneled his vision so that he was looking at the island lighthouse in the distance off the starboard side.

The stranger got up and followed. He stood at a distance that wasn't worrisome. "Ever been to the keys?"

"Just Crystal."

"I couldn't help but overhear your conversation with your mother..."

Reggie glanced over. What was this guy's deal? As soon as his eyes left the lighthouse, his stomach reeled and he was quick to return his attention to that tiny patch of land on the horizon.

This stranger disturbed him. Someone had beaten him to a pulp. It happened to Reggie once when he was eleven, a fistfight with two fourteen-year-olds who tried stealing his Air Jordans out of his locker before gym. He'd fended them off, but not without catching a few clocks to the face. The swelling had been similar.

"Why are you in my business, man?"

The stranger smiled and raised his hands. Reggie noticed the bandage on his left middle finger. The wrapping was brand new, pure white, and without a speck of dirt. Might be a fresh wound. Guy was deep into something, best to steer clear of him.

"Just being a Samaritan," he said. "Sea travel is hard for some, and I don't want you suffering the whole way."

"Yeah."

"I know how I must look to you. I wouldn't trust me in your shoes, either. I'm gonna be over there. If you need anything, just ask. Otherwise, have a good trip, my friend."

"Appreciate it," Reggie said after a minute. "I don't do this enough to get used to it."

"You will."

"Man, I hope not."

"Crystal Key that bad?"

"Not if you like to fish."

"I don't," Samaritan said.

"Then why go there?"

"Looking up an old friend," he said. "And you're visiting your Dad?"

"More like being unloaded on him."

"I'm sure he does the best he can."

Reggie's mouth twisted into a frown. The ferry was almost past the island that had served as his centering point, the rebellion in his stomach nearly quelled. He gave it another second to be sure and then went back to his seat.

Samaritan didn't follow. He stood with his back to Reggie, head following the Florida Keys as the boat left them behind. "Nice meeting you," he said and then headed to the back of the boat.

"You too," Reggie said and plugged the buds back into his ears, thinking about his newest Insta follower, plotting the ways he could impress her with photos of this trip.

It was going to have to be skillful, though. No room for error—squirrels was still a strike.

His mind went to work while Crystal Key became more than just a white line on the horizon.

Manuel waited until everyone had cleared the ferry before disembarking onto Crystal Key.

The offboarded arrivals were scattered around the Island Hoppers parking lot, reuniting with loved ones. The kid with the upset stomach stood by the metal guardrail, trying to play it cool with his father, shaking his hand but keeping his distance as the old man tried to get a hug. Poor bastard seemed grateful for any affection.

It was difficult for Manuel to watch.

A couple of the tourists headed into town by way of the sandy bike path that separated the shoreline from the inland, while others hopped a golf cart emblazoned with a logo of placid water racing off in two separate directions, the words *Shifting Tides* arched around the illustration's curve.

That's where Manuel wanted to go, though his grumbling stomach proposed alternate plans.

He found a hot dog shack a quarter mile beyond the Island Hoppers booth. A handwritten sign taped to the sliding window promised high quality surf n turf. He believed that like he believed the Earth was flat but ordered a small plate of fried clams with extra tartar sauce anyway. Then went for a Coke once he saw they stocked the Mexican kind.

"Hearty breakfast coming right up, hon," the woman inside the booth smirked.

At Manuel's age, his stomach couldn't easily handle fried foods, but he enjoyed them so much he was willing to risk indigestion. Worst case, he'd be like that kid on the ferry, puking somewhere in the shallows, then spending the rest of his morning staring at the lighthouse out in the distance.

He carried his tray to a picnic table that overlooked waves of golden sand, where seagulls served as the Crystal Key equivalent of homeless beggars, gliding through the low sky and squawking with the cutesy hope Manuel might fling a couple of scraps in their direction.

He did.

He ate to fill the hole the vodka had left in his stomach and sucked down the Coke in a few swallows. He asked the teenager wiping down the unused picnic table beside him how far of a walk it was to Shifting Tides.

"Little over two miles."

Manuel looked up at the beating sun and couldn't remember the last time he'd seen it. He was familiar with its light only when it crept in around the edges of drawn curtains. That's how he preferred it, though today he felt like a vampire being allowed to walk in daylight for the first time.

Anne could be anywhere on Crystal Key, but the photo in his pocket was taken at Shifting Tides, the resort sign visible in the distance behind her.

Once he finished eating, when much of his strength had returned, Manuel took Anne's picture in his palm and stared at her. Until he couldn't. Until every life he'd ever envisioned for her ended in the same place. In ashes. This wasn't about finding a missing girl. To Manuel, it was how he got clear of this life. It was about reconciling his failures. As a husband. A father. A man.

And what does it change once you find her?

"It's not too late to make it right," Manuel whispered.

You'd better hope so.

"What was that, sir?" the teenager sponging the tables asked.

Manuel thanked the kid for the directions and headed for the island's south side. The terrain changed from loose sand that skittered across the thin road each time the wind blew, becoming swaying blades of long grass. The sound of crashing waves soothed his roiled psyche, and the breeze rushed his hair, restyling it into a wind-burnt surfer's do.

His swollen features ached beneath the beating island sun and he crossed the barren road to move beneath the tree line. By the time Shifting Tides was visible, sweat dotted his forehead and his Hawaiian shirt was a couple shades darker beneath the arms.

The resort was impressive, even at this distance. A dock extended out from the lobby's central hub, propped up by struts that disappeared into the water. Cabanas lined the pier all the way out, and the immediate beachfront was fortified by several smaller structures. There were two restaurants, four bars, Jet Ski and surf rentals, as well as a combination convenience store-gift shop.

Manuel had to climb a sand dune to reach the last wing of his march. His ankles slipped beneath the sand as he headed down the other side, kicking off his shoes as the terrain flattened. He hot stepped along the beachfront, carrying his moccasins toward the steel drum music emanating beneath the straw roof of the bar where he was at least a decade older than the next youngest person.

Two girls looked him over from across the way. Wrinkled foreheads. Squinted eyes. Smirking lips. He ordered a double shot of vodka and turned away, didn't need their scrutinizing bullshit, wasn't going to be their afternoon mark, preferring instead to look across the beach to the crystal water rushing up against it.

Something glimmered in the distance. A little white dot became a bigger white dot that morphed into a boat, far out to sea but growing larger all the time. Getting closer.

Three men sprinted across the beach, signaling the glinting speck with waving arms as if the driver was somehow oblivious to the approaching landmass that was Crystal Key. They splashed into the Atlantic up to their hips as the GoFast Boat barreled straight toward the bar.

Manuel took his drink and headed for the commotion.

"Frank, Sam, out of the way," one of the men shouted. "He's landing right here!"

"Coming in hot!" barked another.

The speedboat sliced through the shallows like a torpedo. The three men back waded onto the beach, their shouts drowning beneath the approaching engine's growl. They dove gracelessly away from the hull as it barreled onto the sand, carving a deep indentation across the muddy beach, slumping, and then stopping where the grains were drier.

"Doctor! Now!" the driver screamed. He turned to the girl sprawled across the rear seats as the men converged on the boat. The effort to debark her was less than graceful. The driver lifted her legs over the side while the others reached for her ankles. There was a miscommunication among them, and the bottom guys didn't have a solid grip on her when the driver released her shoulders. She dropped face-down into the sand, laying like a corpse.

"Christ!" the short man with a crew cut snapped. "That's Beth."

"Where the hell's Colleen?" another man wondered.

"Get her up... up!" the crew cut shouted. He wasn't helping, only conducting. He noticed the scattered crowd down beach, closer to Shifting Tides. They had gotten up off their towels to watch the action from afar. "Shit," he sighed. Had to be the manager because no one else would care that much about spectators. "Okay, listen. Put her between the two of you, like she's drunk, you know? Then walk her around the back of reception."

"I don't know," one of the other men said. "What if she's hurt? Maybe we should bring her over there..." He gestured toward Manuel, to the bar at Manuel's back, while helping the woman up, looping her arm around his neck.

The manager ignored the suggestion. "Sam, would you give Frank a hand like I asked?" He pointed to the large glass hub that was the Shifting Tides' central building. "Call it sunstroke if anyone down there asks. Then you keep her out of sight. Understand?"

Manuel was surprised to see the one called Frank still staring at him, eyes locked from beneath his wide-brimmed hat, fingers toying with the dangling chin cord, sizing him up. Frank's other hand rested on the top of the bladed hilt on his belt, an island gunslinger who threw knives instead of bullets and wasn't keen on outsiders.

Manuel finished his double vodka and tipped the empty glass to him.

"Will you move?" Rand gave Frank's shoulder a hard shove and then the men went on the move, dragging the girl *Weekend at Bernie's* style as the driver hopped down into the sand.

"Think some of your guys can give me a hand getting her water-born again, Rand?" He spoke in a thick Jamaican accent.

"Head up to the office," Rand said. "I'll have my guys take care of it."

"Thanks."

"Least I can do, Odell."

Odell flashed a wry smile. "Girl's in shock. Dehydrated. Sun was beating on her for a few hours, but I think I found her in time."

"Thank God you happened to pass by," Rand said. "Where were you going?"

"Here," Odell laughed.

"For what?"

"Boss wanted me to syphon some of *your* damn customers for a change, man."

"Son of a bitch."

Odell gave Rand a familiar tap on the shoulder and then jogged off to catch Sam, Frank, and the unconscious girl whose feet carved little trails in the sand as they dragged her away.

"Excuse me, sir," Rand called out, moving gracelessly over the beach terrain toward Manuel. "I'm very sorry for the disturbance." He motioned to the bartender and waved one finger in a circle. "Next round's on the house, okay?" That netted a hollow cheer from the two girls who were already ordering shots of Patrón.

Manuel watched the manager hurry to catch the procession of flunkies marching back toward Shifting Tides as he attempted to process all the action.

"What are you having?" A waitress stood at Manuel's back. Behind her, a trail of small footprints tracked all the way from the bar.

"Double vodka," he told her, then motioned to the boat with his thumb. "Catch the show?"

"Doesn't even chart on this week's weirdness scale."

"What's that mean?"

"Been an eventful couple of days, let me tell you."

"Sure. Tell me."

Her courtesy smile faded, figuring him for just another asshole who couldn't distinguish between professionalism and genuine affection. "I'll get your drink."

"I'll walk with you," he said. "You can tell me all about the weirdness scale."

"I'm sure you've already heard about the red sky."

Manuel shook his head.

"Hell on Earth," she told him. "If you're a church going type, I suppose. Looked like someone was trying to burn down the night."

Manuel was too drunk for metaphors, massaging his temple as they walked.

The waitress noted his confusion. "A freaking rock the size of a planet smashed into the water. How's that?"

"Sounds bad," Manuel said.

"Not as bad as this weekend's going to be."

"Worse than hell on Earth?"

His question provoked a soft chuckle in her throat and suddenly there was a smile more authentic than that of her transactional hospitality face. "Wont' be any better," she said. "Next two days are what's standing between me and a week off. Quality time with my son but... I've talked enough."

Manuel grabbed a stool at the bar. The two girls who sized him up earlier had migrated to a booth with their Patrón and were now sitting with two guys of closer age. One of the girls caught Manuel looking and shrugged her shoulders. *You snooze, you lose.*

Manuel shrugged back as the waitress placed his double shot in front of him. He handed her a $5.

"Comped, remember?"

"This is for the long weekend," he said.

She stuffed it into her uniform's front pocket with another smirk that acknowledged his slyness. Now that her defenses were down, her warmth more genuine, Manuel realized how beautiful she was. Mid-fifties, he guessed off her age lines, though her uniform accented impressive curves while her blue eyes sparkled with youthful exuberance, framed by shiny blonde hair that ended at her jawline.

He enjoyed looking at her.

"Bob," he lied and extended his hand.

"Barbara." She shook it and noticed his wedding ring. "Where's the family today... *Bob*?"

"I'm alone. Any vacancies at Shifting Tides?"

"There's a front desk way over there that can tell you."

"What about Anne Munro? She working today?"

The question brought a sledgehammer's end to her cordiality. Barbara rolled her eyes and started for the nearest table. "Let me know when you want another drink."

"Whoa," Manuel said. "I've offended you. And I'm sorry. Anne's a friend."

Barbara nodded. She'd heard that one before. Manuel considered showing her the photo, but what would that prove? That he was a pervert who kept Polaroids of barely legal teenagers on hand.

"Look," he said. "I knew her father. Ray. I just stopped by to look in on her."

Barbara studied him, eyes falling on each cut that graced his battered face. She could've concluded that Manuel was some degenerate, here on the island looking for a good time with a bad girl. Instead, she seemed to interpret his injuries as harbingers of loyalty, the kind of guy who dove through plate glass for a friend.

A trace of warmth returned to her eyes. "Haven't seen her in a few days," she told him. "Nobody has. It's why I've been stuck here since Wednesday. She was supposed to work the weekend."

"To be honest, I wasn't really sure she worked here."

"She does, but like I said, no one's seen her."

Manuel slammed his shot back and lifted the glass. "Another one, please?"

"You in a hurry?"

"Not exactly."

"I mean, you should pace yourself."

"What I meant to say is, one more question." Manuel held out a twenty.

Barbara snatched the bill from his hand with a smirk. "Fine."

"When you're working, where do you stay?"

"Unless you're local, you stay in the staff quarters. There." Barbara pointed to the resort's lobby. "But Anne rents a room downtown. From Mrs. Blankenship."

"Got the address?"

"I think I've said enough. I mean, you seem like a good guy. Weird but…" She studied his face again and nodded, affirming her previous conclusion. "Good."

"I'm not here to make trouble for her," Manuel said. "Already told you I knew her father. I'm here as a promise to him."

"We're not friends, I—"

"Point me in the right direction." Manuel smiled. "I can do the rest."

"Pretty sure she lives on Biscayne Road. Don't know the number." She described a gray house with circular windows on the attic. And then she walked off to wait on the girls in the booth who had convinced the young men to buy them margaritas.

Manuel left another twenty beneath his glass, then started walking inland.

When he reached town, he skipped the main strip's seafood smell and cased the residential streets. Crystal Key's homes were scattered around the inner island on narrow dirt roads. Very few people here had cars. Most of the houses were within walking distance of town, and nearly everyone he passed was pedaling a bike.

Each person waved, none of that stranger's suspicion that Frank had greeted him with back at the resort.

Biscayne Road was right off the downtown strip, and Anne's house was even easier to locate. The Gothic construction was almost out of place among the rest of the summer shacks. It had two floors and an attic marked by those small circular windows just as Barbara had described. Black curtains were drawn on both floors, and Manuel walked around back. There was no motion from inside.

He went up the wooden stairs and pulled open the screen door. He knocked but the gesture returned only silence. Peering through the glass revealed shoes scattered across the linoleum.

With four to five hours until nightfall, Manuel went back into town and used his stipend to get a pair of binoculars, a beach chair, and some knockoff Oakley sunglasses spelled Oakie. He lugged all of it into Lashonda's Bar and bought himself another double vodka. Three double vodkas.

The wait staff there wasn't as courteous or as pleasing as Barbara.

Once he reclaimed his buzz, however, he headed back to Biscayne and unfolded the beach chair in the overgrowth across from Anne's backyard.

There was a clear line of sight to the rippling Atlantic,

which is what he was watching, should anyone ask. All he needed was to swivel in order to get a full view of the stairwell right to Anne's door. He was curious to see if the girl would come back, but wondered with even more eagerness who else might come looking for her.

She was hiding out here, after all.

Man, it was difficult to focus.

Reggie supposed it was good to see Dad, but when they got back to his little seaside shack, the reality of this vacation was clear.

He stepped outside after a few minutes of *How are your classes?* small talk, hoping his phone could catch a 5G signal. He was thinking about that Instagram notification again, wondering if he should respond. His heart pounded with helplessness.

BeckyTheSaintG is now following you.

The long-sought St. George gates had been thrown open, making it impossible to enjoy all this island "charm." He tried to forget about the ground he *could've* been losing to Bieber Lite, but the more he dodged his paranoia, the harder it itched. The stakes had never been greater.

And he was a thousand miles from Boston.

"Hey," Dad said from the doorway. "I upgraded the accommodations since the last time you were here. Maybe take another look before you write it off."

"I wasn't—"

"I get it," Dad said, smiling. "We're all just bumpkins out here."

"It's not that," Reggie said, dragging himself back inside the dark and shuttered living room. Sure, he was willing to look, but this was a waste of time. He needed to be exploring, finding something interesting he could talk about once he got home. Insta would serve only one purpose this week: lay foundation for the potential conversations he would have with Becky St. George.

There was no Crystal Key Adventure if all he did was sit around Dad's place moping.

At least Dad wasn't lying about the accommodations. A gigantic plasma was bolted to the living room wall, lording over the dark brown paneling. Dad had been watching a 19" tube last time, so the progress couldn't be ignored. A stack of Blu-rays were piled on the stand beside it. *Assault on Precinct 13, The Thing, They Live, Vampires*. Dad's nostalgia, but cool stuff all the same.

"I figured we'd take in a Carpenter or two for old time's sake," he said.

"Cool."

"You see that?" He pointed to the bottom shelf. An old Xbox 360 looked like it had been taken out of the box and placed down without ever being connected. "I know you like to game, and since I might have to do a little work this weekend..."

Reggie didn't have the heart to tell him that he was gaming on newer hardware now. The 360, classic that it was, was yesterday's news. Still, a nice gesture from a guy who grew up without any such luxuries.

"This is awesome," Reggie said. "Nice work, Dad."

"Mean it?"

Reggie smiled, said thanks again, and assured him that he meant it. But the prospect of wasting a week on Crystal Key continued to defeat him. Bieber Lite was on the front lines. *BeckyTheSaintG* may surrender to him.

"How's your mom?" Dad asked. He went to the kitchen and carried two bottles of Red Stripe back.

Reggie stared like it was a trap.

"Nah, man, go ahead. You ain't driving anywhere. And don't pretend you aren't drinking back in the city."

The only pretending here was Reggie making like he enjoyed beer. He drank it, masking the winces that followed each sip. The bottle was half gone when Dad asked again how Mom was.

"You guys talk, don't you?" Reggie said.

"I mean, I know what she tells *me*. But that ain't reality. It's pleasantry."

"I get that too, you know."

"She could lose her leg to diabetes and she'd still tell me she was never better. What do *you* think, man? I told you you gotta take care of her. You doing that?"

"Always," Reggie said. "She's good, I guess, but I haven't seen the guy she's taking off to Europe with."

"I don't care about that. Just want to make sure that everything's cool back East. She happy?"

"She's going to want to know the same about you."

"That a fact?"

"She's always asking if I hear from you. I think she wants to know how you're doing without asking you how you're doing."

"Shit." Dad chugged the rest of his beer. "That's the game. She gets the intel from you, she don't gotta talk to me. Know what, though? Your Mom's good people. Probably just wants to make sure I'm taking care of myself."

"Yeah," Reggie said. He figured maybe that was the truth but hadn't given it much thought.

"So," Dad pressed. "What are you gonna tell her?"

Reggie looked around. Dad was living in a bachelor's pad for sure. But everything here was like that Xbox in the cabinet:

open but untouched. The furniture had that factory fresh smell. The television's border was still covered in glossy plastic. There wasn't a crumb on the floor that he could see.

Mom talked about keeping up appearances, but this was the first time he understood what she meant. Dad lived here, but he wasn't *living* here.

"I guess you're doing okay," Reggie said.

"I'll take it," Dad laughed. "What say we take a walk and grab some lunch?"

Reggie's stomach was still queasy from the morning's cruise. His gamer's instinct thought this was the perfect opportunity to kick back and burn daylight in front of the Xbox, but the Wi-Fi situation had slowed his phone to the point it couldn't even refresh TikTok. It would be even more merciless to Xbox Live.

They headed toward town to grab food. Reggie paused at the sight of an old broken shipwreck on the beach. It had been turned into an oceanfront bar called The Captain's Patio. Reggie ran onto the sand. "Hey, take a few pics of me in front of this?"

"Thing's been here for years. What's so impressive about it?"

"It's something you don't see every day," Reggie said.

"I see it every day. Literally every day."

"C'mon, Dad." Reggie strolled into the opened hull. The broken wood had been sliced away and the sharp edges filed down for safety. The upper deck was mostly gone, leaving a clear view of the deep blue sky. He crossed his arms and leaned against the busted wall.

Dad shrugged and took a few snaps, adhering to Reggie's direction. There were no doors to the patio, but the section that had once been the captain's quarters was outfitted with a locked metal door. Dad told him all the alcohol was on mobile carts and was stored in there during off hours.

They resumed their march to town while Reggie fiddled with Insta filters, occasionally glancing at the nondescript buildings as they passed. "There's really no Dunks out here?"

"Don't remind me of the things I'm missing."

"How do you get iced coffee then?"

"You know Dunkin' doesn't have the market cornered on iced coffee, right? We've got places to eat, man." Dad pointed to a little breakfast place. "They got iced coffee in there that's better than Dunks. Best omelets ever, too. Want one?"

"I guess." Reggie was too busy posting his photo to really consider it. "Do you ever miss the mainland?"

"Hell no. Miami traffic will kill you."

"Can't be worse than Boston."

"Ain't any better. It's like... imagine Route 128 during rush hour... but all day."

"Damn."

"No suit and ties out here, either. None of that commuter shit. People on my boat work 'cause they want to work."

Reggie kept forgetting his father was a captain. Back home, he always told people Dad was a fisherman. Didn't know why. Ship captain sounded way cooler.

"Can I see the boat before we eat?"

The question made Dad swell with pride. "The dock is back by the ferry. You cool with walking that far?"

Reggie said that he was more than cool with it, though by the time they reached the harbor, he *was* starving. He stashed the urge, telling himself that Dad would order him all the burgers he could eat later on.

Dad's boat, *Eve*, bobbed at the end of the longest dock in the harbor. One of his crewmen stood on the deck, spraying the hull down with a hose as they got there. Dad introduced him as

Breyer, and the guy smiled and nodded and then got right back to his task without speaking.

"I thought Taffy was helping you," Dad said.

Breyer pointed below deck, just as another man appeared there. "Cap," the one who must've been called Taffy said. "Just got off the radio... not good news."

"The hell's that mean?"

Taffy looked Reggie over, reluctance rippling through his wrinkled face. "We should talk privately."

Dad got the gist. He motioned for his men to step inside the cabin and then closed the door. Reggie walked to the ship's bow. Up front, you could really feel the *Eve* nodding up and down on the Atlantic. He pressed his back against the cabin wall to eavesdrop on the conversation and spotted that island lighthouse in the distance. It made him wonder briefly about that blasted-ass guy from the ferry, what he was doing right now.

"Frank was just here," Taffy said. "There was an accident this morning. One of Rand's girls was found stranded at sea. She swears up and down a shark attacked her last night. Her friend fell overboard and the damn thing ate her."

"I knew it!" Breyer sounded overjoyed by the news.

"So it's definite," Dad said. "Call Parker and Zane. Get them here. We need to move fast."

"There's more, Luther," Taffy's voice wobbled as he said it.

"Okay, tell me."

"Coast Guard says they got a report of a second boat out there... somewhere between the Key and Miami. Smashed to pieces. Parker's boat."

"No," Dad said. "No way Parker goes out like that."

"Frank doesn't know what happened yet," Taffy told him.

"He just went zipping out of here ten minutes ago, headed for the coordinates the Coast Guard gave."

"They couldn't go?"

"Not with the hurricane coming. Not for a while. Luther, if there's no sign of Parker and Zane *and* we've got confirmation of a shark in these waters..."

Sharp silence settled inside the cab while Reggie's eyes drifted out across the ocean. He caught himself smiling at the thought of a shark. How's that for excitement? But a million *Shark Week* clips flashed through his mind, rinsing that smile off his face.

Nothing can happen while you're on land. He wasn't taking this lightly, not with people missing, presumed dead. But even with that, the excitement was attractive.

"How much of that did you hear?" Dad appeared on the walk space between the cabin and the rail.

"Everything."

"Let's go."

"If you gotta go do some stuff, I can..."

"Don't worry about that," Dad said. "Let's just get off the water for now."

There was a change in Dad's demeanor as they walked back. He was quiet and guarded. Friends of his were likely dead.

That had to be weird.

Reggie's phone buzzed, but he was too busy thinking of the predator out there. The ocean was everywhere they walked and he glared at it as though it was conspiring against him.

They were almost back to Dad's place when he remembered to check his phone.

BeckyTheSaintG had liked his patio pic. And that should've made him happy. It did make him happy.

Even though it had only been taken an hour ago, he

looked far happier in that picture than he felt now. Because there was something terrible in those waters, Reggie knew.

And he knew something else.

More people would die.

SHARK NIGHT

Wade Parker's boat had somehow capsized on relatively calm waters.

That's what Frank figured as he killed the *White Knife's* engine and floated toward the upside-down wreckage, his thumbs hooked into his pant pockets to prevent them from shaking. He felt sweat running down his face, and couldn't tell if it was from the heat or anxiety.

White Knife floated forward and bumped gently against the overturned hull to reveal worse surprises.

The foredeck had been eaten—at least in part. A section of the fiberglass was ripped completely away and something like a small, serrated dagger was embedded deep inside the remaining piece.

Luther Bradshaw was right.

"Goddammit," Frank hissed. He had allowed Rand Hamilton's deep pockets to encumber his judgment. Open beaches were in the best interest of Crystal Key's tourist economy, and every dime Rand paid went unreported to the IRS, making it an even sweeter deal.

But this wasn't supposed to happen.

Parker had gone to his grave because Frank hadn't wanted to believe Crystal Key had a shark problem. It wasn't like he'd been deliberately negligent. Sharks simply weren't drawn to the Keys. Sub-adult sharks often passed through as they migrated toward the Gulf, and maybe they'd wind up doing a few laps just to load up on spring fish. But this shark was a first. An unwanted tenant that haunted these waters like a poltergeist.

Frank grabbed the MF/HF marine radiotelephone, figuring he was too far out for the VHF receiver to reach the Coast Guard, and fiddled with it until he found their channel.

"Mayday... mayday... mayday. This is *White Knife*, FL 3717. Mayday. This is *White Knife*." He offered his magnetic bearing and stated he was ten miles out of Crystal Key, and that the nature of distress was a shark attack. Two persons missing and presumed overboard.

When there was no response, he repeated it again and again at two-minute intervals.

White Knife rose on the attacking swells, easing back down into agitated water only to be lifted again. Frank felt vulnerable as he stared at the wreckage that bobbed demolished atop the blue void. Its torn hull streaked with thin strands of blood that probably belonged to a man he knew.

He looked for a way to give the boat a tow, provided he could get the double braided lines around it somehow without having to jump into the water. But that wasn't going to happen since the *Louisa* was overturned. Nothing to grab onto.

He reached for his cell phone, thinking Luther should know about this.

"Tell me you have good news," Luther answered.

"No eyes on Parker or Miller, but I've got the *Louisa*. Capsized. Nearly sunk. It's been chewed through and there's blood on the hull."

Luther's quiet anger bubbled from the handset. "Once this gets out, there's going to be full blown panic on the island. Three people dead..."

"They could still be..."

"Yeah, Frank, they swam all the way to the fucking Keys."

Frank didn't press the issue further.

It was a little after four. A whole lot of daylight left. The trick was getting this boat to the authorities. Frank had been waiting on the arrival of the Monroe County medical examiner since this morning. Nester Hudson had two crispy stiffs to examine. Not only was he a no-show, he wasn't answering his phone.

"I'll be back as soon as I can raise the Coast Guard," Frank said. "Luther, keep people out of the water. Tell them whatever you need to tell them, but keep them calm. Keep them dry."

That wasn't a responsibility Luther Bradshaw should have, but what other choice was there? With two of his guys missing, Luther was likely to collect a watery militia and head out to hunt the shark himself. Bastard's temper ran so hot, Frank braced for a burn each time he shook his hand.

Whatever quality Anne saw in him was unique to her perspective.

Next, Frank dialed Rand and offered the same heads up. "It's about to blow wide open."

"Shit," Rand said. "What can you do to make sure that it doesn't?"

"Bodies are adding up. Nothing to be done about it now. Keep your guests out of the water."

"Not an option."

"Make it one."

"Shit, Frank—"

"Look, I just talked to Bradshaw, so get him in the loop and present a united front. The beach is closed until further notice, understand?"

That was the end of the call.

Frank tried placing a third, to his contact at the Coast Guard, but the phone refused to connect. He repeated the radio mayday, hyperaware of his isolation. On the starboard side, an upside-down boat taunted him with the deaths of two islanders. On the port side, a tiny speck floated in the distance.

Frank squinted through the sun, figuring it for driftwood. It might've been more than that.

Was there someone out there?

He started the engine and cut the wheel, humming toward the drift and slowing to a sputter as he neared. It was nothing but a barbed mess of seaweed tangled in a torn button-down shirt. It hadn't come from the *Louisa*.

Frank spotted another piece of drift in the distance. He drove toward that while repeating his maydays, finding a busted plank of floating wood knocking against his hull. And another after that. Then one more. Nautical breadcrumbs scattered across the Atlantic.

The trail led to Granite Island. The lighthouse sat on a paltry acre of land and had once been the tip of a really thin Key, but the rest it had eroded over time, leaving just the structure, with its paint long-faded and lookout windows gunked by decades-old soot as the only reminder that anything had ever been out here.

Frank slowed the boat and floated toward the small dock on the far side. Water around the island was a hundred feet deep. No danger of running aground.

Sprawled across the rocks was a man in sandals and khaki shorts—facedown and unresponsive. Frank called out, but there was no motion. He cupped his hands around his mouth and shouted again. One of the arms stirred. The head followed, lifting off the granite like a waking dog.

"You okay?"

The man shifted into a sitting position, searching out the sound of Frank's voice, squinting against the blinding sun. He flinched as though every muscle in his body screamed out. He touched his hands to his chest repeatedly, in disbelief, it seemed. "I'm alive," he said.

"How'd you get out here?" Frank called.

A long spell of silence took the man. He stared out across the ocean, jaw pulsing as unspoken memories returned. His face ignited in surprise as he spotted the *White Knife* floating against the dock—his first time noticing Frank.

"It came up fast," he said, nearly muted in the sea breeze. "Like a heart attack."

"The shark?"

The man nodded, speaking up. "It, uh... Pushed our boat through water like we were flying. Like we were caught in a woodchipper."

"Who's *we*?"

"My wife. I, uh, she—"

"Shit. I'm sorry."

"—got dropped into a meat grinder." He put his head into his hands and convulsed.

"Hey, buddy," Frank shouted. "How long have you been out here?"

The man's spasmic sobs had tinges of hysteria, sorrow and laughter becoming indistinguishable.

"Buddy." Frank clapped his hands and the man snapped out of it.

"What day is it?" he asked.

"Saturday."

"Been here since yesterday morning."

"Nearly two days? You're dehydrated, possibly delirious."

"It hurts to speak," the man said, his voice desert dry. "Sun beating the shit out of me this whole time."

"You try to get in the lighthouse?"

"Padlocked. Had nothing to break it with."

"I need to get you onboard," Frank said. "I'm from Crystal Key. Less than twenty miles southeast of here."

"I'm not getting back in the water," the man said, his panic returning to a boil. "I... can't do it. Those teeth... when I close my eyes..."

Frank lifted his arms out in front of his body and moved them up and down in a calming gesture. "You'll go from the dock to the boat deck. Those teeth won't get you." He remembered the dislodged tooth stabbed through the hull of Parker's boat, and figured he'd keep that one to himself.

The distress rinsed off the man's face. "You got a radio?"

"Right here." Frank gave the device a reassuring tap.

"Put a call into the Coast Guard?"

"Normally that'd be a done deal, 'cept I can't get anyone on the horn."

A terrified laugh escaped the man's throat. "I was in the Coast Guard for five years. Someone's always home."

Frank grabbed the radio and did the mayday call again, then put the receiver down and let the silence speak for itself.

"Got the right channel?"

"Channel nine. Could be that the coming storm has put more of a strain on their resources than expected, but it's still strange."

The man shook his head. "Not strange. Wrong. Storm ain't here yet, and even if it were, well, like I said... someone's always home."

"You should come with me now." Frank's hand hung nervously over the throttle. He pushed it forward and guided the *White Knife* along the dock so the castaway had less distance to travel.

The guy rose to his feet and his knees wobbled. Arthritic steps to the dock, feet shambling along the thin column of rickety wood, all of it oscillating and creaking beneath him.

"Hold on," Frank said. "Don't board until I'm ready for you." He inched the throttle forward and the boat ebbed further, brushing against the island rock. The entire boat vertical with the plank now.

The guy was eager, eyes dancing with that *I'm going for it* look.

"Not yet," Frank said, more forcefully. There was still too much of a gap between the boat and the dock.

The man didn't care. His knees bent, then he leapt. And came up short. His hands clamped down on the wall of the *White Knife* while the rest of his body splashed into the Atlantic. His eyes popped wide in shock—a silent plea for help.

Frank closed his hands around the man's chapped forearm, attempting to pull him from the ocean.

"Oh, God," the man cried, his body thrashing. "It's going to get me!"

"Not if you work with me."

The man gave his arm over to Frank and used his other one as leverage, pushing down so to hoist his body out of the drink. In a moment he was up and over the brim. Laying on the *White Knife's* floor, gasping. "You... saved... my... life..."

Frank started the engine again and threw the boat into reverse. They could introduce themselves later, once they were back on the ground at Crystal Key. He never wanted to be there so badly.

"White Knife, White Knife, Octagon over."

Channel sixty-seven. Frank had to think for a minute about what that even was. The bridge-to-bridge channel? Generally, ships used it to communicate with each another about the particulars of nautical life: navigation, weather advisories, or general caution. He hadn't thought about it since getting his ship radio license years back.

He keyed the mic and brought it close to his mouth. "*Octagon*, this is *White Knife*, over."

There was nothing else. Who was *Octagon*? He looked across the vacant ocean. The only vessels he'd seen today had been decimated by their shark problem.

And yet, someone out there wanted to talk.

He pushed down on the orange transmit button. "*Octagon*, this is *White Knife*, over."

The boat continued to sputter away from the lighthouse, but the radio was shy.

The man's breathing stabilized, and he was settled into a seat now, arms folded across his chest and stop from shivering in the breeze. "Where's that ship calling us from?" he asked.

Frank ignored him.

"Hello, *White Knife*," the radio said.

"*Octagon*, six-eight?" Channel sixty-eight encouraged open chatter, and Frank hoped the mystery vessel would be open to taking things public.

"Six-eight," *Octagon* confirmed.

Frank turned his radio knob. "You there, *Octagon*?"

"Right here, *White Knife*. Can we get your coordinates, please?"

"Depends on who you are."

"We are here to help."

That didn't make Frank feel any better.

"I think we've got visual, *White Knife*."

Frank turned back toward the lighthouse and watched the open ocean beyond it. The Florida Keys were maybe ten miles from there, but he couldn't see them. What he saw was a speck on the horizon, increasing in size with alarming rapidity.

"There you are, *White Knife*," the radio crackled. "We'll be seeing you soon. *Octagon*, out."

The ship grew out of the distance, a glistening jet-black sheen that somehow advertised sinister intentions.

A warship. Combat-ready. Headed straight for them.

Frank took the opportunity to throttle it back to Crystal Key, but he didn't feel good about leaving that behemoth to follow.

Manuel pulled a Phillips-head screwdriver from Mrs. Blankenship's open work shed. He carried it upstairs and went to work unscrewing the doorknob from Anne's door. Breaking the glass was faster, but he couldn't afford to rouse suspicion, and based on the way Wyatt Earp had looked at him on the beach earlier, he guessed he'd already done a bit too much of that.

Night had come to Crystal Key, and with zero activity around this house, Manuel decided he could risk this much. Working out in the open like he was supposed to be there. Criminals weren't usually this casual.

The knob came off easy. He placed two knuckles inside the hole to push the locking mechanism out. The door creaked open and Manuel accepted the ghostly invitation.

Anne's place was like any teenager's first apartment. Mismatched furniture and appliances. So sparsely decorated you didn't know if anyone currently lived in it. The refrigerator was one of those lead things from the fifties that somehow still functioned. Anne kept caramel-flavored coffee cream in there, along with a head of lettuce, a half-pound of sliced turkey, and a sixer of Corona along with two limes.

On the countertops were Ramen, a few boxes of Lipton tea, and a loaf of wheat bread. Either Shifting Tides wasn't paying the bills or she lived close enough to the market that every night was an impulse meal.

Manuel wanted to believe the latter.

In the living room, he found a MacBook Pro on an old coffee table that had several initials carved into it. Forgotten assholes who thought the world needed to know they'd been here. A fallen ashtray lay face-down on the heavy wood floor, grey dust scattered, half a footprint stomped into it.

Manuel lifted the laptop screen. The blue light blazed, asking for a password. He keyed in Ray Munro. His guess was rejected. The machine might as well have been a brick in his lap.

It felt wrong to invade her bedroom, but he was lacking in all modesty these days. A few sex toys were tucked under the bed: a black strap on and a pink dildo with more crafted veins than a bodybuilder's arm. At the bottom of Anne's underwear drawer was a small yellow notepad, the pages packed with scribbles. A diary.

The bed was neatly made and smelled distinctly feminine as he sat on it—some scented body scrub or berry conditioner. This was a different Anne than the little girl he remembered. A stranger. As he sifted through her penmanship, however, the familiar girl returned. Funny how handwriting never changed. Funnier how the brain allowed memories to lay dormant for years.

This was the same bubbly cursive that had once penned a Krebs Cycle essay at Manuel's kitchen table. Only this notepad wasn't interested in Biology. It was the outline of a novel featuring a protagonist called Sharon.

Sharon is a disinterested college student by day. By night, she prowls the S&M scene to pay for school, determined to find a man who can inflict on her so much pain that she might finally begin to feel alive.

"Oh honey," he said, knowing that he and Ray had done this to her. They could've traded in their guns for a food truck at any time, had spent enough time dissecting that dream to make it a reality. But dreams were for sleeping, and neither man had wanted a life of honest work. That was the truth of it. Manuel wouldn't allow himself the comfort of excuses.

Sharon thinks she's finally found salvation in the arms of an ex-solider called Wesley, running from his own war-torn demons, but a jilted lover known only as the Bleeding Eyes Man has other plans.

Manuel read through everything Anne had charted, wondering if her manuscript was on the MacBook. Sharon's story had no ending yet, according to these notes. Was it because her creator was still trying to find her own way?

The material depressed him. An endless sexual odyssey of increasingly violent and angry encounters. Sharon growing more terrified of this *Bleeding Eyes Man* who "lorded over dominion."

Manuel recognized Catholic guilt when he saw it. His back was permanently curved from carrying so much of his own.

He stuffed the notepad into his pocket, then swept the place for anything else useful. When that was all there was, he headed back to Shifting Tides.

The teenage girl at the counter greeted him with a smile so bright and genuine, she belonged at the Ritz Carlton Miami and not at the ass-end of Florida.

Manuel had to hand it to the place. Its lobby was as classy as anything you saw in the Bahamas. Ocean water ran through an interior moat that circled the room, filtered straight in from the Atlantic. Fake palm trees graced either side of the entryway, and the reception desk was a gigantic circular setup in the middle of the room—your gateway to the entire resort. On the radio, Jimmy Buffet sang about a cheeseburger in paradise, and that was all the incentive Manuel needed to hurry up and get out.

The check-in process was painless because he paid cash and used the name Bob Torres. The desk clerk didn't ask for identification, which was a refreshing change of pace. She hammered the keyboard, eyes dotting back and forth as the monitor spoke to her. She looked up with an even wider smile to report there were two rooms left. "We were expecting guests this afternoon," she said, "but the hurricane must've given them cold feet."

Manuel took the waterfront room. A teenager in khaki shorts and a green Shifting Tides T-shirt offered to help with his bags, but Manuel didn't have any. He asked for the room key, then assured the staff that he could find his own way and what he really wanted was to stop off at the bar first.

He headed down beach to where his day on the island had started. The bar there was much busier now, with a half dozen kids going hard at lime-stuffed Coronas. Those same grifter girls still there, plastered and licking Patrón shots out of each other's bellybuttons to a chorus of whoops. They could hold their liquor. Manuel would say that much.

He chose to sit in one of the lounge chairs that faced the beach.

"Well, what do you know?" Barbara said, suddenly behind him, looking like she hadn't slept in days. Her hair was tousled, and the vibrant sparkle that had lived in her blue eyes was blunted by the reality of a double shift. "Back again?"

Manuel lifted the keycard.

"Welcome," she said, a smile at the corners of her mouth. "Take it you haven't found my replacement?"

"That why you're still working?"

"I'm stuck here until Monday. What else am I going to do?"

Manuel glanced at the bar. The spring breakers had convinced the bartender to do a shot and he was looking up and down the beach to make sure the coast was clear before pouring a splash of tequila across the girl's golden belly.

"Do they tip good?" Manuel asked.

"When they get drunk enough," she said. "Or maybe I just overcharge them so it evens out. What are you having? More vodka?"

"Seven and seven," he said. "I've had too much vodka today."

"Do you think you've had too much in general?"

"How much of a tip do you expect if I order a water?"

"I'll just overcharge you."

Manuel laughed and Barbara placed a hand on his shoulder. Her gentle squeeze exorcised some of the bad energy nesting inside him. It had been there so long he just figured it was part of him.

"You're right," she said. "Seven and seven coming up."

She returned with the highball glass, and Manuel handed her a twenty. To his delight, she sat down in the chair next to him and stretched her legs while yawning. "Where do you think she is?"

"Wasn't home."

"Told you."

Manuel took a sip, sucked half of it down in a swallow. Barbara's eyes blinked with disappointment. A real alcoholic's move, she decided. Manuel didn't bother denying it. "When I asked you about Anne earlier, you jumped to a whole bunch of conclusions."

"She had a way about her. I shouldn't judge... I mean, who among us makes good life decisions?" She waited for a second and then unleashed an infectious grin that forced the corners of his mouth to push upward in reflex.

"*Least* of all me," he corrected her, then swallowed the rest of the seven and seven. "I hate drinking alone."

"You're going to have to," Barbara said. "I'm a professional."

"Your shift has to end sometime," Manuel said. His smile kept stretching. "Or, knowing you, maybe it doesn't."

"I'm always here. I'm actually a ghost."

"I've been haunted by worse."

"A ghost who's sorry if she offended you today." Barbara blinked and her eyes were refreshed, brighter than the bar light at their backs.

"Takes a lot more than that to offend me."

"So, what now?"

"I keep looking for Anne."

Her eyes roved his face, questioning his swollen features, wondering in silence what he'd done to deserve the beating. He was buzzed enough, and she was disarming enough that he might have told her, but instead she said, "I know someone who might be able to help. That girl they brought in off the ocean this morning..."

"What happened to her?"

The college kids called for another round like it was a battle cry. The bartender called to Barbara and she stirred with a groan. "She's waiting to see a doctor. I hear she's in shock. I need to go."

Manuel reached out and touched her forearm, but didn't grab. "Let them wait."

Barbara looked at the crowd, then back to Manuel. There was hesitation on her face, but the lure of a paycheck prevailed and she started back toward the bar. Manuel stared as she left, admiring her curves in those short shorts. He was a little embarrassed when she turned back around and caught him staring.

She might've been smiling in that pocket of darkness just before the bar light. "I get off work at midnight," she said. "Maybe I'll see you around."

Then she went back to work, leaving Manuel alone with his empty glass.

❧

"Bacteria," wasn't the right excuse. Nobody believed that.

Owen Bowles did a double take from the deck of his boat as Dad told him to stay on land. He added, "Frank's orders" so that he didn't have to listen to a rival fisherman accuse him of sabotaging his season.

"*Virbrio vulnificus*," Dad said, as if anyone would know what that meant. It sounded like a damn Harry Potter spell. "Nasty, flesh-eating stuff."

Bowles sulked off, mumbling beneath his breath, occasionally looking back like he expected to see father and son rushing headlong to their own boat in order to steal the ocean for themselves.

Gary Dennington was only slightly more receptive to the warning, telling Dad that he wouldn't cuss him "out of respect for your kid." It was Reggie who smoothed it over, asking why he wanted to spend a Saturday afternoon on the water when he could be home watching the Marlins spring training.

"Because the wife don't nag me when I'm night fishing," he laughed. "My phone always dies out there."

No one else on the docks put up much fight, and that was good, because Dad was more worried about the western beach. He and Reggie talked strategy together as they walked inland.

"It'll be tricky," he said. "People don't live here 'cause they like being told what to do."

"Like you?"

Dad smiled and took a minute so that topic would dissolve. "The people here... they're already on edge because of that damn meteor that dropped on us the other night."

"Seriously?" Reggie said. "That's pretty cool."

"Not to me it wasn't," Dad said. "Scared me shitless."

"You saw it?"

"I was out on the beach by the resort when the sky cracked open... I mean, that's how it looked. Then I see this... damn planet smack the water. Shit was biblical."

The entrance to the western beach was behind Lashonda's Bar where four women spread out on beach towels, baking in the late sun. Reggie admired their generous displays of golden flesh, his stare perfectly obscured behind tinted aviators. His attention narrowed to the leggy brunette closest to him. Probably just north of forty—a little chicken neck, sure, but with a body that glimmered in tanning oil. The way she used her big toe to scratch her other ankle was oddly seductive.

"Afternoon ladies," Dad said.

"Hello Luther," the brunette said with sing-songy playfulness that Reggie envied. He'd never had a girl talk to him like that.

"Frank wants the beach closed. For your own safety."

"Then go over to Shifting Tides and let Hamilton know," the brunette said. Not only slammin', but sassy, too. Reggie liked her a lot. "We're not even swimming."

"Tides is my next stop, Maura," Dad said. "I don't have time to make sure you heard me, so listen… Frank says there's bacteria in the water. Boats are grounded, people are beached. Way it is. When's Frank ever raised a false alarm?"

The women barely acknowledged that question, just shifted and stretched across their blankets.

"I trust Frank," Maura said. "We all trust him."

"That's right," Dad said. "And with the hurricane bearing down on us, he doesn't think we should be taking any unnecessary risks. Wants us to shelter in place and stay safe. We can't stay safe when people are swimming in bacteria-infested water."

"Infested?" Maura said. A few *tsks* from others echoed her concern.

Truth's worse, Reggie thought.

"So you'll stop anyone who comes down here looking to swim?" Dad said.

"We'll pass the message along." Maura caught Reggie

looking in her direction and flashed a smile that made his insides flutter.

Dad thanked the women and Reggie echoed him, realizing how stupid his parroted authority sounded as soon as they set off. He might as well have asked them about squirrels on the roof.

They walked further down beach and spoke to everyone along the way. A guy flying a kite with his son told them he had no intention of going in the water. A teenage girl with pasty skin lay beneath an umbrella reading an old school paperback by some author called Michael Slade. Six people from Shifting Tides had wandered out this way to toss a football around. They, too, agreed to stick to the sand.

Next stop was to turn the downtown shops into megaphones. If anyone came in looking for bathing suits, or sunblock, or anything else that screamed *beach day*, they were to be told "sorry, no swimming until further notice." It was already early evening and shouldn't be a problem until tomorrow and by then the storm panic should start kicking in.

"This will buy me enough time," Dad said as they walked to the resort.

"Time for what?" Reggie asked. The immediacy of his question faded beneath their crunching footfalls while they crossed a sand-strewn road beneath palm trees that flapped in the gently roiled night.

Even at Shifting Tides, there was zero resistance to Frank's edict. Timid looks from the staff, maybe. But each of them claimed that Mr. Hamilton had already closed the beaches here.

"Can we eat now?" Reggie asked. "You owe my stomach lunch and dinner."

Dad laughed. "As soon as I hear it from Rand myself."

He went inside the lobby to find the resort's owner and

told Reggie to walk the shore. Make sure they were doing what they claimed.

There were no swimmers that he could see.

The bars and restaurants were beyond capacity, the sheer number of bodies stuffed beneath the tiny structures produced loud voices and louder music. Techno beats peppered with samples of carefree laughter.

The Atlantic tide washed over the dark, compacted sand at Reggie's feet. A chill moved up his ankles, icing his blood as he considered the ferocious animal that haunted the very same water in which is feet were planted. A monster searching out prey while mutilated human remains digested in its bowels. Husbands and daughters, an indiscriminate notch on the food chain.

The shark should be easily avoidable, right? Stay out of the water and you don't get killed. The prospect of this bloodthirsty creature excited Reggie, though. Not because he wanted more death, but because he was guaranteed a picture of its body once his father killed it.

One hell of an Insta exclusive.

Dad could avoid the topic all he wanted, but he had that determined look in his eye. He was about to go hunting.

Last time Reggie had seen that look was after Mom had thrown him out. He'd stopped by and found another man at the dinner table. It was only dinner. Thai take-out from shared boxes. Didn't matter, though, because Dad's temper blazed. A table got flipped, a face punched, an ambulance called.

He left the state shortly after, swearing that Mom had done terrible things to his soul and he needed to get away. He had that look again tonight—a guy planning to do something crazy.

"How's the stomach, *amigo*?" The stranger from the ferry rose out of a lounge chair and came down from the last bar on the beach, a tropical drink inside a hollowed-out pineapple cupped in his hand. His face was still messed up and the finger bandage was freshly rolled again. Either he was neurotic, or the wound was still so fresh that it had to be changed regularly. Everything about this guy was kinda wrong.

Yet Reggie liked him.

"Still ain't had no ginger, but it's empty."

"What did I tell you about greasy food?"

"I'm trying man, it's just… I'm here with my Dad and…"

The stranger looked around and then huddled closer. "What brings you two to this side of the island? It's adults only over here… you might see something you're not supposed to."

"Like what?"

The stranger laughed and stepped aside, giving Reggie a clear glimpse of the bar. Two girls on top of it, their bathing suits pulled up into thongs, giving Miley Cyrus a run for her money by twerking to one of her shitty songs. Neither of them had much booty, but not a bad sight for a couple of skinny girls anyway. Nice enough to quicken Reggie's heartbeat.

"Okay," the stranger said. "Head back to your Dad before he thinks I'm a bad influence on you."

"Don't go in the water, man. We're closing the beach."

"*We're?*" The stranger found Reggie's deputized authority highly amusing.

"Locking it down."

"We have already heard, sorry to say." They watched as a circle of guys sprayed bottles of champagne on the dancing girls' asses, whooping and hollering so everyone around them knew *this* was the life. "Why do you think the bar's so full now? They can't float out there on alligator rafts, so they've decided to drink Shifting Tides out of alcohol."

"Looks all right to me," Reggie said.

"To you, it should." The stranger dropped his voice to a whisper. "But why are they closing the beach? Really?"

"Bacteria," Reggie said, selling the lie worse than his father did.

The stranger didn't seem to care. He was calm as he stared out at the water, his mind occupied by thoughts he didn't intend to share. He snapped out of them with a smile and nod. "Of course," he said. "Bacteria. Consider us landlocked. Tell your father that we would not dream of disobeying."

"Cool," Reggie said, watching the girls gone wild until the stranger gave a gentle nudge that inched him back the way he came.

"One more thing," he said, extending his hand. "We should be properly acquainted. Name's Bob."

"Reggie." They shook.

"I'm staying here, if you… ever need anything…"

"I'm good, man."

The stranger smiled. "I know. Stay safe, Reggie." He headed back to his seat with a slight wobble in his step.

Reggie stole a few final glances of the clapback girls and then jogged back to the lobby. Was nearly there when a scream came out of the ocean like a catapult, a human record scratch that locked him into place while plunging the bars and restaurants into immediate silence. All eyes on the water.

"Under the pier!" someone shouted.

It took a second for Reggie's brain to process what his eyes were seeing. A girl clung to one of the support struts out there. Reggie was closer than anyone else, and he was certain that his eyes were locked onto hers. Her hysteria funneled into a single, elongated word aimed squarely at him.

"Help!"

It was all she could say before a gigantic shadow burst from the surface and engulfed her lower extremities. Whatever it was struggled to push itself up out of the water, inching past her waist, along her torso. The girl screamed as the thing continued its ascent, jaws gnashing up and down, hundreds of stab wounds drawing fountains of blood that went spilling into the Atlantic.

The poor girl surrendered her grip on the strut and fell atop the water without going under, pushing off something that Reggie couldn't see. Her blood-soaked body launched toward the beach, slipping away from certain death.

Trying to escape the shark that followed.

The fish lunged for the board tucked beneath the girl's stomach, catching the foam tail in its mouth and lifting it straight into the air.

The girl tumbled off it, into the water, splashing for her life, swimming desperately as she pushed toward the sand. People spilled out of the bar, cell phones in hand to capture the action. Everyone clustered along the beachfront, cheering her on.

The fish's head flopped from side to side as it slammed the board around in tantrum, breaking it in half. Scattered pieces drifting on either side of its dark, serpentine body.

The animal bolted forward, disappearing beneath the waves, its small dorsal fin zipping toward the girl, closing the distance to her in mere seconds. Everyone on the beach jumped back, as if it might somehow begin slicing through the sand next.

The girl sensed the fish was behind her, craning her neck in time to see a massive bullet-like frame rise out of the water alongside her. A head Reggie could only describe as demonic in appearance, the unnatural fusion of fish and reptile, its expression tuned to permanent, involuntary delight.

The monster dipped beneath the water and its body began to follow, resurfacing on her other side, rising, then falling across her shoulder blades, coiling around her body like a snake.

Her eyes met Reggie's again in that moment. They popped with a kind of searching desperation. When there were no answers or solutions, but you didn't want to believe that life could end like this.

Reggie shook his head as if to apologize to her, and then the fish, the creature, whatever the hell it was, pulled her beneath the waves, leaving the terrified spectators to gasp in unison. Cell phone lights swept along the Atlantic, finding only etches of blood that rested atop the water like oil slicks.

The commotion lapsed into cemetery silence. A makeshift wake for the swimmer's untimely passing. Until finally some asked, "Does anyone see her?" A stupid question that went unanswered.

Except, there was a sudden splash just beyond the reach of the phone lights, followed by a piercing cry. The girl had shattered the surface in one final surge of life, the shark still coiled around her body. Its grip seemed to tighten—one final squeeze as breaking bones echoed all the way on shore.

Her body went limp.

Then, both she and it were gone, leaving behind patches of blood that were somehow darker than the shifting onyx water.

"Jesus," Rand Hamilton said, realizing that he was in trouble. "She was a guest."

The entire resort had watched the island's boogie shark make its long-awaited appearance, dragging nineteen-year-old Taylor Gordon to her death. The Nevada native was vacationing with her boyfriend and another young couple—the four of them sharing one of the cheaper cabanas on the far side of the resort.

The girl's friends were outraged. Threatening to sue. Luther understood that. He had walked them back to their rooms and urged them to stay inside. For their safety. He also conceded that they had every right to sue Shifting Tides into oblivion, only recommending they worry about once they got home.

Hamilton's resort had been negligent. No denying it. When clearing the beach, the idiot kid working the rental desk had somehow forgotten about his one board rental that afternoon.

Once a tiny sense of order was restored across the clientele, Rand and Luther retreated to his office. Reggie sat on a bench in the hallway, badly shaken but silent. He assured Luther he was okay, just wanted to throw himself into some iPhone game to get his head clear.

Rand closed the door. He leaned on the palms of his hands which were flat down on his desk, arms looking like they were on vibrate.

"I'm ruined."

Luther didn't know how to respond so he poured two glasses of whiskey.

"Tomorrow's ferry," Rand said. "The one that's going to take all these people home before the hurricane hits… It isn't coming."

"What?"

"Had four separate groups tell me today the Island Hoppers booth is unmanned."

"Probably had a couple sick calls."

"Gets worse," Rand said, swallowing the whiskey in a single shot. "We can't contact the mainland. No one can."

"My son did it this morning."

"Things change fast, Luther. Service has been a mess since early this afternoon. The guests are discovering this uneasy fact one-by-one. None of their cell phones can connect a call."

Luther downed his own whiskey and refilled their glasses. "Goddammit."

"They'll revolt once they realize they're trapped," Rand said.

Luther fished his cell from his pocket and dialed a few friends in Miami. The phone beeped in futility without connecting each time.

This was bad.

"I'm telling them that communications on the island are always a bit finicky. That this is business as usual."

"So we're on the clock," Luther said. "Tomorrow morning things go from bad to worse once these people realize they're not going home."

Rand took another shot. "We're telling them the ferry will be arriving on schedule—"

"You don't know that it won't."

"Come on, Luther."

Luther nodded, conceding. The time for optimism was past. Two of his men had died out on that ocean today, and there hadn't been a second to mourn them. Had to swallow his panic for the sake of his son. For the sake of the island. But he felt it now, dissolving his nerves like there was acid in his bowels.

Best now to begin anticipating the worst.

"Anyway," Rand said. "Telling them the ferry's still coming is the only thing that helped us get a handle on tonight. Thank God nobody tried leaving on this afternoon's boat because that one didn't show up either."

Luther wouldn't have minded the sight of squirming

Rand Hamilton on most days, but these problems were the island's problems.

"Where's Frank?" Rand said. "Of all the times for this fucking guy to go missing."

Luther didn't like it either. He opened the office door to make sure Reggie was still where he left him. The kid didn't even glance up from his game. Luther was glad for that, envious of his ability to escape.

When Reggie was a baby, there was nothing better than the sight of his innocent face, no sweeter song than his joyous laughter. For Luther, that purity was underscored by a sense of indescribable sadness. He eventually realized why he felt that way. It was dread. Dread for the day his son's purity got sacrificed on the altar of a cold and unforgiving world. He would've given anything to prevent it, but learned too late that fatherhood meant being there to nurture those moments.

Bad shit was gonna come. Luther, of all people, should've known that. It was how you helped your kid weather it that made you a real man.

Luther shut the door carefully so not to disturb Reggie, then kept his voice low. "This is fucked, man... missing people, zero cell phone reception..."

"We have a shark," Rand said. "The shark didn't eat our reception."

"It's connected. Too coincidental. Fireball drops out of the sky, then we got shark attacks, failing cell phones..."

"Come on," Rand said. "I thought you were smarter than that."

"Could be the ferry's just grounded because of weather."

"For a storm that hasn't hit yet?" Rand said. "The ferry isn't the only thing that hasn't shown up. The medical examiner was supposed to be here today. I have two bodies at my place, remember? They're about to decay and if that happens, the whole island will be wanting to know what I've got in *storage*."

The island was going to lose power in the coming storm. It happened to Crystal Key so often that no one batted an eye. At least half of the residents had generators, and those who didn't were always invited in by those who did for hot meals and warm showers.

If the power did blow, Luther could ask one of the restaurant owners if the bodies could be stored in one of their walk-in freezers. It was as sanitary as making soup in a toilet, but any port in a storm.

"If that happens, I'll come over to your place and move them."

"That'll be one problem dealt with. But I have another."

"We're about to have a shitload, man."

"The girl who works for me... the one who watched her friend get eaten by that shark? She's in hysterics. I'm keeping her medicated but..."

"What are you, a doctor? What do you mean, *medicated?*"

"Valium."

"Shit, you trying to do more damage? Know how many side effects you might be forcing on her?"

"What other choice is there?"

"Let her freak out," Luther said. "She's earned it."

Someone knocked on the door and then a young woman in a Shifting Tides polo appeared in the jamb. "Sir, you really should see this."

She brought them up to the lobby's second floor, past the indoor pool, small gym, and vintage arcade. On the far side was an observation deck, every railing displayed a sign that warned against drinking there. The young assistant manager gestured to the coin operated telescope that was pointed out over the water.

"Through there," she said.

"Why is everyone so nervous?" Reggie asked from behind them, having followed them up and out.

Luther's first instinct was to assure him that they weren't, but then he glimpsed himself in the kid's face and realized that he would've wanted the truth at Reggie's age. Luther's father had lied so much he didn't trust him to report the weather. Wouldn't be able to stand it if Reggie came to think of him that way.

Rand dropped a quarter in the slot and peered through the visor. "Jesus, what is that?"

"I think it's the ferry," the night manager said, breathing easy. "Better late than never."

"No way." Rand passed the viewfinder off to Luther. "It wouldn't be coming from that direction."

Luther placed his one functional eye on the eyepiece.

The profile of a large ship sat on the horizon, and he didn't need a second look to know it wasn't a ferry. He had a friend in the Navy who often waxed poetic on nautical technology. *"If you only knew what we were doing with it, you'd sleep better at night."*

Luther had always doubted that statement.

The boat out there was a modern design, resembling the Navy's Littoral Combat Ship—independence variant—that Luther's friend talked so much about. It was easy to remember because of its narrow front, like a bird's beak, that widened out at the bridge and extended to the ship's rear. The thing was capable of high sprint speed, while shallow draft and propulsion systems made it a floating fortress with endless maneuverability.

The sight of it alarmed him.

"This isn't good," Luther told them, watching the ship

crawl across the horizon, all the pieces of this puzzle clicking into place at last.

"What do they want?" Rand asked.

"It's a one ship blockade," Luther said.

Just before the lights went out.

❧

Manuel pulled out of Barbara and she collapsed onto her stomach, gasping straight into the pillow. He fell beside her, the two of them lacquered in sweat, reclaiming their breaths as the suite's central air sputtered its remaining gusts of chambered coolness, and then stalled.

"Jesus, you fucking hurt me that time." Barbara rolled onto her side and reached for something on the bed table.

"Sorry." Manuel placed a hand on the curve of her ass and gave a squeeze like he was ready to go again. "I can't control myself with you."

Barbara came back with cigarette papers and used the flat of Manuel's back to roll a joint. "You can't possibly want to go again. Three times?" She used a pink BIC to light it, then took a few deep tokes and offered it to Manuel. He waved it away.

With the joint pursed between her lips, Barbara nestled against him, draping her inner thigh across his ass as her fingers wandered his thick hair.

"I can," Manuel told her, beginning to grow against the bed sheet. "I do."

"Way you fuck, I'm glad."

"You bring it out of me."

She scoffed at that, and Manuel turned onto his side so that they faced each other. The room was already beginning to overheat in the air conditioner's absence. Barbara's body, glossy with perspiration that he had the sudden urge to lick. "I'm the one desperate enough to go to bed with Scarface," she said.

"The world is yours," he told her, then pulled her close and licked her breasts.

She laughed and pushed him away. "Okay, just... let me smoke first."

Manuel wasn't expecting to be so *willing* after tonight's horror show. Less than a week ago, he'd beaten a pedophile's brains out of his ears and sort of enjoyed the experience. It wasn't violence that unnerved him. It was how it sometimes unfolded. How that shark had somehow wrapped itself around its victim. Something no human was supposed to see.

Each time Manuel closed his eyes he saw that young girl dragged down into a cold blue hell and was desperate to feel something other than terror.

He licked Barbara's naked shoulder, savoring the saltiness of her slicked skin. Determined to please her as many times as it took to convince her of his interest. There was a semblance of guilt here, yes, that he could find satisfaction in the wake of something as terrible as that attack. But what was life if not these little moments? Happiness wherever you could find it.

Perhaps another woman somewhere could fill the void just the same, though certainly not the younger waitresses and bartenders at Shifting Tides, as Barbara's mockery implied. All of them blandly attractive, indistinguishable from the millions of spring break faces that infested Miami's beaches each year.

Manuel was no saint, would never pretend to be above the simple chemistry of physical attraction, but an experienced partner was desirable beyond animal instincts. He preferred mature women for the distinction of their age lines, and the character of their wisdom. Pillow talk. The connectivity he'd come to crave long after his body was spent and his mind continued to hunger.

A woman like Barbara had lived, made bad choices and learned from them. Knew what she wanted out of life and brought that agency into the bedroom where she was an equal partner. She was also stunning, crystalline eyes and platinum blond hair that smelled of citrus with hints of floral. A goddess, whether she believed it or not.

Manuel thought he could make her understand.

And he envied that she'd missed tonight's show. While the entirety of Shifting Tides had migrated to the beach in disbelief, Barbara had been out back fighting the padlocked liquor cage because those college kids had run through two bottles of Patrón and somehow wanted *two* more.

"Tell me about the girl who was brought in off the sea this morning," Manuel said.

"Beth."

"How is she doing?"

"She's at Hamilton's place."

"Of course she is."

Her joint had already sizzled down to a nub, every puff making her a bit friskier, her thigh pushing against him, stirring an erection. "He wants to keep her comfortable until the doctor can get out here."

"A humanitarian."

"He likes Beth 'cause she looks the way she does and 'cause she's willing to play the game to get what she wants."

"Ever play that game?"

Barbara slapped his hip like they were old lovers and then pushed her knee against his balls. "Just 'cause I'm in bed with *you* doesn't mean I'm a whore, asshole."

"Hey," Manuel said. "Just taking an interest."

"Is that so?" Barbara crushed her joint out on the bed table, then pushed Manuel onto his back and climbed on top of him.

The press of her soft thighs against his hips.

The brush of her hard nipples on his chest as she leaned down and kissed him.

That distant floral smell that danced through his nostrils.

These sensations were a resurrection. Just days ago, Manuel had been a dead man walking. His life nothing but a series of failures. And when he'd taken that fire extinguisher to DJ Muto, or Buto, or whatever the fuck, part of him had hoped Garcia would put him down for good.

Only tonight had changed everything. He stared up at his straddling angel like she was heaven-sent and felt more than physical relief coursing through him. He felt his soul. He wanted to see tomorrow.

Long, passionate kisses blotted out the world. He pulled his tongue away and lifted her head so their noses touched. Her eyes were hazy, mouth popped into a desperate o. This simple, lustful look was enough to ignite his own. Barbara felt him throbbing against her thigh and grinned as she understood the extent of her power.

Maybe now she believed him.

"Does Hamilton play *the game* with others?" Manuel asked.

"Really," she said, cooling. "Why?"

"I want to know the kind of person you're working for."

She came down for another kiss. "I'll tell you... if you satisfy me."

"I'm just getting started," Manuel said, and arranged himself so that he could enter her. Barbara slapped his chest, *no*. She had other plans, sidling up his torso until her thighs were clamped against his ears.

She came twice, palms against the wall, hips writhing on Manuel's face, her entire body engulfed in tremors, then she dropped beside him and rolled another joint. Manuel partook this time, sharing the same pillow, heads resting against each other as they passed the cigarette back and forth.

"You're really happy here?" he asked.

"Why? You gonna steal me away?"

"I couldn't steal hotel towels."

"Bet you stole more than that to get your face all cut up."

Manuel took a long hit in order to dodge the topic. "I don't exactly live in luxury back on the mainland."

"What *do* you have on the mainland?"

"An apartment... some books..."

"My dream man." Her voice was a whisper, but still somehow laced with humor. She closed her lips on his Adam's apple and sucked until a splotch of blood came to nest beneath the skin. With his defenses ground into dust, she lifted her mouth and asked, "What do you do for work? Really."

"This and that."

"Stop," she said, lifting his bandaged hand gently in between fingers, stroking the back of it. "What happened to your finger? Your face?"

"I'm in talent booking," he said, searching for an answer that was at least a little honest. "Had a high maintenance client. Asshole DJ blowing coke off my dashboard. Took my eyes off the road for one second to tell him to stop, and we got sideswiped on the Palmetto Expressway. Car went into a tailspin, smashed cement... He was okay, of course. I... I went through the windshield."

"Oh, God," Barbara said, tracing a finger down his torso to his flaccid cock, feeling it stir.

He moaned. She giggled.

"If you're in *that* business, why do you care about *me*?"

"You're a real person."

"Everybody's real."

"Not true. But you're headstrong, can give as good as you get. I need that." His body tensed beneath Barbara's touch as she continued to stroke him.

"Probably why Hamilton never wanted to play the game with me," she said.

"Won't put up with his shit?"

"I mean… I'm fifty-three," she said that like she was confessing. Manuel didn't want to say that Barbara looked good for her age because that implied concession. For her age. He simply thought she was gorgeous and hated that she felt the need to apologize for getting older. Life was one perpetual march into old age. All we could hope is that we didn't become bridge trolls.

"So what?" he said.

"Okay, look, this sounds weird, like I'm complaining because Hamilton never invited me to his place for dinner… but that's how it starts."

"What starts?"

"The preferential treatment."

"Figures."

"I've been here since we opened. Six years. Even then, forty-seven was too old for Hamilton. Asshole has always looked at me like I've got cobwebs in my cunt."

Manuel laughed and pulled her close so he could get another taste of salted flesh, licking her neck and shoulder. Barbara giggled and tugged him harder. He moaned to let her know that he approved.

"Don't think I'm complaining," she said. "I mean, yeah, in some way, I guess it's a blow to my ego that he's never so much as slapped my ass. Twisted, right? I know I'm better off, 'cause it never works out for his conquests."

"Apparently not," Manuel said. "Beth is lucky she wasn't lost at sea."

"Beth is lucky to be alive," Barbara said. "We don't send people across the ocean alone. That's the closest thing Hamilton has to a policy. Scuttlebutt says she went with Colleen. And Colleen never came back. After tonight, I'm pretty sure I know what happened to her. Why Hamilton isn't letting anyone get near Beth."

Manuel lay back, embracing Barbara's confident touch.

"God, you've got a huge dick." The weed made her giggle uncontrollably over that observation, but the humor was fleeting, her face tightening back into admiration. An expression Manuel found achingly erotic.

"I need to know how to find Beth," he said.

"Unless you're going to break into Hamilton's house while he's in it, your best bet is to wait until daylight."

"I can live with that," he said and stretched out.

Barbara swung a leg over him and slipped him inside of her in one quick motion. Manuel pushed his hips upward and they moaned in unison. "I *did* think you were looking for Anne because of her... reputation," she said. "I'm sorry if I misjudged."

"I'll try and forgive you." He stared at her silhouetted curves, only faintly lit by the moonlight reflected off the ocean.

"Although now you're fucking me, so maybe you're just content to be getting it," Barbara giggled.

"Are we fucking or talking?"

"This is your third time, thought we might slow it down." She gave his chest a playful slap.

"Anne got invited to dinner?"

"Oh yeah," Barbara moaned. "Everyone on the island wanted her."

"Where'd she disappear to?"

"I really don't know. Ask Beth."

"It's possible the shark got her."

"That'd be a coincidence."

"Why?"

"For the resort to lose two employees to that shark? I mean… lots of people are out on that water every day."

"You didn't see that thing."

"Night before she went missing, Anne, Beth, and I were on a smoke break… right out there, actually." She gestured to the bay window overlooking the ocean. The tiny stretch of space beyond it that edged right up against the pier railing. "Anne liked to talk about her guy problems."

"Hamilton?"

"Someone put a stop to that fling."

"Who?"

"Never met him," she said, starting to find her rhythm alongside Manuel's gyrations. "But he was here today. Tall black man with a scar through his eye. Good-looking, if kind of intense. Had his son with him."

"I know the kid," Manuel said. His old man was involved with Anne? He thought about the journal tucked into the drawer across the room. The pages outlining her prospective novel. A young woman's S&M adventure. The father could've been the inspiration for Anne's solider character, Wesley. The soft-hearted man who couldn't quite make her love him. Except Manuel wondered now if dad wasn't more appropriate for the *Bleeding-Eyes Man* on account of his damaged eye—Anne inadvertently leaving clues to her disappearance.

The *Bleeding-Eyes Man* was the one who terrified her main character, after all.

"Do you think the dad is dangerous?"

She shrugged. "You're all dangerous when you want to be. Can you shut up and fuck me?"

Manuel rolled them onto Barbara's back and fucked her, determined to savor this night. Business in the morning was bound to be unfortunate. Whatever Beth would have to say about Anne wasn't going to be uplifting.

So he decided to lose himself in his thrusts, in Barbara's moans. The two of them grunting and sweating and kissing and licking. Barbara taking him all the way to heaven before his world went to hell.

The frilled shark slithered through the darkness at two hundred fathoms.

He felt the passenger wiggle from somewhere inside his body, taking away another piece of his limited consciousness. The evening's kill was fresh in his stomach, but the need to eat again had returned at his passenger's demand.

The lure came, not from the island, but from the sea. He swam toward the sprawling abyss and caught pings that informed him of several men entering the water.

Through seaweed haze, it glided, paying no mind to the school of bluefish that broke around its momentum, knifing toward the intruders.

These men were unlike the others. They dove for deeper fathoms, and every trespassing kick enraged him. The shark no longer felt encumbered by a survivor's instinct. The passenger did not allow for self-preservation, it was changing him, growing his abilities while reducing his nature.

All that mattered was that he ate.

The divers came into view, and the shark realized that several were waiting for him with spear guns pointed. Other men continued to descend into the surrounding gloom, but he could not worry about them yet, cutting to his right as a flurry of spears propelled forward in bubbling haze.

Their assault enraged the shark, who opened his mouth and zig-zagged toward the nearest diver, the man unsheathing his blade, preparing for contact. The shark's head wound back, his body assuming the shape of an S as it readied his strike. The man's knife hovered overhead, but the shark ignored it, going for the other arm, raised defensively over his face.

The shark lunged and, with all three hundred teeth, trident-shaped and pointed inward toward his throat, frayed the diver's flesh down to the bone before cleaving his forearm off in a single bite.

He did not circle back, but focused instead on the next diver, coiling around the human's torso as it had done to the girl on the surfboard—an ability the shark did not inherently possess. Whatever passenger he carried in the bowels of his body and brain had granted it, enabling him to twist in ways he found surprising. A complete contempt of its evolutionary history.

The man gave a muted grunt from behind his mask, his blade sinking into the shark's skin with frantic stabs. The fish looped the diver's body, scales squeaking along the rubber suit, tightening his squeeze until he felt the human's bones buckling beneath the pressure. The subsequent crunch was fatal, the diver's rib cage shattering. The shark allowed the body to drift down toward a continental shelf where lesser predators could claim him as he unspooled himself and darted toward the next diver, who had managed to reload his gun.

The spear caught the fish through one of his flippers, sinking clean through and hindering his maneuverability, leaving a chemtrail of drizzled blood behind his charging body.

The diver dropped his weapon and swam forward, blade in hand. The shark flanked left and swung in behind the attacker's raised arm. He sunk his teeth into the human's stomach, stealing a meaty bite from his side, turning part of the diver's body into a cavernous recess that spilled with chum, the water turning into a clouded red mist dotted with morsels of floating meat.

The shark did not care about leaving the food behind. He dove in pursuit of those who had gone further below in search of something. The passenger conveyed its frustration to its host, for it was trapped in the shark with no place to go. And though it would lay eggs through the shark's feces, they would wither and die almost instantly in this water.

The passenger hated the fish, believed his body to be its prison.

The shark descended to the ocean floor and found two divers working on a pair of electrical pipes with a blazing cutting torch. Quick bursts of blinding light were a contradiction at this depth. He slowed his advance so not to foreshadow his arrival, choosing to approach their backs.

These men had a job to do and were focused on doing it.

His motionless glide carried him close, mouth hanging in anticipation. He caught the diver's head between his jaws and took it off at the neck. The body snapped limp and drifted upward.

The last man screamed through his breather and flailed for the surface. The shark caught his foot in his mouth and took his entire leg with a single bite. Another bubbly scream escaped through his breather as he clawed at the water.

The frilled shark got his other foot next, and when the diver was just an upper torso and two outstretched arms floating like a frozen specter, the shark headed back toward the island now that the thumping, irritating music was finally silenced.

HURRICANE DAY

Crystal Key bustled on Sunday morning.

Reggie was up early because Dad's place had seen a steady stream of visitors since before dawn. Reggie was cool with that, having suffered one too many nightmares about sharks, and was glad for the excuse to get up and move about.

He headed downtown to the diner for an omelet and iced coffee. The line outside Lane's Market bled onto the street, and most of the tourist shops had decided not to open at all. Their owners outfitted hurricane shutters to the front windows and packed sidewalk displays into the storage rooms out back.

Power was still out all over the island. Humming generators could be heard up and down the street, but nervous chatter was everywhere because nobody could contact the mainland. Phone and Internet were out, so Crystal Key didn't know for certain whether it was even in the storm's direct path anymore.

Dad said he was headed to the docks to use the ship's radio, thinking he could get an update that way, while his guys—Breyer and Taffy—led groups to each side of the island to keep constant eyes on the mystery ship that circled them. Fire off a flare if it, or anyone from it, got any closer to Crystal Key.

That boat was here for a reason, and everyone agreed it would eventually send a boarding party ashore. The popular theory was that it was blocking all mainland communication.

That made it an act of war.

Frank the sheriff, or whatever the hell he was, had also been by this morning, telling Dad how he had managed to evade the ship all night as it moved into the bay, trying several times to raise him on the radio. *Lure* him.

"Whatever differences we've got, Luther, now is not the time for a pissing contest," Frank had said. The two men stood in Dad's kitchen, speaking in harsh whispers with a sliver of dawn light spilling across the table between them. "I don't know what that ship wants, but I had to drift into Balmer's Cove to get away from it. My hull's scratched to hell, and I'm lucky I didn't run aground there. They're here for a reason, dammit, and it's not good."

Dad had agreed with him.

Frank volunteered to recruit volunteers. They were going to need every able body to look sharp, and with communications down, he had to go off and do it the Paul Revere way. *"The black vests are coming!"*

"Those motherfuckers don't have to answer to anyone," Dad said just before leaving for the docks. The tone in his voice, the genuine fear that lined his words, had spooked Reggie. If Dad was worried, there was good reason to be scared.

The diner was closed and boarded, so Reggie wandered without aim, nibbling on a protein bar he'd swiped from Dad's cabinet while snapping a couple pictures of storm preparation and wishing he could post them to Insta. His phone battery was at thirty percent because he'd played too much *Relic Run* last night and was now living on borrowed time. His 4G coverage was in play but continued to state NO SERVICE.

The guests of Shifting Tides were gathered at Island Hoppers, tired faces eager to catch a ride back to the mainland. Tension thrived among the crowd because the booth was empty and even the snack shack down the road had been boarded up.

"They have to send a ferry, they can't just leave us out here."

"They don't even know the trouble they'll be in... my uncle's a lawyer and this is, like, a violation of our rights or something."

"What do you mean I can't get a lobster roll?"

Reggie snapped a few pictures to document the suffering, then tucked his phone away, best to save his juice for when it was needed. To charge up, he'd have to find a house with a generator, or ask one of the few residents that had vehicles on the island.

He hurried over to the docks and found Dad sitting aboard his ship, at the controls, tinkering with the radio.

"They're blocking everything," he said. "Every damn thing."

"You can't call out on that?"

Dad put the receiver back on its cradle and shook his head.

"Excuse me." Behind them, three college-age girls stood on the dock, their rolling luggage behind them. "How much would it cost to get a ride back to Miami?"

"I'm not going to Miami," Dad said.

"Please, mister..." The girl who'd asked started to cry, sheer hysterics at the drop of a hat.

"There's a bad storm on the way," Dad said. "Everything's slowed to a crawl because of it. Best thing for you to do is get back to Shifting Tides, okay? They're putting all you up free of charge, so go hunker down."

There was more protest, offers of way more money, but all Dad had to do was point to the black gunship crawling the water on the horizon. "No one's leaving until they decide to let us go."

The girls looked out at the ocean with empty stares. They couldn't grasp this because it wasn't real for them. This was a vacation, and how could they suddenly be in danger? Reggie could read those thoughts across their stunned faces.

"Look, maybe you're stuck here another day," Dad said. "It's not the worst thing in the world."

The girls wandered off, each of their frowns more severe than the last.

Dad stepped off the boat and folded his arms across his chest. He stared at the dark ship that seemed headed in the same direction as the girls—back toward Shifting Tides.

"Maybe they're here to kill the shark, Dad," Reggie said. "Do you think that's it?"

Dad didn't answer. Didn't even try to pretend Reggie might've been right. The time for comfort was long past.

❧

Barbara's naked body was wrapped in a bed sheet, mottled hair moist from an evening well spent, her pillow daubed in sweat. No better sight on Crystal Key.

And Manuel was leaving it.

This trip wasn't about starting over. No, *cabrón*. It was about finishing strong.

It was sun up. He grabbed his blue Hawaiian shirt off the floor and put it on before sliding into linen drawstrings and tucking the semi-auto into the elastic waistband. On the way out the door, he glanced back for a second, watching Barbara's side rise and fall in contentment.

Maybe there was a way to do both. Quit this life with his head held high, do the job Garcia needed done, then swim for clearer waters. Manuel wouldn't have thought that possible, but last night's encounter with Barbara had exhumed in him emotions long buried. Everything was different now.

Shifting Tides was abandoned as Manuel walked up the pier. Nearly every door was ajar as the maid staff cleared away mountains of empties and vacuumed hangover food crumbs out of the rugs.

He headed past the lobby and moved for the trees that banded around the southwestern side of the island in a half-crescent. According to Barbara, Hamilton didn't live far and the *skinny forest*, as it was known, would take him all the way there in anonymity.

Hamilton's place was new construction. It wasn't blatantly extravagant, but a larger, more current home than any other on Crystal Key. It was affixed with every modern trapping, from automated lawn sprinklers to a grid of solar panels on the roof, and A NORAD-size radar dish in the front yard that was sectioned off by waist-high fencing.

It must've been used to provide the resort with its boast-worthy selection of cable channels, and it made sense to keep it away from the frequently drunken rabble.

A stone building brushed against the tree line—something old on Hamilton's property alongside all the new. The wooden door affixed to it seemed to be original. Faded black hinges across its front, and a knob that was a rusted, ringed latch. The small structure had no windows as Manuel walked its perimeter.

He thought he heard a flapping in there, a bird that had someone found its way inside, perhaps, but then spotted Hamilton on the vinyl porch across the yard. He closed his front door and went for the Shifting Tides golf cart that was parked on the lawn. A ten-minute walk to work, and the man was still too lazy to make the effort.

Manuel watched the cart putter off from behind the stone building and, once the coast was clear, he crossed the grass toward the house. He might've worried about being seen, about nosy eyes, but the island was too busy fortifying against the coming storm. Perfect camouflage today.

It was too easy to expect the front door be unlocked. He tried anyway and it didn't budge. Unlike the old doorknob fastened to Anne's apartment, this one didn't have screws. He went around the house, searching for vulnerabilities. There was motion in the kitchen window as he passed it, a woman in a Shifting Tides uniform wiping down the countertop, tossing a plate of half-eaten sausage into the garbage, then changing the bag.

Of course Hamilton used his help this way.

Manuel returned to the front and trotted up the porch steps, knocking. The maid answered and Manuel asked if she spoke Spanish. She did. He told her he'd just run into the boss man and there was some emergency at the resort. Hamilton needed her to get back there right away.

Manuel told her to leave everything, assuring her that he would clean up. She went rushing across the grass, toward Shifting

Tides, and Manuel slipped inside. He started a ticking clock, knowing he might only have fifteen minutes to get what he needed.

Beth was in the spare bedroom at the end of the hall. The door was open, and she was laying beneath a thin sheet—out cold and breathing heavily. A bowl of uneaten and now soggy cereal sat on the table beside her. A creased John Saul paperback folded open on her stomach.

Manuel whispered, "Beth." There was no movement at first, but he was patient. He whispered her name a second time and her body stirred, eyeballs rolling back and forth behind closed lids.

"Hey," he said, doing his best to sound like a father waking his child for Saturday morning scrambled eggs. In this moment, he could almost remember what that had been like.

Beth's eyes cracked, then fired open when she didn't recognize his voice.

"It's okay." He nodded.

"Shark!" she screamed, her face registering pure terror as her body bolted upright and the sheet tumbled off her shoulders, revealing a thin white t-shirt that stopped at the midriff.

Manuel guided her back to her pillow and reapplied the blanket. "Relax," he whispered. "You're safe."

"It was horrible," she said through bubbly sniffles, chest heaving in spastic rhythms.

"I know," Manuel said. He gave a reassuring smile while trying not to think about that monster, understanding full well her trauma. "We are going to kill it."

"It's my fault she's dead. I..."

"No one thinks that," he said. "Okay?"

"S-sure." Beth collected herself, sitting up, attempting to reconcile her emotions with Manuel's words.

"Anne Munro is missing, too," he told her.

"Can you get me out of here?" she said. "I just... can't stand this another second."

"I'll take you into town."

"Hand me my clothes?"

The only clothing was a crumpled white bikini on the dresser. He handed it to her and waited in the hallway, his back turned.

"Last time I saw Anne was, ummm, Wednesday night," Beth said, bed springs squeaking as she climbed out of bed. "We got off work at the same time and she wanted to go to Lashonda's... that's a dive bar downtown, super easy to catch free drinks in there."

Made sense. The girls that Hamilton imported were maybe a dime a dozen on Miami Beach, but not here. Here they were goddesses, and who wouldn't want to be in the presence of Aphrodite? Of course they got free drinks. It also meant that Crystal Key was an island full of Mr. Greens, Professor Plums, and Miss Scarletts—provided Anne was dead.

"Anne was into one of the regulars there," Beth said. "Older guy..."

"One eye and a facial scar," Manuel said.

"He sat with us like he usually does."

"Did Anne go out with him?" Beth shuffled across the room somewhere behind Manuel doing God knows what while he stared transfixed by a painting of a naked girl bent over a bathroom counter, about to be taken by a grizzly bear with a nuclear erection. Manuel might've laughed at the absurdity of the illustration, except it was a reminder of the type of person Anne had become involved with.

An extension of Manuel's failure. *I failed you, Ray*, he thought. *I failed us both.*

"Yeah, I guess she did go out with him," Beth said. "We partied with him sometimes. Lighthouse jams."

"That old lighthouse the ferry passes?"

"It's pretty cool at night," she said. "Gives a nice view of the Keys. Except it's dingy as hell and my asthma flares up after ten minutes. Anyway, used to go out there on Luther's boat… till he got weird."

"What's weird? Violent?"

"Nah, more like… attached."

"Obsessed?" Manuel asked. Because that might explain why, if you were Anne, you'd create a character called the *Bleeding Eyes Man* who "lorded over all dominion." A guy in your life who couldn't stand to let you go.

"He wasn't really like that," Beth said. "Just dramatic. And it's like… whatever. The guys here… old men who act like they're taking us to France when they're really just inviting us to drink cheap whiskey in an old lighthouse."

"Who else partied there?"

"I dunno… a bunch of people. Guys from the resort. A few locals… I don't know their names."

"Then tell me how Luther got weird…"

"The other night at Lashonda's, I got the sense that Anne and Luther wanted to be alone. Except every time I got within earshot of the table, they were arguing. And that's how he gets sometimes. Nice guy, but…"

"Nice guy until it's time to beat on women?"

Beth tapped Manuel on the shoulder. She had changed into her bikini and had a Shifting Tides towel draped across her shoulders, hanging down to her hips. "He just got hella jealous."

Manuel figured Hamilton might be headed back this way any time to see who was in his house. That was a confrontation he didn't need and suggested they hit the road.

They were on the front lawn, moving toward the stone structure, when Beth said, "Frank was there that night, you know. At the bar. He told Luther to stop making a scene."

"Frank's the tough guy who runs security for your boss?" Manuel asked. "Likes knives, has an allergy to sleeves?"

Beth giggled, touching his shoulder as they approached the tree line. "You're funny."

"I'm not."

"Okay," she said. "Thanks for getting me out of there. Rand has a way of making me feel like a prisoner. Pretty sure he was keeping me drugged... guess it never occurred to him to just talk to me. Calm me down that way."

Manuel forced a smile. His cheek muscles had atrophied years ago, grinning now more difficult than burpees.

"Frank's alright, though," she said. "Nice to have someone around who can keep the peace."

"Know where he lives? I'd like to swing by and see him."

"Yeah, we've all had to drive his ass home on occasion. Often has too many while at the resort. He's on Gillett Road. You'll know his place by the old muscle car he's got on cinder blocks. Always talking about how he's going to restore it..."

"After Frank told Luther to relax that night, did he?"

"Like I said, Luther got jealous, but sometimes he had a reason to... when Anne knows that she has you, she twists the knife every way possible. Flirts with other guys... talks openly about the ones she's screwed... even messed around with Luther's crewmate. She thought that would *really* fuck him up."

"Who's his crewman?"

"The guy who mixes up all his letters. Don't know his name."

They were at the trees when the unexpected flapping from inside the shed returned, what sounded like a fluttering wingspan. It startled Beth into yelping, and they traded looks of mutual confusion. Manuel reached for the latch, pulling open the door. Daylight pushed across the floor, revealing a small workbench on the far wall flanked by two Army cots.

On top of each was a body bag.

Manuel's heart raced. He stepped instinctively inside, worrying that Anne was inside one of them.

Beth tugged his elbow, a futile attempt to yank him back. "Hey, no—"

Manuel tore his arm from her grip with a ferocity that startled her. Hysteria brought a nervous tick to her face and he forced another smile to prevent it from sticking around. "It's just that I have to check. Wait in the trees so no one sees you."

"Hurry," she whimpered.

Manuel crossed the room and unzipped the nearest bag. A rush of fetid decay punched him in the nose, bile rising through his throat while he moved to the other bag. Two bodies. Both crisp, skin that was nothing more than flaking char. If one of these were Anne, he would never be able to tell. He pulled the zippers back up and covered his nose with the pit of his elbow.

He was almost back outside when the restless flapping sounded again, a crinkling bag right behind him.

The hairs on Manuel's neck understood before his brain could reach the same conclusion.

The bags were moving.

The gun found its way into Manuel's fist as two fingers the color of black and bone poked up through the zipper trail, forming a V shape as they pushed down, reopening the bag, the stench of rotten garbage blooming.

The burnt body rose out of the bag, sitting up on the cot, eyes locking on Manuel, igniting in his presence. Beside it, the other bag shifted, the corpse inside seemingly entombed inside the vinyl.

Manuel's finger rubbed the trigger, paralyzed in this moment, his free hand instinctively performing the sign of the cross.

The charred body touched down and began to shamble forward. Its distended jaw hung lower than a mouth could naturally open, and for a second, Manuel thought this poor bastard was still somehow alive and trying to communicate.

That would've been preferable.

It reached for the sledgehammer resting on the workbench. The body didn't have the strength to lift it, so the weighted end dropped to the floor, making its entire body go lopsided as its shoulder angled down with it. A tormented groan escaped into the air, and soon it was dragging the weapon across the floor, slowing its pace like an anchor.

Behind it, the other zipper finally broke, and a visibly female body sprung from her plastic prison, waving skeletal arms around like a morning stretch.

Sledge was less than ten feet away, glaring at Manuel through eyes that were like two scoops of white jelly. Just wobbly, shimmying globs. Its tongue poked out between still-white teeth, the muscle somehow slithering around in front of its scorched face. Once the body shambled into the daylight, Manuel realized the strange, animated tissue had blinking, reptilian eyes. And that its attention was homed in on him.

It wasn't a tongue at all.

The female's knees buckled as her hand scooped the screwdriver off the bench, lifting it into a menacing position. One of her eyes was still blue while the other socket was a recessed, empty hole. It was enough for Manuel, though, because Anne's eyes were green.

Manuel lined Sledge in his sights, gun trembling as he aimed.

"What is—*holy shit*," Beth screamed, her presence in the doorway suddenly blotting out the light.

Manuel fired a shot at the lumbering silhouette. The bullet caught Sledge in the neck and sent his body spinning. Blood pumped from the wound like a water bucket in an old western.

"Out!" Manuel shouted.

Beside him, the sound of Beth tumbling gracelessly in the dark, tripping and smacking down on the stone floor.

One-Eye noted this vulnerability and surged forward, moving faster than Sledge. Manuel leapt back and squeezed off two more shots, ears ringing as the corpse's head bolted back and then slowly fell forward, a thick gob of red tears gushing from the bare socket where he'd blasted through to her brain.

It didn't matter. One-Eye kept coming.

The gun swiveled back to Sledge, but One-Eye lunged forward again. Her blackened body collided with Manuel, mouth dropping, the wiggling pink appendage in her throat attacking. The slug, far wider than any tongue, snapped forward, desperate to get Manuel. He retreated against the wall.

Sledge continued to advance while One-Eye perked on Beth's whimpers, pivoting, then storming for her. Beth was crab-walking out the door, too startled, too terrified to get to her feet.

One-Eye threw herself down on top of the girl, her weight knocking Beth flat against the stone. The corpse's gnarled body struggled to assert its dominance over the flailing, hysterical girl, pinning her arms with her skeletal limbs. Beth cried out and the slithering tongue creature lapped one side of her face, leaving a thick trail of crusted slime behind.

The worm leapt from One-Eye's mouth to Beth's stomach, crawling up between her bikini breasts like a landing strip. Her hands grabbed for it, but the sucker moved fast, and her scream was an invitation to let it in through the front door. The creature disappeared into her mouth, Beth's throat flexing and pulsing as whatever the hell it was slithered straight down inside of her.

One-Eye glared at Manuel, her blue eye blazing with triumph. Her lower body bulged as another one of those things dislodged itself from whatever part of the body it was nesting in, her stomach rippling, then her chest. It slithered up through her throat, assuming the same posting the other one had held. The living tongue waved tauntingly to Manuel as the corpse started rising to her feet.

Manuel fired at Sledge again, another bullet to keep it back. The bullet caught him between the eyes and didn't so much as knock him off step. The brain wasn't driving anymore.

In the puddle of daylight, Manuel glimpsed the length of Sledge's body, where what remained of his genitals had melted into the side of his thigh. Neither of these corpses were Anne.

Sledge was nearly to him, and One-Eye was back on her feet. If they converged on him, he'd be trapped. Manuel lowered his shoulder and threw his weight into a charge as he stormed for the thin latch of sunshine.

He knocked One-Eye aside, hopped over Beth's seizing body in the doorway, and was back in fresh air. Over his shoulder, the primitive stone shed was something out of a nightmare, and the pulsing Crystal Key sun seemed alien now. The world, suddenly different.

Manuel threw his weight against the door and it clicked

into the jamb. There was no lock. No way to keep them inside.

The sledgehammer scraped across the stone floor. Nails on a chalkboard. There were *three* gravelly groans inside now. Three shrieking whines from the creatures living inside their hosts.

Manuel couldn't burn a stone shed, and he had nothing with which to light the bodies. His first instinct was to run back to Shifting Tides, but most of the people there had cleared out for the day.

The town was far more vulnerable, even if they weren't going to want to hear doomsday cries from a stranger.

This was a crossroads, and the decision was harder than it should've been. All he cared about was Barbara.

But if he didn't make the right call, things were going to get much worse. And nobody was going anywhere for a while.

"Shit," Manuel said, and rushed toward town, his eyes catching sight of the military ship gliding across water in the distance.

The shark circled the island, aware of the large ship above him, floating endlessly along the surface. A constant irritant.

Instinctively, the fish believed its presence to mean danger. He might've preferred to avoid it altogether, but his passenger was curious and forced him to ascend to ten fathoms, bulleting back and forth along the inclining ocean floor, tips of coral tickling his underbelly as he swam.

The passenger filled its host with impatient rage. Its pincers reaching further into the shark's basilhyal cartilage, causing him to twist in pain while new urges filtered through his thoughts, telling him to attack the vessel above.

Over his thirty-year lifespan, the shark had never felt so helpless. This betrayal of long-honed survival instincts made his anger pulse. The passenger, this invader, wanted him to get caught.

To the shark, this meant death.

He swam up the continental slope, arriving in the shallows, determined to ignore these new and intrusive thought patterns. The passenger realized there was a struggle. Didn't seem to care.

Because the fish was already hungry again. And would do anything to eat.

❧

Dad set up a lookout at Crystal Key's highest elevation, a hillside that sported a couple of newer residences in a cul de sac at its top.

They blocked off the narrow and winding road with two SUVs, forcing any invading army onto the trail that ran along the north ridge where a couple volunteers crouched in wait with assault rifles.

Dad's command center was on the flat roof of Joe Gottlieb's garage. This vantage point allowed him to watch his guys spread along the coast in every direction to ensure the proverbial invaders never got further than the sand. They had their orders: blast some fire into the sky at first sight to call the cavalry.

Breyer was tucked into some rocks along the northeast cove while Taffy sat perched on a lifeguard tower in the northwest. They had recruited locals to the cause, so the Lookout Militia was dispersed in all directions: center north, east, south, and west, with a few bodies patrolling the shorelines as fail safes.

Frank had signed off on the plan. They would swap bodies every eight hours. Had to keep people fresh and on point. A solid strategy for now, but once the storm got underway, flares would be as effective as farting in a blizzard.

"That's what they're waiting for, you know," Dad said.

"We don't even know if the storm's going to hit, right?" Reggie said.

"That boat is telling us all we need to know." Dad looked out across the island, at the treetops dancing in the wind. "We're taking a direct hit, and once we do, they'll be coming ashore."

That sinister calculation terrified Reggie more than any shark. He walked down off the roof and went into the garage, looking at the collection of guns spread out on the folding table before him. Frank came in and placed two more pistols on the end.

"That's the last of them," he said. "Everything our people are willing to hand over, that is."

"It's a lot," Reggie said.

"Enough for us to arm every man in our well-regulated militia," Frank said.

"Didn't realize so many people would be glad to hand over their shit."

"They see that ship out there just like we do," Frank said. "They know what it means."

Here was one way to stave off panic. Execute a plan. The arsenal was their last resort, Crystal Key holding the high ground if it came to that. Last thing Frank wanted was a panic, so he whispered into the ears of people he knew could handle it, telling them to get everyone up to Joe Gottlieb's place if things started going sideways.

Dad disagreed, felt everyone should come up immediately. Safety in numbers. But, again, people lived on Crystal Key because they didn't want to be told what to do. Not even in an emergency.

A gunshot tore through the sky from the south. Overhead,

Dad's rapid footsteps crossed the roof to investigate. Then he came downstairs and hovered in the side door. "Did you hear that?"

"I'll go check it out," Frank said. "Just take care of our guest."

Reggie turned toward the mainlander slumped in the corner, splayed out in a tri-colored beach chair. Frank had picked him up on Granite Island, hardly conscious. He wheezed like his lung had been punctured and shouted warnings about sharks whenever he was conscious enough to do so. Didn't matter how many times Reggie told him they all knew about the fish. He screamed anyway, like a man whose soul was on fire.

That's how Dad described it. Reggie thought it was too dramatic. He crossed the garage and readjusted the mainlander's thick blanket so that it covered him shoulder to foot, hoping comfort would keep him out of commission.

Dad pulled a bottle of Red Stripe from the cooler and flung the cap. He swallowed half of it and sat in silence for a long time. "Sometimes, man, I think I'm cursed. Nothing I do is ever the right thing."

The heavy look in his eye dragged the rest of his features into a slouch that made him look years older than he was.

"When you were born," he said, "I used to stay up with you at night while your mom slept. She was the one studying law, trying to make the family stronger. And I didn't mind 'cause I got to hang with you." He chuckled at the presence of some private memory. "Hell, you weren't any bigger than a loaf of Italian then. Still can't believe you were ever that small."

Reggie had seen pictures. It never fully sunk in that he was looking at himself cradled in Dad's arms. A concept too abstract to reconcile.

"They tell you that you gotta be careful when you bring

a baby home from the hospital. And you don't really know what's up, 'cause you're in a daze. Feed him every couple hours, don't let him go on his stomach. Let him cry, but not *too* much... Too much means shit's wrong. Know what, man? Through all that, what some might call inconvenience, I looked at you with nothing but appreciation. 'Cause for as much work as I had to do to keep you alive, keep you healthy, you were the one saving my life. Corny shit, right? I know that, but it's true."

"Why you saying all this?"

"I got no idea, man. Look around you. I don't know how any of this'll go, and I need to clear the air."

"Clear the air," Reggie said.

"It means... I'm sorry for leaving you and your mother." Dad's eye blazed for a second. "You got older, started figuring things out for yourself and I... I guess I self-destructed when I should've fought. That was the wrong lesson to teach you, man. That's what your mother says, and part of her job is to read people for a living. I worried so much about protecting you from a bad world that I got sucked into its misery machine instead."

"Mom's got an answer for everything."

"That's the truth," he said, forcing a laugh. "But, man, I really thought I was going to make this a great vacation for you. For us."

"It started out okay," Reggie said. "Not sure any of this is your fault."

He laughed again. "When your mother asked if I could watch you, I was more excited than I've been in a long time. Spent weeks planning for your stay and then——"

He realized he'd gone a few minutes without a drink. For some reason, it was easier for guys like him to bare their souls over a procession of empty beer bottles. He took another from the cooler and didn't resume his thought until after the cap was popped. "I've been going through some stuff."

The *stuff* turned out to be some girl called Anne. Dad was pretty sure he loved her. Yeah, it was awkward because she was nineteen years old—just six years older than Reggie, but it was different. She had a hard life and grew up fast. They found each other through shared memories of terrible decisions and regret. Misery fucked company.

"So where is she?" Reggie said.

"That's the question everyone's asking." Dad emptied his Red Stripe in a single glug.

"What do you think happened?"

"I think she went for a swim," he said. "Only thing that makes sense, given what else we know. That's the feeling I've got, anyway."

"That's why you didn't want me visiting at first? I heard Mom talking to you on the phone about it."

"Absolutely." Dad grinned, a momentary flash of pride for his perceptive son. "But I figured even if it was a shark, you could still come. I mean, yeah… we probably weren't gonna go snorkeling or whatever shit, but it'd be cool."

"I don't know about that."

"Your Mom works hard and needed the getaway. I thought you coming here would be a good thing for the both of us. I need to do right by you. Can't be like my old man. I can't—"

"It hasn't worked out too well for me either," Reggie said.

Dad cracked a smile and took two more beers out the cooler. "The doctor is in, my man."

Reggie paced the garage, carrying the sloshing bottle, finding it difficult to open up. Dad had never really been a *Dad*, but more of a weird, older friend. That meant he could probably help. So Reggie told him all about Becky St. George with the same kind of admiration that he used to describe Taylor Swift.

"I'm guessing you like her."

"A lot," Reggie said.

"Then you'll make it happen," Dad said. "Last thing you should do is let a girl know just how much she means to you... at this point. Not saying you play games, just don't be desperate. Going radio silent for a few days, whether it's by choice or not, is the best thing you can do right now. Trust me."

It might've been good advice, but it wasn't what Reggie wanted to hear, so he felt no comfort. He gulped down his Red Stripe as he looked out on the dead end street.

"Guess I should check the roof again," Dad said. He grabbed his rifle and headed for the stairs.

"Where's the ship now?" Reggie asked, hoping it was still out there somewhere. That everyone was wrong about its intentions.

Dad had the binoculars up to his face when Reggie came up. There was a long spell of silence as he scanned the ocean in every direction. "Don't see it anymore."

It was early afternoon, but the storm was coming and the sky had turned gunmetal grey.

Cold air breezed off the Atlantic and Reggie shivered. Below, Frank's mainlander began to scream about the water again, about his wife coming apart in the shark's mouth, and Reggie looked out on rushing waves with a crushing sense of dread.

Frank dropped his walkie-talkie as he pulled onto Rand Hamilton's property and saw the stone shack door hanging off its hinge.

Oh shit, he thought, his cart skidding across the grass, leaving riveted tracks arched across it. He sprinted for the shed, catching motion in his peripheral.

Beth stood on the porch, leaning over the vinyl rail in a white bikini top, plentiful breasts nearly spilling from the fabric. Frank was so startled by the unexpected sight it took a moment to notice fresh cuts on her stomach and cheeks.

"What happened, Beth?"

She flashed a tight-lipped smile, almost naughty.

Frank went to her on the porch and her smile stretched wider as he approached.

He saw that her thighs were scraped and bleeding. Charred flakes dusted across her skin like when he and Luther had moved the burnt bodies from the reeds.

Frank glanced at the shed door behind him, then back to Beth, putting it together. "Why'd you go in there?"

She shook her head and reached behind her back. In a second, her top came free, the smeared white fabric of her bikini gliding down her battered arms. Her breasts offered a liberated bounce and Frank stepped back, stunned by the gesture.

She was more dazed than when they'd pulled her off the ocean. And what had she done to those bodies that hers was covered in burnt crust?

"Let me get you back inside."

Frank opened the front door and Beth followed him inside. He was on his way down the hall to find her some clothes when the lock clicked. The unexpected sound stopped him in his tracks. Beth leaned against the door, one finger raised to her mouth. She kissed it, signaling the need for silence, then shimmied out of her bikini bottom.

Hamilton's place was the only house on the island with

a permanent generator. The light above the kitchen was on, meaning it still had juice. Beth moved forward, hips slamming in a seductive saunter. Frank thought about getting her under the stream of a warm shower. Whatever had caused her to go inside that shed, she was in shock from what she'd discovered.

And if she still wanted to play after, well, at least she'd be clean.

"Come on," he said and reached for her hand, warming to the idea of giving her what she wanted.

Beth nodded and accepted his fingers. Her eyes narrowed and her lips pursed.

Frank couldn't resist this tender piece. His decorum slipped away as his blood flow shifted downward to his hips. Her body stepped to his, a gentle ebb as he took her in his arms. His hands glided across scuffed but lovely flesh. He brought his mouth to her neck, licking and sucking.

Beth's throat chirred. He felt it vibrate. Something on the other side of her skin, pressing, stretching her throat outward.

Frank pushed her away as Beth's smile became a gaping grin. Her tongue squeezed between her lips like a child blowing raspberries. The chirring grew louder as her mouth widened and the tongue wavered out in front of her face, rising vertically like a charmed snake.

A guttural wail passed through Beth, some part of her protesting the pink slug that dangled from her mouth. Tears streaked down the sides of her face and her eyes shimmered with desperation. She fell to her knees, but her arms did nothing to assail the gliding creature.

It was as though she'd given up. Or couldn't fight.

Frank pulled his gun, which did nothing to curtail the creature's striking motions.

"Shit," he said. "I'm sorry, girl." Then he fired.

❧

The streets of Crystal Key were so empty it could've been Thanksgiving morning.

The only place still unshuttered was Lashonda's, and nobody there was hearing anything Manuel had to say. He kept going back to that stone shed on Hamilton's land. A pivotal moment in his life, like finding out at nine there's no Santa Claus and the guy at the mall is really just some unemployed actor.

Rising corpses and controlling worms could jangle you like that.

Make you feel less in control.

"Frank's gone over there to check it out," the guy with the mesh trucker hat said. "I just talked to him." He had a walkie-talkie on the table. "You picked the right day to give us a campfire yarn, I'll say that."

"It's no yarn."

"I know," the trucker hat said. "I'm saying we're in a believing mood."

Manuel threw back the Stoli double, hoping he could burn the memories away. But when had that ever worked? His eyes kept clocking the entrance to Lashonda's, expecting intruders. Those *things* had probably already escaped the shed. What could Frank do against them? His gunslinger shtick wasn't going to scare slugs.

Still, if anyone was going to sound the warning bell on this island, it would have to be Frank. This wasn't the type of place that listened to brown-skinned strangers, believing mood or not.

Manuel's ears tuned on the chatter coming from the tables. The locals were quick to debate everything from the mystery ship to Frank's gun collection. They weren't happy about any of it.

An island without power meant lukewarm beer on its way to skunktown. Since you couldn't bring ice-cold beer back from the brink, and because Lashonda was too cheap to get a generator, she was giving it all away. Two for the price of one.

Tempers were already soggy.

The regulars traded conspiracy theories like watercooler gossip: this was a government experiment, Frank was doing some of the dirty work for them by disarming everyone, the shark was a kind of military drone. It got crazier as each table became a bastion for depleted longnecks.

Manuel asked the bartender for a Stoli refill. She placed the rest of the bottle down with a *do it yourself* smile. If this was *the* Lashonda, then he liked her management style.

"It's a goddamn extermination party," someone said. "You watch."

"The government would never do that to its own people," another said.

Manuel laughed. He had no love for the government. Uncle Sam didn't give a shit about anyone, and some people still needed to learn that lesson.

"I'm talking to you, mister."

The locals had gotten bored with their speculation and turned their attention to Manuel.

"I said where'd you come from?"

"Shifting Tides," he said, and sipped his vodka.

"You seem a little too old for that place."

"Nobody there carded me when they took my money."

"You're on vacation... alone?" The interrogator in the trucker hat took the opportunity to stand. He brushed his walkie-talkie aside and shuffled forward. A deep beard obscured much of his face, and there was no shirt beneath the camouflaged vest, just Brillo pad chest hair. He carried an armful of empties across the room and placed them on the bar, swiveling his attention toward Manuel.

"I am," Manuel said.

"Where from? Why here?"

"Sarasota," Manuel said. "Heard Crystal Key was a good place to get away from it all."

"No doubt." The man extended his hand. "Owen Bowles, friend."

"Bob," Manuel said and shook it.

Bowles gave it a hard squeeze, looking him in the eye and judging his reaction. Manuel let him have the grip.

"Bob what?" Bowles said and let go.

"Bob Torres," he said.

"What kind of work do you do, *Bob Torres*, that you gotta get away from?"

Manuel drained his glass, knowing that Bowles was looking for a reaction. Wanted to see shaking hands, hear a wavering tone. Anything that could brand him a liar.

"I'm a chef," he said, drawing on long-dormant career wishes. "Had a little taco truck outside of Sarasota for fifteen years. *El Hupil*."

"Damn," Bowles said. "How much would it take to get you to do that here? When I want tacos, it's an hour to the mainland."

"Sold the truck," Manuel said. "Looking for the right place to settle."

"See, people don't usually look this far south. We're on the literal edge of the United States, and when you settle down on Crystal Key, it's usually because you're trying to leave something behind."

Manuel asked Lashonda for another glass. She lifted one onto the bar's surface. He filled both and pushed one over to Bowles.

"What are you running from, Owen?"

"Everything." He laughed and took the glass. "Thirty years in law enforcement makes a man hate everyone the same. Got my own business now, my own crew, and I get to spend my days doing what I love. Catching fish. Getting paid for it. That's the American Dream right there."

"Amen," Manuel said.

"I gotta ask you this, Bob. No one ever got rich selling a taco truck. You ain't affording real estate on that dime."

"Was only looking," Manuel said.

"Settle a bet," Bowles said. "A few of us think you're legit. See, we get perverts like you every once in a while. Guys hiding from their wives, pretending to be someone they're not so they can take advantage of the drunk single girls staying on the other side of the island. You got wild oats to sew, that's not any of my business. And maybe you stumbled across some weird shit on Hamilton's land just like you said but… maybe not."

Manuel tensed, feeling the noose tighten.

"I don't think that's the case, though," Bowels said. He downed his vodka and slammed the glass on the bar top. A test to see how wound up Manuel was. He'd been intimidated by much, much worse and didn't so much as flinch. "You come in here with a story about… infections, and I start wondering if you're not trying to start a panic."

"I was just here to relax," Manuel said.

"I doubt it. I told you I'm coming off three decades in law enforcement, so don't talk to me like I just carried my fishing pole in from the bog. You don't get as far as I have without picking up a trick or two. I thought I caught it when you first walked in, but I wasn't looking that closely then."

"Caught what?"

"See, you're pretty comfortable about it, and now that I look you over, I see a bunch of other tells. Your bandage, for one. Your swollen face for two. And just before I put the bottles down, I saw you adjust your shirt. It's a tell, Bob. So now I'm wondering what a former taco truck chef is doing on Crystal Key with a handgun stuffed into his pants like some two-bit thug."

Manuel finished off the vodka, needing every last drop to keep his heart rate tempered. "I'm here for the reasons I said. And there's nothing illegal about a conceal carry."

"Am I talking to you about legalities? If you're here to fuck drunk college girls, you don't need a weapon. If you're here to fuck drunk college girls, you're sitting alone in a bar on the other side of the island. Now some of my friends think you're legit, but I don't. You just happened to arrive before the ship did. Now you've got a story about Rand Hamilton's place... and you're sizing us up, that it? See what we've got before your men move in."

Manuel wanted to tell Owen Bowles, and all the rest of them, that he was mistaken. But panic had seized them, and Manuel was the outsider who would inevitably bear the brunt of their aggression. So he saved his breath, watching as Bowles reached behind his back. A click signaled the unsnapping of his holster flap.

Manuel went for his own gun a second too late. Bowles' hand swung back around with a Beretta in it.

"Okay," Manuel said. "Listen..."

It was too late for that, though. Bowles' drinking buddies were invested. They moved toward the bar and surrounded Manuel.

"A bit of free advice," one of them said. "Keep your fucking mouth shut." He reached into Manuel's waistband and confiscated his pistol.

"We should talk somewhere else," Bowles said. "Like your room at Shifting Tides. If I'm convinced you're telling the truth after we search your shit, I'll build you a house on here myself."

"I get the sense I wouldn't be welcome," Manuel said.

"I got an instinct about these things, mister, and your timing's too damn coincidental."

No shit.

They pulled Manuel off the barstool and escorted him to the door, pushing him through it, into the streets of downtown Crystal Key. The Bowles procession spilled out around him, and then the door to Lashonda's slammed and clicked.

They headed for Shifting Tides beneath a sky that was almost black. The wind swirled and blew so hard they had to lower their shoulders to move against it.

The storm was coming.

ISLAND OF THE CREEPS

Kathy Roth woke from an early sleep. A stir of commotion in the distance had denied her a trip to dreamland, where she hoped to pass the majority of Hurricane Margot's rage.

This was not the first time she had been awakened by raucous kids boozing their way through spring break. That damn resort. This was exactly what she told them would happen when the island's board decided they wanted to be in the Rand Hamilton business.

Whatever boom to their private economy Shifting Tides had guaranteed, she hadn't wanted it at the expense of tranquility.

Without electricity, there was no way to tell time. It was late, or it looked late because the only color outside Kathy's window was shadow. It reached through the pane, spreading darkness across her floor and walls. She rolled onto her side and grabbed the second pillow to stuff over her head, wishing she hadn't procrastinated on ordering those earplugs.

It wasn't any distant shouting that riled her, she realized.

It was scratching somewhere downstairs. Same way the family dog used to paw at the door when he wanted to come in for the night. Maybe it was some poor stray looking for storm shelter, but Kathy was so damn allergic to the beasts she wasn't willing to ride out the hurricane with one.

She wrapped the pillow around her head, then realized the scuffing wasn't coming from the street at all. Whatever was down there was already inside.

Her nightgown billowed out behind her as she flew across the room and lifted the baseball bat stuffed behind the dresser— an old habit from when Warren was alive. Whoever was down there was guaranteed a crack across the face for scaring her half to death. After that, she'd decide whether they could stay.

Downstairs was her antique shop, tables overfilled with knick-knacks and scattered décor from local woodworkers. The front door thumped against the jamb, conjuring a loud rattle with every wind gust. Hers was the only shop on the island without a glass window front, so Kathy never had been compelled to deal with storm boards. Might've bought herself a good night's sleep if she had.

She touched her fingers to her thumping chest, beginning to calm as she scanned the room for any shelf or table light enough to push in front of the door.

The intruder stood in the far corner. A dark figure with its nose to the storage cellar door. It didn't seem to notice Kathy at the foot of the stairs as it pressed its face up against the entrance, teeth scraping along the wood. Trying to eat its way inside.

There were no police to call on Crystal Key. Kathy was on her own. And it wasn't enough to scare somebody like this off. You had to hurt them.

Her fingers curled around the bat, solidifying her grip as she snuck forward. The howling wind camouflaged creaking floorboards as she approached.

The intruder turned in time to see Kathy lift the bat. Muted moonlight crawled through the small window and lived high on the flower wallpaper. Rustling branches hovered just beyond the pane, rendered as skeletal fingers pointing to the trespasser, drawing attention to its smoldered, bleeding face.

Kathy screamed.

Soulless white eye sockets glared through her. Teeth without lips chattered. Dried blood ran a trail from the bullet hole between its eyes to the frayed tip of its chin. Bone hands reached out and clasped her cheeks, pulling her right up against its deathly visage.

The bat tumbled from Kathy's fist and rolled out of reach with a clatter.

Her chest constricted, piercing pain rushed through her shoulders and arms. Breath became a commodity she could no longer afford. All of this was before the intruder's tongue crawled from its dead mouth, slithering through the air toward her lips.

High-pitched and enthusiastic humming filled the room like a night bird tweeting from some high flung power lines.

The creature's slime-crusted head brushed against Kathy's chin, frosting her flesh with thick goo. It latched onto her bottom lip with a bite. A sharp pinch in the loose flap of skin there, warm blood spurting free. Another delighted whine as the slug rappelled up her sheer face, forgoing her gasping mouth in favor of a twitching eye.

Teeth that Kathy couldn't see chomped through her conjunctiva's protective layer, then the slug went burrowing straight through her cornea. Searing discomfort, as if someone had submerged their thumb in a tub of Vaseline and pushed it straight through her eye.

Her vision fell away like the flick of a light. And then those squeaks were living inside her head.

❧

"Are you feeling better?" Colby called from down the hall.

Maura stared at herself in the kitchen window, where her reflection was half-formed—a ghost peering in from the spirit world.

The question passed through her head like a dream. There for a moment, gone the next. She frowned. Her entire afternoon had been like this. In fugue. At lunch, she'd ordered a half size of raw oysters from the Crystal Thyme, then brought it back home to continue storm proofing.

They must've been spoiled, she thought. Great. Now they were spoiling her plans.

Last Maura had seen, they were projecting a long storm. Nothing to do in weather like this except stay cozy. That's where Colby came in. His big arms and broad shoulders, specifically.

She didn't want to be distracted by breaking glass or falling grills, meaning the windows got reinforced, the yard swept clear—everything thrown hastily into the shed—so that she might enjoy her evening.

Yeah, she thought. *You're feeling better. You're going to enjoy your evening.*

There was an empty wine bottle in her hand and Maura

stared at it. Did she just down this? Or had she come out here to grab a refill because she and Colby were drinking too much of it?

Maura shrugged and grabbed another bottle off the counter, carrying it back through the house.

The bedroom was pure ambiance. Mood oil burned in ceramic trays atop the dresser and bureau, filling the room with a relaxing sandalwood scent. Flickering candles were strategically placed, throwing shadows across the ruffled mattress where Colby waited, naked and harder than a math problem.

Screw it, she thought and popped the cork. She tossed it at Colby and it bounced off his erection, which made her double over in a fit of hysteria. "Pin shot," she snorted.

Colby barely reacted, smirking with his hands behind his head. King shit at twenty-four, completely accepting of his place here. Maura's boy toy.

The wine sloshed in Maura's fist as she climbed onto the bed, got on her knees, and handed it off. Colby rose to meet her, stealing a couple of quick swallows, mumbling something about "fuel injection" as she slid her robe from her shoulders and reclaimed the bottle. She poured it against her collarbone, letting it cascade down between her breasts, giggling again as rushing liquid ticked her belly.

Colby slapped his hands around her ass, locking Maura into place as he slurped the flowing wine like an animal. She eased him back against the bed and grinned, her hands wandering his hardened pecs, squeezing, appreciating his sculpted body. No end to her admiration.

Her head throbbed. Even worse, her stomach felt loose, something pushing on her intestines, keeping her in perpetual discomfort. The raw oyster lunch, a terrible idea.

Colby stretched his mouth and sidled his jaw to show

that he was capable and willing. That he knew precisely what she wanted. Maura glided up, her thighs scuffing his cheeks as she sat on top of his face. No amount of discomfort was going to prevent her from getting *hers*.

Except her bowels retched, this time accompanied by the sensation of something passing through them. She bucked, not because of Colby's eager mouth working between her legs, but in reaction to the slither that filled her stomach, ascending her esophagus, crawling into her throat. Her tongue erupted into pain as a dozen needle stings sank through the muscle at once.

Between her thighs, Colby was retching too. Maura hopped off his mouth, reaching into hers, grabbing for the slimy intruder that was currently eating away her tongue.

A quick snip of pain followed. The tips of her fingers fell down her throat like gumdrops.

She gasped, pulling back a maimed and spurting hand, then catching sight of a pink worm tail as it disappeared into Colby's gagging mouth, his eyes rolling back in his head.

Maura tried to scream, but something inside her suppressed the instinct.

This is what happens, she told herself with blithe acceptance, the pain in her hand beginning to recede.

Maura abandoned the room, abandoned the struggling Colby, suddenly more interested in what was happening elsewhere on Crystal Key. She hurried to the front door and watched as her hands grabbed for the storm barricade, tearing through reinforced plywood with newfound strength.

Her thoughts began slipping away in quick flashes. She remembered lunchtime. Oysters on a plate. The bottle of Corona stuffed with lime slices. Eating and drinking in between storm proofing.

Then those thoughts were gone for good.

Maura recalled barricading the back door. Had memories of a young girl stumbling over her knee-high fence, dropping face-first into her freshly cultivated spice garden. Maura, running over to check on her. A rotted face looking up, wiggling worms dancing inside vacant eye sockets.

Those memories were the next to go.

Maura remembered her own tumble into the grass as those creatures glided along the ground, finding holes in her body, slipping past them, igniting seismic pain.

Then there was darkness. Sparkling star fields. Flashes of creatures that her human brain could not process. A stranger's memories trespassing in her skull, belonging to the monster that had whittled her tongue down to a nub in order to take its place, nesting comfortably inside her mouth.

Maura threw the door aside and stepped into the whipping wind. Her body bristled, but she didn't care. In a moment, Colby appeared on the empty street too, standing beside her, saying nothing. He didn't have to. He was like her now.

On the hunt for another host.

Craig Taffy stretched out on the lifeguard tower, watching eager Atlantic waves break across the jetty. He had a thermos of hot coffee tucked between his legs, a pack of Camel non-filters in his coat pocket, and a walkie-talkie in his fist. All emergencies covered.

"I'm in place for another twenty," he told Breyer. "But if Luther needs me to stay out here, I can do it. I'll just have the wife run me down a pint of SoCo if that's gonna be the case."

"You mean *Beeping Sleauty* doesn't need his rest?" Breyer said, unable to control his laugher.

"We're going to get your weird ass speaking habit diagnosed one of these days."

"Plenty of great men in history have had it."

"Yeah," Taffy said. "And you," Together, they agreed that they would stay in their lookout positions for the time being. With that boat out there, the whole island on edge, nobody was sleeping tonight.

He went radio silent and fired up a smoke.

Hurricane Margot had found Crystal Key. In Taffy's mind, these rampages were Mother Nature's right. With everything his species was doing to the planet, she should be riled up. They were the shittiest tenants ever.

Storms were always humbling. Margot had intensified, turning the sky darker than space. The Atlantic hurled endless swells at Crystal Key, each one breaking against the shore with a violent sizzle. Slanted rain reduced visibility to zero, making Taffy feel like he was trapped inside a snow globe as he tried to get a visual on the ship.

Their mystery boat had gotten harder to find.

Taffy reached for the Remington 700 nestled against the seat backing and pushed the scope to his eye. The residue of the Rem Oil that he regularly massaged into the rifle to keep her firing like new tickled his nostrils. It never failed to relax him.

Only his Nikon Buck Master scope couldn't see a damn thing out on that angry ocean.

The lifeguard tower rocked against the wind. Soon it would be unsafe to perch here, and Taffy decided he should hoof it down beach before he went spilling into the sand. There was an alcove down there that he could take shelter in while keeping an eye on things.

He gathered everything into his duffel, flung the rifle over his shoulder, and started down the ladder. His radio coughed out a couple of indiscernible and crackling voices.

"Luther?" he asked once he was sprinting against the wind, moving along the beach. "You trying to raise me?"

"I'm here, man," Luther said, voice wrapped in static. "See any movement on your end?"

"Whatever the ship wants, they're sitting tight."

A cluster of erratic shadows grabbed Taffy's attention as he passed an alleyway. He yelped, stunned by the human outlines nestled between the two beach houses.

The bodies eased back in one rehearsed motion as he came forward. Their movements timed.

"Who's that?" Taffy asked, unslinging his rifle as his bag dropped to his boots.

The people filtered back through the alley. Taffy followed them to the road and found they were joined by even more bodies, all of them standing shoulder-to-shoulder. Motionless.

"Jesus, if everyone's going to be out in this mess, I'll go home and get warm."

No response. Less motion. Glares he felt but couldn't see. A mechanical hum taunted his ears, somehow amplified by forceful winds. Taffy unclipped his military flashlight and clicked the switch, revealing a sea of yellow grins. Friends and neighbors beamed, but their expressions were wrong.

He lifted his rife and stretched one finger over the trigger. He wasn't going to shoot but felt the urge to protect himself from this sea of unhinged smiles.

"Craig," Luther buzzed from the radio. "Get over to the marina…"

The walkie-talkie provoked them, and the twisted faces

converged on Taffy through one unanimous step. Everyone leering. A deranged funhouse nightmare.

Mouths dropped lower than any jawbone should. The sound from every throat, inhuman but united. A chirring insect noise that somehow encouraged their actions. That's when Taffy saw the worms, launched from their hosts, propelling along the ground, across Taffy's shoes, up his legs, straight for his crevices, knowing exactly where to go.

Taffy screamed and kicked his leg out. On it, he saw a lump moving beneath the fabric, scurrying up his thigh. Another worm was at his hips, slipping under the fold in his shirt, chewing on his stomach. He felt a bite on his ear, another on the round of his ass. Taffy grabbed for the one attempting to force its way into his hearing canal. It grunted as he yanked it away from his head, half his ear coming off in the creature's grip.

His head hit the pavement and for a hazy moment, Taffy stared into the face of the worm lying beside him. Little black eyes stared back, deep recessed pinholes looking him over. Then it shot forward, chewing through his mangled ear, expanding the tunnel to accommodate the rest of its wiggling body.

The worm coursed through Taffy's head, feeling like a squirming Q-tip pushed further and further inward. The one on his thigh was now a rising bulge. His hands dipped beneath his belt and he took it in his hand, ripping the invader off his skin, smashing it across the pavement with an opened palm.

It broke with a textured crunch, a splotch of neon pink blood staining like a spilled glow stick.

Friends and neighbors reached down, taking Taffy's hands and legs and stretching him out. Worms slithered all along his body, some of them creating their own entrances.

The one in his head seemed to look out from behind his

eyes. The pain might've been blinding, but the chirring convinced his flailing limbs relax as his breathing lapsed into calm acceptance.

Friends and neighbors lowered Taffy back to the ground, the impromptu induction ceremony completed to their satisfaction. Taffy's cheek brushed the glowing blood, and the creature inside his head billowed its displeasure over the loss of one of its own.

The friends and neighbors shuffled away from the spilled light, disappearing into Margot's crushing darkness.

The struggle was over.

Alex waded into the shallows as the world behind him descended into chaos.

The only sounds left on Crystal Key were sporadic screams. Terror that overpowered the perpetually howling wind.

Alex had made his way to Bernard's Market to grab batteries for his emergency radio and found the old clerk sitting on the floor in front of the ice cream cooler, a severed head in his lap, the skull cracked open, blood pouring from the ears and nostrils. And the old shop owner, just stuffing hunks of jellied brain into his mouth.

The last straw for Alex after a series of close shaves. Crystal Key had fallen and there was nowhere to run. No place to hide. There was only those who were already dead and didn't know it.

Alex was going to swim. He knew the chop would be bad, but it was so much worse. The Atlantic, just a spectacle of frenzied waves rising and crashing in tantrum. The ocean roar, overpowered by lashing rain. If Alex could at least make it to the lighthouse, he'd be okay. Ride out the storm and then hop a boat to Miami once the Coast Guard came to check on Crystal Key.

Pretty big if…

More screams ignited. Alex spotted shadows moving across the beach, hunched backs and limped gaits moving toward him with deranged glee.

He trudged into the water past his hips, waves lifting him higher, bringing him further out, pacifying what indecisiveness remained. Nature forcing him to get a move on. This was a bad idea for a million reasons.

And yet, he was glad to take his chances.

A chance was more than what the people on the island got.

Out here, a chance was a chance. The storm's chaos made things hard, but also camouflaged his trespass, making it harder for the shark to find him. He dove headfirst through the oncoming wave, swimming harder than he ever had.

Waves crashed against the hulls of boats, metal twisting and banging as Alex pushed harder, clearing the harbor, knifing through open water.

"Alex, don't!"

At first, Alex was certain he'd imagined that voice. It was somehow louder than the roiled ocean and the whipping wind. Curiosity got him to flip over onto his back, and he spotted shadows standing against the shore. Three bodies lit by chance in pallid moonlight. The quickest glimpse, right before the storm clouds overhead rushed to obscure them.

The voices might've continued shouting but Alex couldn't hear anything save for the high-pitched trilling. An insect's warble that somehow circled the tumultuous air around him.

Alex pushed harder, finding that he couldn't outswim the noise. It followed, growing louder, as though it was already inside his head. Panic threatened to overwhelm him, but he was exerting himself too hard for it to take hold. He just swam.

There'd be time enough to worry whether he had one of those things inside him once he was basking in the lighthouse warmth.

No chance, he thought. *I've been careful.*

A sharp sting caught his legs, but he didn't stop. The pain never materialized. But then Alex was paddling through water that had become even darker. He kept going because nothing else mattered. Swim or die.

Except his body reoriented into a vertical position and he floated helplessly atop the rising waves, unable to locate any forward momentum. He kicked against the water, but didn't move, figuring that he'd gone numb, realizing with sudden horror what had happened.

His lower body was gone.

The insect chirp rose to a high pitch, its tone morphing, becoming a burst pattern that Alex somehow intuited as mocking. Cruelty that barely registered as the ocean erupted into an apocalyptic splash.

The world went from ash grey to pitch black as Alex's flesh got flayed right off his bones. His torso raked along the razor walls of the creature's jaws as it darted up from the depths, closing its mouth around him. Its teeth chomped down, cracking Alex's bones, severing his arms.

Alex felt his skull crack open, the shark's mouth popping his brain free. He died fast, and the last thing he heard, even louder inside the fish's mouth, was that terrible insect chirp.

As the darkness extinguished him, he understood what had happened. The ones on shore had communicated with the ones inside the shark.

They brought the fish right to him.

DESPERATE HOURS

They dragged Manuel back to Shifting Tides and took the long way.

Owen Bowles made sure the prisoner caravan used the route least likely to have witnesses. Silly, given that the whole island was in self-preservation mode, everyone on Crystal Key doing their best to brace for the worst.

By the time they reached the resort's pier, moving through a sedated crowd of college kids, it was early evening.

The patrons were overtaken by dejection, sitting outside, watching the ever-darkening sky from their balconies. Storm clouds cast long shadows across the beach. Conversation was sparse. The mood, sullen. Nobody could believe they'd been abandoned here.

"All the way to the end," Manuel told his escorts, hoping that his cooperation might count for something. "Key is in my wallet."

Bowles waited until they were both in front of the door before he flashed the gun. "Swipe it," he told Manuel. "Do it slow."

Manuel didn't believe that Bowles would be stupid enough to shoot him in front of two dozen tourists. Then again, the kids didn't seem all that interested in the hostage crisis underway at the pier's end.

He slid a hand into his pants and fished the card key out of his wallet. He swiped it through the reader and the authenticator light flashed green.

"Allow me," Bowles said, entering first and sweeping the room as Manuel followed. Once it was clear they were alone, Bowles balled a fist and punched Manuel in the nose.

He went spinning to the carpet and lay stunned by the old redneck's strength. The rest of the posse snickered as they filled the room, then the lock chain rattled somewhere overhead as it scraped along the door, clicking into place. Manuel stayed on his elbows and watched Bowles reach into his waistband. In a moment, the cold steel of a Beretta was staring down at him.

"Last chance to come clean about the boat."

"It's not me," Manuel said. A slow trickle of blood rolled through his moustache stubble.

"Bullshit." Bowles kicked him in face.

Manuel fell back to the floor, mouth filled with blood. One of his molars slipped out of place and floated like a lone oyster cracker in a cauldron of tomato soup. He spat it out onto the feet of the nearest posse man, some *Cheeseburger In Paradise* wearing a Hawaiian button down and leather moccasins suddenly hot-stepping at the string of splatter across his toes.

"Shit," Moccasins barked. "Fuckin' blood all over my feet, Owen."

"How long do we have?" Bowles said. "I know your people are coming ashore, only we're not going to let that happen." The gun barrel hovered against Manuel's face, threatening to spit. The man holding it wasn't any cooler, and when nerves were frayed, people made mistakes.

"I can't tell you because I don't know," Manuel said. He allowed his voice to climb toward panic—a show of vulnerability he hoped these vigilantes might buy. "You're basing your suspicion on the fact that I carry a weapon. Do you think the government would send a busted-up Latino as their undercover agent?"

Bowles' face tightened into a sneer. "Learned long ago never to underestimate the stupidity of my government."

"You think I blend in here?" Manuel said, allowing his words to wobble. "If anyone was going to infiltrate this godforsaken island, they'd send a fresh-faced rookie to mingle with the rest of those spring breakers out there."

Bowles chewed that over, hostility disappearing from his face with the suddenness of an off switch. Maybe he believed Manuel, though he didn't seem like the sort of guy who would cop to making a mistake. "Empty out his pockets."

The goons swarmed Manuel and lifted him off the rug. A flurry of hands excavated his pockets. They flung his car keys down on the bed comforter. His wallet beside it. The photograph of Anne missed the mattress and went flapping to the floor.

Bowles rifled through the wallet.

"Manuel Redondo," he said, unsheathing the driver's license and reading it aloud. Then he flung the plastic back in Manuel's face. "Not Bob fucking Torres. Know what that tells me? You are hiding something. And don't say *El Hupil* was a lie, my brother, 'cause I want to believe in the magical taco truck."

Manuel remained silent while Bowles searched his belongings. Nothing in his wallet would betray him. The only thing of value was a folded picture of Marie and Sanson hiding beneath a credit card. Bowles zeroed in on it, waving it around like he had discovered a smoking gun.

"Wife and kid?"

"Was," Manuel said. The only card left to play was honesty.

"What happened?"

"Wife and kid were visiting Dad in the hospital," he said. "My boss happened to be visiting too, only he had a target the size of Jupiter on his back."

"Ah, shit," Bowles said, more than a little ashamed.

"A few *pendejos* showed up, thinking they could hit that target. Happened to catch mine in a burst of panic fire instead."

Bowles placed the picture on the bed face up in a display of respect. He gave his men a single nod and the surrounding posse loosened their circle, dispersing throughout the room.

"Tempers are hot," Bowles said. He might've been aiming for a soft apology, but his tone remained entitled. "Don't change the fact that nothing you've told me checks out."

"Look at *that* photo," Manuel said, pointing to the floor.

One of Bowles' friends picked it up and handed it over. Bowles studied it for a long time and then asked, "Who is she to you?"

"She's why I'm here," Manuel said.

"You're looking for her?"

"Know her?"

"Manuel," Bowles said. "If you had only just leveled with me from the start, none of this would've happened."

"Is that so?"

"This... well, this I can believe. Everyone on the island wants some of this."

The room shook, a severe and unexpected rumble got the bed hopping up and down, dresser drawers clacking, vibrations that knocked decorative paintings clear off the wall, frames shattering at their feet. Everyone was looking at someone else, as if one of them was responsible for the plaster raining down on them from the flaking ceiling.

It stopped as suddenly as it started, but before anyone could speak, the shaking resumed with even more severity, the rumbling tethered this time to what sounded like a tolling bell.

"The hell is that?" Bowels shouted over the commotion.

Outside the cabana's thin wall, resort guests stirred with rushed around and spastic voices. Their chatter drowned immediately by something louder, what Manuel thought was a striking gong radiating with deep and shifting echoes.

Large cracks began to cut through the ceiling, hunks of it dropping down onto them while the floor splintered between their legs, busted wood planks swiping up at their ankles as everyone dove for impossible safety.

Manuel attempted to sidestep the plummeting hole, but the floor fell away as the ceiling pushed down. The eager Atlantic Ocean was there, pushing up, saying hello as the pier collapsed into it.

Cold water was a shock to Manuel's system, oddly refreshing on his bruised and bloodied face. He didn't swim for the open ceiling as much as the raging water shoved him straight through it. He swallowed the current as he paddled through the gloom toward lighter darkness, breaking the surface and finding the screams of a dozen people splashing around him in the raging storm.

Manuel swam along the collapsed pier toward the Shifting Tides beach. Half the structure was collapsed and underwater now. People clung to the vertical section of the broken dock, using it as a ladder to reach safety. The lucky ones at the top of the wharf were screaming for the climbers to move faster, helping those in reach.

There was commotion all around Manuel, and he suddenly thought of the monstrous fish, probably twisting through the waves to get him, panic materializing in his throat as a kind of whimper.

A body floated through the rising swells up ahead, a small red bathing suit ridden up on hairy thighs. Manuel reached for him as he swam past, hoping to help, but catching a dead gaze instead—unblinking eyes boring straight down into salt water. A piece of dock wood spiked through his neck, blood spreading through the surrounding water.

Manuel pushed faster toward the shore, but the beach was far enough away to be Miami. More screams. Splashing. Too much chaos to focus.

"Swim, dude!"

Somehow, Manuel knew that was in reference to him. Knew better than to look, though he did anyway. Over his shoulder, a fin breaking the surface on agitated water, knifing toward him, distance closing like a missile.

His mind's eye projected images of that monstrous head and constant smile, and he screamed in terror as he expected to feel those teeth snap through his kicking legs at any second.

"Swim, Bob!" Barbara's voice cut through the commotion from somewhere above. In Manuel's jumbled thoughts, he wondered if he was already dead.

He wasn't going to make it but fought against the weather harder than he'd ever fought against anything else.

How was the beach still so far?

❧

Dad came down off the roof as the rain picked up. He walked inside and bolted the door. For a second, there was silence as the deluge battered the building from all sides.

"Get ready to go," he said, filling a duffel bag with all the bottled water in the cooler.

"Where?" Reggie said. "I thought we going to keep watch here..."

"Just get ready."

"Is it the ship?"

The windows on the garage door shattered, answering his question. A flurry of arms lunged inward, fingers opening and closing, desperate for purchase. A swarm of bodies in the driveway, each of them eager to get inside.

Behind them, the rear door splintered open, a sledgehammer smashing through, lifting out and then crashing back down, sending the wooden slab rocketing across the floor. A dark figure shambled into frame.

"The generator called them here," Dad said, as if Reggie was supposed to know who *them* was.

In the low-level garage light, Reggie saw the intruding figure wasn't dark, but actually *burnt*.

Dad scooped the dirt shovel and charged the trespasser with a roar. The cutting edge caught the burnt man's chest bone and knocked him against the wall. The blade cleaved through his neck and took his head clean off.

Reggie screamed at the unexpected outcome.

There was no blood, and the headless body shambled

on, changing directions, toward their dehydrated bunkmate—the man Frank had rescued off the lighthouse, and who he'd tasked them with caring for—his face twisted in a terrified, silent scream.

A squirming pink snake blasted up through the burnt man's neck cavity, dancing back and forth in the air as it prepared to abandon ship. The body dropped to its knees in front of the castaway as if presenting itself. The castaway shrieked at the sight as the creature wiggled free of its hidey hole, its host body falling spent and motionless across the slab floor.

Dad was stuffing guns into the bag dispassionately as Reggie watched the worm wiggle its way into the castaway's screaming mouth, disappearing as a bulge down his throat. His eyes rolled back in his head and his body convulsed. Dad grabbed Reggie by the arm and pulled him toward the broken door.

"But we gotta help him!" Reggie said.

"Forget it," Dad shouted. "He's gone."

They sprinted through the backyard and moved into tall grass along the hillside. The generator's grinding hum retreated into the howling wind, but they heard a dozen others as they made a dash for downtown. Dad explained how that was good. How those things would go toward whatever noise they could easily hear.

Loose hurricane boards skittered across the ground like terrified animals. Broken branches whipped past their heads. Heavy rain obscured their vision, steadily worsening as they got closer to the shore, where washed up shells and hollowed out crabs pelted them constantly.

Reggie assumed they were headed home, but Dad took them across the beach instead, running past the Captain's Patio toward a cropping of rocks in the distance, a jetty hammered by so many waves that the breaking water looked like a series of soggy explosions.

Dad scaled the rocks first, dropping to his stomach, then reaching down to help Reggie climb up. Instead of rushing out over the ocean along the thin path of rocks, Dad ushered him in the opposite direction, to where the rocks were higher.

He climbed them and reached back for Reggie again. "Careful here," he said. "The surface is slippery." He said something else too, but his mumbles were lost in the whipping wind.

Reggie kept his head down and took it slow as they moved into the razor thin space between two rocks. The cavern was a tight squeeze, scraping both his stomach and back as they pushed in out of the storm. The freezing stone made him shiver, and the gusting wind that followed them in was like hearing a ghost scream in your ear.

The entrance constricted, pressing on his chest, challenging him to breathe. He turned his head to his right and could barely see Dad up ahead struggling with the same narrow pathway. Then he slipped from sight and Reggie thought he might've heard him calling out, but the howling wind was in surround sound, couldn't hear anything but that whistle in his ear.

A hand reached back through and clamped around Reggie's elbow, tugging him the rest of the way, until he squeezed through and found himself inside a larger cave. His body was sore, rubbed raw by the natural structure on the way in.

"Holy crap," Reggie said, bending over to catch his breath. Images from the garage flashed through his mind. He found them impossible to process and spun the trauma by telling himself at least he'd have some stories for Becky St. George that were more exciting than his squirrel hunt. "How do you know about this place?"

"It's a small island," Dad said. "Only so many places for kids to sneak off to."

"You ain't no kid."

"Couple times a year kids get stuck up here 'cause they think we don't know this is their lovers lane. One of the only places to smoke and drink in anonymity. Speaking of which, you'll have to excuse the spent condoms and empty Natty Ice."

"Gross," Reggie said, checking around his feet.

"Natty Ice ain't bad in a pinch."

"Not what I meant."

"Relax, we clean it out every couple of months. It'll work for us now. Keep us out of sight."

There wasn't much room here. Enough for four or five people to maybe sit in a circle and puff puff pass.

"What the hell was that thing?" Reggie said after they'd taken some time to assess the situation.

"Stop talking so damn loud," Dad said. "We're hiding from… whatever's happening." He dropped the bag between them and began rummaging through it.

"I thought everyone was dependent on you?" Reggie said. "Now there's no one to watch for signals."

"It got real bad, real fast," Dad said. "No one left after that." One by one, Dad's team had gone radio silent. The assault on the garage had made Reggie realize that Dad had been right to assume the worst.

"Maybe the boat people won't come," Reggie said.

"All this is a guarantee they will."

Dad lifted a gun out of the duffel bag and placed it against Reggie's palm. It felt heavy, physically and emotionally. The amount of damage he could do with this… it was almost unthinkable. The longer he held it, the heavier that responsibility became. It made him feel tired and sick. He put it on the cold ground between his legs and pushed it off.

"That's your liberal mother," Dad said. "Always talking about the violence behind a handgun. Never the protection."

"I don't feel safer with that in my hand."

"'Cause you never learned to shoot. Look, man, it's not a power thing. Believe me, there are plenty of guys in the world who think a gun in their hand makes them Charlie Bronson, but not me. Right now, where we are, that might be the only thing that helps us survive."

Reggie's eyes fell on the weapon again as the winds surged and a sheet of water cascaded down the rock wall. He shivered and pulled his knees against his chest, ready to cry, desperate to blame Mom for this hell on earth. Only there was no anger. Other people were dead. This was more than some petty inconvenience, and Becky St. George felt like a minor problem on another planet.

"Pick it up," Dad said. "At least let me show you how to handle yourself."

Reggie hadn't taken his eyes off the weapon. In most circumstances, Mom wouldn't want this. She was uncomfortable when there were too many guns in movies or television and certainly hated watching him fire endless ammo into *Halo* n00bs. But she'd raised Reggie to know the difference between fantasy and reality. That was a line he had no desire to cross.

"You want to forget everything I showed you as soon as we're home, go for it. But for now..."

Reggie lifted the gun.

"Okay," Dad said. "Welcome to Handguns 101. For when you can't call a policeman to come save your ass."

The driest of jokes. Reggie didn't laugh. Just listened as Dad rattled off rules, most of which were common sense. Handle every weapon as if it were loaded. Train with it all the time so you don't forget how to use it. Always point it away from people. Whatever.

"Now," Dad said. "Show me how you hold it."

Reggie pointed it at the wall and curled his finger around the trigger.

"Stop. Don't ever touch the trigger until you've got your target in sight. See, firing a gun's no easy thing, especially if you intend to take another life. People get emotional and your trigger finger might catch Poison Sumac. Get real itchy. Get me?"

"Then what?"

Reggie centered the weapon in the web of his hand which, according to Dad, was the correct grip. He placed his thumb low, beneath the slide-mounted safety.

"Nope," Dad objected. "You do that, and you gotta flip your thumb up then waste time returning it to the correct grip before you shoot. In an emergency, you may not have a chance to get your thumb back into place and you'll forfeit accuracy. Or worse. So put your thumb over the safety and bring it down with your knuckle."

Reggie did, and the slide clicked free with alarming ease. This sucker was now armed, and it felt to him like he was holding a nuclear bomb. He glanced at Dad and caught traces of a proud smile in the dark.

"Go on, man, give it a shot. Point it the way we came."

Reggie drew on the entrance, finger crawling for the trigger.

"There's going to be recoil," Dad said. "So... just squeeze it gently."

Reggie did. The gun barked. A shot louder than thunder. His hand jerked back with alarming ferocity and he dropped the weapon to the ground.

Dad laughed and gave an encouraging pat. "Pick it up

and put the safety latch back in place until it's time for us to move."

"Can I fire again?"

"Just remember how to do it for now. One shot in this storm is okay. Nothing's gonna pinpoint it in that wind, but we don't have to make it easy for them."

Reggie's grin became a frown. All that power in the palm of his hand. The satisfying blast. He wanted to feel it again.

"I had hoped to show you how to bait a hook and catch a fish first," Dad said. "Just tell your Mom that's what we did, okay?"

Reggie nodded, something in this moment provoking additional courage and curiosity. "Why'd you leave, Dad?"

"Really?"

"I mean, I get why you *left* after what you did to that guy's nose, but why'd you come all the way out here?"

"You know how your mother and I met?"

Reggie opened his mouth to answer, then stopped. All these years and he was surprised to realize he didn't. He had always just taken their marriage for granted. One day, he could be with Becky St. George, having this conversation with *their* kid. But that was even weirder to think about.

"I guess I don't," he said, fishing his cell phone from his pocket and pushing the power button as he listened.

"I was a punk kid," Dad said. "Pretty lucky that I didn't get blown away by some trigger-happy cop back in the day. I mean, I wouldn't have deserved *that* for the shit I did, but you know how it goes. And I did live north of the law. Thought I was going to be some expert tagger... do people even do that anymore?"

"What's tagging?"

"Like when you do graffiti on a building. Come up with your *tag* and then find an artistic way to write it out with a can of Krylon."

"Like… vandalism?"

"Yeah, I guess they don't do it anymore. But I used to, and at worst I'd boost bikes, steal beer. Kid shit, 'cept I grew up in the Bronx and you can get killed there for doing less. Anyway, some of the neighborhood crew liked my stuff… my art and my ability to score top shelf liquor on Friday night. Wasn't long before I was being courted by the neighborhood guys for a little pushing. Carry junk into the ghettos, expand their markets, whatever. I never did it myself, okay?"

"Uh, that's good… I guess."

"The only reason I didn't… I think, was 'cause I met your mom at some college party I shouldn't even of been at. She was so damn smart, dual enrolled in high school and Manhattan College. *And* prepping for law school. I'm there talking to her about the art of tagging and she looks me over and says, 'You know how much it costs to paint over that after you've done it?' I didn't have an answer. Never once thought about it before."

Reggie's face was buried in his phone, staring at pictures of Becky St. George, trying to get a few last looks in, in the event he never made it back. Man, what he wouldn't give to feel her lips on his mouth just once.

"I talked to her the rest of the night," Dad said. "The playful way she challenged me was like a drug, and I wanted more. Always having to be on my game… not every girl gets you thinking that way. I begged for her number and couldn't wait to call. We started up and stayed hot. Eventually she had to move to Boston to go to Suffolk and I knew I wanted to come with. School wanted her admission so bad they hooked me up with a job as part of the deal. I was grateful to your mom for the opportunity… until I screwed it up."

"That doesn't explain why you left."

"Yes it does, man. Once I blew it with your mom, and believe me, I fuckin' *blew* it, I knew I was headed right back to trouble. Running, boozing, fighting. Only they don't tolerate that when you're in your forties. You're a thug and a throwaway."

Reggie looked up from his screen, unsure of the point Dad was trying to make.

"No one wants a sob story," Dad said. "Even if part of that story is that your own dad used to beat the ever-loving shit out of you for no reason. Can't ever escape that damage in full."

"You mean... *your* dad?"

"He sure thought there were plenty of reasons, messy house, smelly trash, leftover spaghetti in the sink... any excuse to put his hands on me. I used to take because I knew it wouldn't last forever. Knew I was getting out. And the whole time, I used to tell myself how I was never gonna do that to my own kid."

"You're not like him," Reggie said. "You guys gave me everything."

Dad was little more than a shadow in the dark of the cavern in that moment, radiating with a silent energy that was difficult to describe, Reggie's words somehow absolving him of a lifetime of doubt and guilt.

"Thanks for saying that," he said after a long bout of silence. "If I stayed in Boston, tried to start over there, all alone, I would've become that bastard. The anger I felt with myself for blowing a good thing, the best thing, would've guaranteed it. I exiled myself here... where I knew I'd have to work to survive. Nobody hides on an island this small. No choice but to pull your weight. Turns out... I'm good at that."

"Seems harsh."

"Nah, sometimes putting a stop to the misery is the greatest gift. I came here. Got a new start."

Reggie took one last look at Becky St. George, her beaming green eyes and sunshine smile the only incentives he needed to get through this. His phone was at seventeen percent power and he turned it off before picking up the gun. It felt at home in his fist now.

"I just showed my son how to fire a gun," Dad said. "Another thing I promised I'd never do."

"Mom'll understand."

"I know she will. Your Mom's the smartest, toughest woman I ever met. If she were here, we'd be out of this mess already."

"So you can tell her yourself how you didn't teach me how to shoot a gun," Reggie said, "but showed me how to survive."

They went quiet and listened to rain as it beat against the natural ceiling while the storm continued its island siege, smashing against the rocks with splashes that never seemed to end. The wind tore through the tunnel like God himself was searching furiously for the two of them.

At first, Reggie thought Dad had taken a second to think, but then he heard a few discrete sniffles in the dark. Any other day, this would've made him feel weird. Not now. Reggie reached out and gave him an awkward pat on the back. No words exchanged.

Then they listened to the rain.

The Shifting Tides survivors had moved off the pier and were huddled inside the lobby. Many of them stood on the overlook, watching the riled ocean through cracked and leaking glass, finding silent pity for the one girl out there who refused to come in out of the weather. She stood alone on the beach, ankle-deep in excited water, calling "Jonathan?" over and over with vocal cords that were next to fried, her cries hitting the air in a toneless rasp.

This seemed to go on for hours while some of the guests debated going out there to rescue her.

"What for?" someone said. "Her mind is toast."

"Very Christian of you," another said.

"I'm a fucking atheist."

Manuel sat hunched on the edge of an interior flowerbed. The entire room smelt like a YMCA locker, damp clothes mixed with strained body odor. Barbara tucked her head against his shoulder.

They were sitting ducks. He felt vulnerable but supposed that didn't matter. Even if by some miracle they made it off this island, Garcia would have him killed. Barbara, too, if he found her with him.

No number of crazed sharks or alien worms could make up for his failure. If anything, those excuses would condemn him to a fate worse than Garcia's usual modus operandi of digging your own grave before being blasted into it.

"We need to go," Manuel said.

Barbara didn't hear him. She'd stopped hearing anything. Her blue eyes had faded to an almost different color entirely. On occasion, she mumbled something about her son, who was staying with his grandmother for the weekend.

"You'll see him again," Manuel whispered. He could barely bother with the effort needed to sell that kind of lie and the next time she mentioned her son, Manuel didn't bother saying anything at all.

She had been like that since the pier collapsed. Half the resort guests had become shark food, including Bowles and his crew. Despite the tiny patch of common ground they'd found at the end, Manuel wasn't sorry to see any of them go. They would've lynched him had the wind blown the other way.

The demon shark stalked his thoughts, but it was the pink worms that could somehow make the dead walk that roiled his Catholic upbringing. Everything had been shit since the bathroom in the Glades. For all Manuel knew, he'd died there and this was hell.

He crossed himself at the thought.

Those worms would be headed this way and what remained of this place didn't stand a chance, all these kids crammed inside like sweating cattle.

"Barbara," he whispered, "you're going to come with me, okay?" He yanked her by the wrist, and they wove through an exhausted crowd of half-naked bodies, half of them sobbing in the other half's arms.

There was some tough talk about swimming to the mainland, but anyone who tried that would drown before they could reach the lighthouse, let alone Miami.

Manuel swiped a resort pamphlet from the flyer wall and stuffed the map into his pocket. He pried the sliding doors open just enough so they could squeeze between them. The hurricane gusts weren't exactly inviting, but he was willing to take his chances.

They headed down beach, which was like running through a Syrian sandstorm. The constant blight of drifting beach powder stung their faces as they darted past the dazed girl who continued to scream for her beloved Jonathan. He steered them toward the shore where the ground was harder, water reaching up past their ankles as they splashed through it.

"Come on," Manuel said, encouraging Barbara over the roaring storm. "We're going to make it." But each time he looked back her empty gaze was cast out across the rolling black Atlantic. When he realized he could just as easily tug her along in total silence, he gave up trying to talk.

The beach rounded and they jogged the corner, moving through complete darkness with only a sliver of ambient light off the ocean to keep them from trudging straight into it.

"Hold it." The voice crashed down on them as if it were part of the storm. The sheer unexpected shock of it stopped Manuel dead, Barbara smashing against his back.

The pitch darkness swirled and became a figure that moved toward them from an inland path. Labored steps. Heavy breathing. Liquored breath so toxic it could strip paint off the side of a farmhouse. All of it so pronounced to be perceptible over the roaring storm. It wasn't an olive branch that reached forward, but a rifle. Manuel went instinctively for the gun that was no longer tucked into his pants.

"Where to?" the voice slurred, taking aim.

"Phoenix," Manuel said, wiggling his fingers to remind the drunkard his arms were, in fact, raised.

"That's like two thousand miles over there. Talk straight."

"You asked. I told you."

The rifle clicked. "If you're not with us, you're against us. Go help me sod."

The gunman's words landed strange, and Manuel realized the fates weren't so completely against him. This was who he needed to find, the guy who mixed up all his letters, according to Beth. There was no time to ask pleasantly. "What happened to Anne Munro?"

The rifle lifted into the air, followed by a bunch of stutters that were the man's inebriated words. Manuel took the opportunity to step in and close his palm around the vertical barrel, yanking it free and throwing it to the sand behind him. He might have told Barbara to pick it up, but she was one step away from becoming that poor girl back at the resort, asking the raging ocean to return her Jonathan.

Manuel stepped toward the guy and repeated Anne's name again, loud enough so the wind couldn't wipe it away.

The guy shrugged.

"She fucked you 'cause she thought it'd hurt someone. Your boss. Now start filling in the rest of those blanks."

"If you know that, then you know the whole story."

Manuel punched him in the stomach, a love tap to show he meant business. He doubled over but took his medicine like a man, rising back up and wiping a grimace off his face.

"I paid her, okay?"

"Careful."

"Everyone else is getting it for free and she wouldn't even look at me. Some liquid courage and I ask her how much it would cost. *'Two hundred and you can cover my face.'* After I paid, she took my money and laughed. *'I would've done it for nothing.'* That's the kind of person she was. Cruel."

"Where is she?"

"Ask Luther," he said with a cut of disdain.

Manuel plucked the rifle out of the sand and then took Barbara's hand. "Let's go."

"Not going anywhere," the man said. "I've got a post to watch."

"You don't have a choice."

"Someone has to keep eyes on the sea," he said. "They'll some for us coon."

"No one's coming, *mamón*."

"No… That's not true."

"Trust me or don't, but everyone inland is dead or dying."

Manuel started off with Barbara in tow. The other man seemed conflicted for a minute, then jogged to catch up. The prospect of living had that effect. "Where are we going?" he asked.

"To find a boat."

DAWN PATROL

The tap on Reggie's shoulder pulled him from dream sleep where he was alone on a private island with Becky St. George.

It was Crystal Key, rendered in dream logic—less populated, more tropical, completely foreign, yet somehow familiar. She wore a skimpy bikini—the exact one he'd ogled Maura in yesterday—and right before Dad's touch had shattered the illusion, Reggie had been trying to find an excuse to keep them on the beach, maintain the vacation, despite the prominent growl from inside the forest, growing louder with every passing moment.

"It's dawn," Dad said. "We should move."

"Is it over?" Reggie said as they crawled from the cave. The warm air felt thin and temporary. Gusts off the ocean were much cooler beneath the ashen sky. The damp morning offered just enough muted sunshine so that night before felt like a terrible nightmare.

"No," Dad said. "We're in the eye of the hurricane."

"Why are we moving? Doesn't it make sense to stay put?"

"Come on."

"We had water and safety. Slugs couldn't get us. The shark might as well be in outer space."

Dad scowled, showing that Reggie's inquisitiveness wasn't appreciated. "I think they might decide to nuke the island," he said.

The ship was closer—a few hundred feet off the coast. A jet-black monolith adrift on temporarily muted swells. People moved across its deck, just tiny specs at this distance.

"Shouldn't we try talking to them?" Reggie said.

Dad didn't dignify that with an answer. He moved into cover, through the thin oak forest that stretched inland. Each time the wind gusted, the leaves gave out and drenched them with pools of freezing rainwater. They hurried on to where the edges of the trees came into sight. Dad stopped there and got to one knee.

"You keep that gun close and ready," he said. It was the way he used to tell Reggie to do his homework.

Right. Reggie *was* holding the gun. He'd forgotten. He looked the pistol over, amazed by how snug the grip felt against his palm just a few hours after being shown how to use it. As natural as a cell phone.

They walked to the edge of the oaks, and Dad put his hand in the air to halt their momentum. The downtown strip up ahead looked like a warzone. An uprooted tree lay across the road, making it inaccessible to vehicles. Folding chairs, a grill, and other items—plastic gnomes and random decorations—littered residential yards, while the only storefront they could see from here had a busted bay window.

A group of islanders shambled back and forth across the tip of Main Street. Their feet scuffed as their necks and backs jerked in erratic patterns, like cutting a few random frames from a 35mm print. Reggie thought they resembled seizing belly dancers or drunks who were close to vomiting.

Two of the bodies lumbered toward each other, shoulders colliding. They spun inward, face-to-face. Their mouths gaped in unison, and what looked like pink slithering kielbasa grew out of the spaces between their teeth. Little round heads poked and prodded one another like cautious animals while the human host heads angled back, eyes toward the sky. The slugs nipped and stirred while their mechanical trilling became piercing ticks of approval. Overjoyed shrieks because the island had been conquered.

Reggie covered his ears and watched the creatures as they retreated into their host throats like someone pressed rewind. Human heads snapped back down into place, resuming their normal positions. The bodies went back to marching through broken glass, stumbling over storm debris like they were incapable of noticing it.

Their shrieks were the worst thing Reggie had ever heard.

"They're checking each other out," Dad said. "Making sure everyone's got one." He tapped Reggie's elbow and they went back on the move. The perimeter road was the easiest way to cross the island, but Dad figured those things would be spread throughout the downtown strip, and in heavy numbers. If they followed the central road in the other direction, they'd have to pass through Shifting Tides, and that option might be even worse if all the guests there had turned.

The best decision was to go up the middle, into sweeping

tall grass that passed through several backyards on an inland corridor. They moved without incident by deserted houses, or at least houses whose occupants were too terrified to come to the window to see who or what was bustling past.

One of the houses hummed with the industrial growl of a running generator as they approached.

"This is Doug's place," Dad said as he lifted out of the grass, peering through the screened-in porch. "Doesn't look like anyone's home..." With cautious motion, he crept against the flaking exterior paint, looking through every window and eyeing his flanks with justified paranoia.

Reggie stayed on their path, too scared to do anything but move forward. His feet slurped through mushy earth. Every step was a potential giveaway, and soon he was too scared to do anything but stand and watch Dad slip around to the front side of the house.

His eyes didn't dare move. Every second felt like a minute. Every minute was a moment to assume the worst. The worst varied, but was always one of those slugs waiting for him out front. Or someone inside mistaking him for one of those slugs, then blowing his head off.

Before pessimism could take over, Dad appeared on the other side of the house, looking like he'd come from a funeral.

"What'd you see?"

"Doug took his own head off with a shotgun," he said. "Front door's busted wide. Don't see his kids anywhere." He resumed his position as caravan leader and moved with even more urgency.

"How'd it get bad so fast?"

Dad didn't have an answer, and they marched for another hour before anything else was said. Each time they heard humming generators, Dad made sure they fanned out and moved well around them.

"Those things are like dinner bells," he said.

Crystal Key had become a ghost town overnight, a procession of empty houses and abandoned lives.

They came upon an open back door and a stuffed Easter Bunny doll submerged in the muck. The swing set at the edge of the yard had fallen over, and a child's body had spilled from the center tower, pinned beneath the weight of the structure. Her four-year-old neck craned all the way around in a frozen, painful glare.

Dad noted it and shook his head, then quickened his pace. Reggie couldn't stand to look away. It felt wrong to ignore simply because it was upsetting. Despite the crushing hopelessness of it all, he needed to acknowledge the tragedy. He veered close to the toppled structure, thinking he might somehow be able to do something for the child.

The little girl's eyes blinked once, and her warped neck looked like a twist of Play Dough. Her arms scratched and clawed the ground, fingers vanishing into loose black mulch.

Reggie yelped—the most cowardly sound he'd ever made—then hurried to catch Dad while that little body continued to flail, mouth popping wide, lips forming around the loud keening sound that exploded into the air.

Reggie didn't look back until they were to the next yard. Her host slug hovered straight out of her mouth, and even at this distance, its seed-colored eyes blinked and glared, watching two potential hosts move further out of reach.

It leapt from the dead girl's mouth, her body ceased flailing as soon as it was clear. The creature plopped into the mud, wiggling helplessly, unable to gain the proper traction for pursuit.

They quickened their pace, Dad leading them on a zigzag path to offset any reinforcements that might respond to the creature's call.

Don't freak, Reggie thought. *You can make it.*

That was easier said than done. Reggie freaked when his teachers assigned difficult homework. He freaked when he thought about dying a virgin. And he freaked whenever he tried talking to Becky St. George. Today, he was holding better than expected.

"Gotta be smarter," Dad said. It was another mile or so before he said anything else, mentioning they were nearing the coast. That's when he leapt at the sight of something on his right, movement along the hillside. The rifle in his hand came up quick and he took aim, stabbing the barrel forward, pointing it toward something Reggie couldn't see from his vantage.

"Drop the gun, man!" Dad shouted.

Reggie rushed to his side, drawing before he had a target to draw on.

"Go!" Another voice competed against Dad's. It was muffled somehow, words filtered through a foghorn effect. Slumped against the interior wall of a lean-to, a man in military gear held a submachine gun on Dad, shouting from behind a metal breather. A black face mask covered his head, and thick goggles shielded his eyes. "Keep moving," he said. "I'll shoot if you don't."

Reggie's hand trembled as he realized his gun was pointed at a living person. And that he was ready to shoot him if need be.

"You're already done, man," Dad said. Reggie noticed the stranger had a red splotch beneath his arm where he'd been shot. Blood trickling out like a busted hose.

The man sputtered as if in agreement. Too spent to argue.

"Is the air toxic out here?" Dad said. "That why you're wearing that?"

He shook his head. "They can't get in my mouth this way."

"You're from that fuckin' ship... tell me what you're all doing here."

His filtered breathing was labored and his shoulders heaved as he fought his weakening body. "Came aground in the storm to collect samples." He lifted a hand and pointed toward the beach. "Got attacked by those things as soon as we landed... they cut us down... I fell back to here."

"Who are you?" Dad's voice cracked a little, ground down by tired desperation. There was no answer from the lean-to. The trooper lowered his gun and closed his eyes. His chest continued to rise, but the energy to speak was depleted.

"Leave him," Reggie said.

They did, finding the island's perimeter road as they cleared the downtown area. It wasn't far to the docks at this point.

The hurricane had completely ravaged the Island Hoppers ferry. Only a jagged metallic base was left where the glass enclosure had been.

The snack shack building was also smashed and dented, with bloodstains dotted across its walls.

It had taken them a few hours to cross the island, but they had only found a handful of bodies. Reggie wondered where everyone was hiding as they sprinted down to Dad's boat.

"Shit, man," Dad said. "We made it."

The *Eve* was at the edge of the dock, looking like a beautiful mirage. It promised safety and freedom, and suddenly the morning's cave dwelling felt like a tomb. Dad had been right.

Reggie allowed himself a quick breath of relief, and that small display of emotion threatened a floodgate of tears for all they'd seen along the way.

"We're gunning it," Dad said, his voice cracking with

laughter. "Straight gunning it. Let that fucking shark chase me all the way to Miami if it wants. Untie the line while I start her up."

Reggie hopped aboard and began fiddling with the knot, ignoring the commotion below deck.

An islander in a fishing vest stormed the dock from off the road, shambling toward the *Eve*, his face twisted and furious. The lures pinned to the fabric of his chest rattled up and down as he moved.

Reggie heard that damn insect chirp from inside the man's throat. He raised his gun without hesitation. After all the horrors he'd seen, dropping one of these fuckers was going to be cathartic.

He squeezed off a shot. The gun lurched and the bullet went wide.

Behind him, the commotion below deck suddenly ceased.

Reggie squinted and used his free palm to steady his trigger hand. He squeezed off another shot, and this bullet caught the walker in the nose. His face burst into a patch of wet blood— the same sound as pelting your buddy with a water balloon.

The islander lost his balance and splashed face-down into the water. The back of his head rose, a lump sliding over gradually loosening flesh like a *Tom & Jerry* head injury, rising and then tearing, revealing the angry slug driver beneath.

The creature scurried across the dead man's shoulders, but as soon as the islander slipped beneath the water, the slug lifted its head and made a mewing noise like a chipmunk in heat, then shriveled like a salted worm.

Reggie realized he'd just heard the thing's death rattle.

"Nice work, Reggie." He turned and saw Bob on his father's boat, looking even more messed up since the last time he'd seen him. A dazed and equally battered woman stood by his side. A couple that had been to hell and back.

He had a rifle of his own, and it was pointed at Dad.

"What are you doing here?" Reggie asked.

"That is a very interesting question," Bob answered.

❧

This guy, Luther, was not stupid.

"Let's talk," Manuel said. "You're gonna see something downstairs you're not gonna like."

"Already saw a lot of blood," he said.

"There is an explanation for that," Manuel told him. "If you come with me."

"Okay," Luther said, handing his gun to Barbara at Manuel's gesture. Judging from her face, she would've been more comfortable holding a neon slug. Just took the rife in her hands and slumped against the boat's interior wall, watching the ocean.

"What do you want with my Dad?" Reggie said.

"To talk." Manuel flashed a reassuring smile. "That is all."

"Then why can't we all—"

"Hey, man," Luther said. "You just keep your eyes peeled." He might've been tempted to resist Manuel, but Manuel had once been *El Rastreador*, and *El Rastreador* took to the world *no* like the Amish took to the city. *El Rastreador* would peel your fingernails off with a can opener if he thought you were being cute. The look on *El Rastreador's* face told Luther, *"I'm not asking."*

"Down here," Manuel said.

Luther wasn't stupid. Only stubborn. He glared at Manuel for a long moment. His functioning eye possessed a fighter's toughness that was misspent here. All this obligatory machismo puffed up simply because you had to act the hero around your kid.

Manuel couldn't fault that. Kids were everything because

you were *their* everything. "Stay up here with Reggie," he told Barbara. "But use the cabin as cover so nothing notices you from the shore. You get into trouble, remember... we're right below."

The ship's living quarters were cramped. Manuel stepped aside as soon as he cleared the door so Luther could see the body slumped in the corner. Best to get that out of the way upfront.

Everything above the corpse's neck was missing. A stream of dried blood hardened like a patch of clay on the wall behind it. The head was a few feet to the left. Between the two body parts, the axe blade was stained pink.

"That's your man," Manuel said. "You need to know I didn't kill him 'til one of those *shriekers* got inside."

Luther's jaw tightened. Manuel braced for a dose of his alleged temper. He wanted to see if this guy was the loose cannon others had described, only Luther didn't pop off. He tightened his mouth, holding something back. "How?" was all he whispered.

Manuel pushed on the door behind him, using his arm to keep it open. The bathroom was a mess of splattered feces. The inside of the toilet, painted red. "It got inside him from in there," he said.

Luther hardly reacted, but it was clear now that his clenched muscles were holding back sorrow, not rage.

"I'm sorry," Manuel said. "There isn't any more time. You have to know something else. I have killed men in front of their families when the situation has called for it. Do you believe me?"

Luther nodded.

"You're going to tell me everything you know about Anne Munro."

"She's fuckin' dead, man. Shark got her like it's getting everyone else."

Manuel had Luther take a seat at the small kitchenette

table. "You were the last person to see her." He pulled the rifle's bolt back and weapon clicked, signifying his willingness to use it. "Tell me why you killed her and it will be quick."

"The shark got her, man." The rising panic in Luther's voice could've suggested innocence but might just as easily be the desperate words of a man who couldn't take the thought of being executed in front of his son. There was no time for a more tactful approach.

"You saw it happen?" Manuel asked.

"Don't you think it's a safe guess?"

"What'd the two of you fight about at Lashonda's Bar?"

Luther looked at Manuel with new misgivings. His interrogator had done his homework. *El Rastreador* was more than one of Anne's midnight rendezvous. "Who is she to you?"

An attempt to make things right, Manuel thought. Whatever that meant. He might've found a reason to live in Barbara, though there was no life without the completion of this task. He had to face his failures and fix them as best he could. Even then, there were no guarantees. He suspected Barbara would tire of him once they were on the mainland. She would go back to the reality of raising her infant son, wouldn't have patience for his degenerate baggage.

More nightmares and regrets were in store for him. All of it, exactly as he deserved. Flagellation was necessary to get right with God. He just had to survive until the sky came calling. Whenever that was wasn't up to him. Nothing was up to him. Nothing except finding Anne.

"An old friend," Manuel said. "That's what she is."

"Don't take this the wrong way, but she could've used one of those."

"And to you she was?"

"At the end, I wasn't sure. We dated. I can tell from your face you think I was taking advantage, but it wasn't like that. She was running from something. Never told me what, but I knew and respected it. Pretty sure she figured the same was true of me. That was our foundation. Two drops of water hiding in a bucket of the Atlantic." Luther chewed his lip, a guilty man with much to regret.

Manuel pushed the gun barrel closer. "At the end?"

"Yeah," Luther said. "Last time I saw her. She was different that night. Right from the get-go. Trying to push me away. Saying I shouldn't waste my time... Shouldn't get mixed up in her issues." His regret turned to tears and he made no motion to wipe them off his cheek.

Manuel took the gun out of his face, took a few steps back.

"I told her I was there for her," Luther said. "But she resented the support. Tried to hurt me."

"How?"

"Starts on about all the guys she's fucking on the island. And I'm not stupid... I knew. She waved her relationship with Rand Hamilton in my face and, yeah, it pissed me off. Not because she was with other men but... she made it sound like I meant as little to her as they all had. It cut, and the deeper she cut, the more she laughed."

"Two of you fought before, though."

"Yeah. So?"

"Why was the last time any different?"

"She shows me this video on her phone. Her going down on that scum fuck, Hamilton. Saying all this fucked up shit. Things that'd make a porn star blush. Whole time the video's going she's staring at *my* face, watching me wrench as I watched it... laughing."

Manuel was partly to blame, as was Garcia and every other selfish prick that might've been a guiding force but instead left Anne floundering as the child of two murdered parents. The troubled path was inevitable.

Once that monkey climbed up onto your back, the fucker nested.

"What'd you do next, Luther?" Manuel's mouth curled into a grin, daring the honest answer.

"I told you I was pissed, man, but I didn't kill anyone. We fought all the way home. I knocked over her coffee table. She laughed harder. I called her a cunt. She asked if that was all I had. Wanted me to beat on her."

"Did you?"

"Fuck no. Never laid hands on a woman and wasn't about to start. I stormed out... last thing I said to her was *'One day you're going to die alone and nobody's going to be there to give a fuck.'*"

"The tape put you over the edge."

Luther sighed. "*We* had one, too... Had no idea she ever recorded us. That was her thing. But she starts flipping through the files on her Mac, showing me how much she loved it with as many people as possible... on the beach, in the reeds, in the bars and restaurant bathrooms at that damn resort. Like I said, she was kicking me when I was down and the look in her eyes... I'll never forget it... pure fucking evil. Like... she hated me for loving her."

"Hey, Bob?"

Manuel didn't hear the question at first. Still had too many of his own to ask. Reggie spoke it again, though, and Manuel had forgotten that *Bob* was this trip's alias. The kid stood in the doorway, shifting from one foot to another.

"What are you doing to my dad?" he asked, eyes darting around the bloody room, barely reacting to the carnage. The concern on his face was for the fate of his dad. It struck Manuel like a dagger to the heart and *El Rastreador* went scampering off like a frightened animal, leaving the shame-filled father stewing inside his skin.

"I'm sorry," Manuel said.

"Get out of here, Reggie," Luther said. "Go above deck. Stay there like I told you. Go!"

The kid was stubborn and refused his father's orders. His heart pounded so hard Manuel could hear it from across the way.

"I knew there was something up with you," Reggie said to Manuel. "Knew it." A flash of steel, then a gun appeared in his wavering fist.

Luther shouted "No!" and Manuel crossed the room with slow, diffusive steps. He reached the center and dropped his rifle to the floor. Once it was obvious that Reggie wasn't going to take a shot, Manuel turned back to Luther, who looked relived at this turn of events. Maybe even grateful. An unspoken understanding passing between them. Fathers on the path.

"If that was the last you saw of Anne—"

"It was," Luther said. "Please, man, we're sitting ducks if we stay here any longer."

"A girl doesn't disappear without a trace."

"She does in an apocalypse."

"She was gone before all this," Manuel said. "On an island I can cross in an afternoon. If you didn't—"

"Hamilton," Luther said.

"He likes to degrade young girls," Manuel said. "But he couldn't kill a snail." He'd known a million men exactly like him in his line of work. Rand Hamilton was much closer to that DJ, *Muto*, or *Buto*, or whatever the fuck...

The agony on Luther's face was raw and unrehearsed. When stories were honed to perfection, they were easy to spot. The dramatic pauses, the flickers of emotion at just the right time.

None of that here. Just remorse for the way he'd allowed it to go down.

Luther regretted the way he'd left things with Anne, probably realizing that she might still be alive if only he'd bottled his anger and spent the night. Wasn't only the *shriekers* that chased Luther, but guilt, too. They also had that in common.

The three of them climbed above deck and went to the front of the boat to stay behind the cabin.

Reggie took a spot against the bow, pistol in hand. Barbara sat on the deck, staring off, lost in her thoughts. The wind was picking up, the sky beginning dim. The boat rocked with increased aggression. The eye of the storm, almost gone.

"Sorry you had to see that," Manuel said as he neared Reggie. "I lost my temper and took it out on your father." He turned to Luther, who nodded in appreciation.

"Whatever," Reggie said.

His dismissal hurt Manuel more than it should've.

Manuel looked at Luther. "What's your plan?"

"I think you know."

"It's risky."

"Risk is our last chance."

"Will you take her?" Manuel asked.

"Still willing to take you, too," Luther said. "Provided I don't ever see you again once we reach the mainland."

"I need to find her."

"I'm telling you... the shark."

"Until I know that for sure..."

"You'll never know that for sure." Luther started for the boat's controls.

"She might still be alive," Manuel said.

"You crazy? Nobody is still alive after last night."

"Then I'll have to settle for the truth," Manuel said. "I don't suppose you know her Mac password?"

"I respected her privacy."

Shit, Manuel thought. This wasn't like the movies where a few quick guesses would yield the answer. He didn't know Anne anymore and guessed her password probably wasn't a combination of her parent's birthdays.

"You don't need her password," Reggie said. "You can reset the whole machine. I do it for Mom every couple of months."

Manuel tore a strip of paper from the boat's handbook and a found a pen in the same compartment. He scribbled out a list as the kid talked.

"You hold Command + R for recovery mode," Reggie told him. "Key in a few prompts until you reach the utilities terminal, then type *reset password*. Choose a new one, then shut the thing down. If you're lucky, Anne didn't encrypt it and you're golden."

Manuel stuffed the paper into his pocket and touched Barbara on the chin, gently turning her head away from the rising waves. "I'll look you up once I get back to the mainland."

Her blue eyes reignited, the first time she reacted to anything since the world had gone to hell. "You son of a bitch," she growled. "You're unloading me? Take care and have a nice life?"

"These are good people," Manuel said. "They will get you to your son faster than I will."

"I don't know them."

"You don't know me."

"Get home to your boy." Manuel disembarked and Barbara must've agreed deep down because she stayed aboard, scowling. It was Reggie who came jogging after him.

"Hey... There's a motor-powered dinghy over there." He

pointed to the beach on their right. "Some of the dudes from the ship came ashore in the night. They got got, but… Well, in case you decide to follow us."

Manuel smiled. "I'll be right behind you." He tapped his pockets performatively. "Though I, uh, don't seem to have any ginger. For the trip home."

It was Reggie's turn to smile.

A spread of warmth filled Manuel. At least he'd won the boy back at the end.

"What's your real name?" Reggie asked. "In case you don't come back."

"Manuel."

The kid glanced over his shoulder. Luther was at the boat's controls, fiddling with some knobs and dials. He turned back to Manuel with a lower voice. "What you said about my Dad back there… do you think it's true?"

"No," Manuel said. "I don't think so. I'll let you know what I find."

"How you going to do that?"

"Finding people is my job. The only one I've ever been good at."

"Just… make it off this island, Manuel." Reggie nodded goodbye and then jogged back along the dock, hopping aboard his father's boat.

Manuel gave the *Eve* one last wave, though nobody was watching him anymore. It was just as well. *You're terrible at goodbyes*, he thought, then hurried inland, wishing he could've stayed on that boat.

They were ready to leave.

Dad waited as long as he dared to start the motor, knowing they would be broadcasting their escape the moment it went off.

Reggie cut the rope from the dock post and the *Eve* drifted out of port. The girl wasn't much help, leaning against the bow, staring at the waves as they floated.

Dad pushed the throttle up. "We'll be planing in six seconds on this bastard."

Reggie didn't know what that meant.

Sensing his confusion, Dad added, "We'll be coasting *through* choppy waves as opposed to getting knocked around by them."

The sky was apocalyptic, bleak for as far as Reggie could see. The air made him shiver as the boat rose to the top of the water and glided along.

"See if you can get eyes on that ship," Dad said and handed his binoculars over.

Reggie scanned the sea. It was too dark to get a visual on anything, save for the frenzied ocean.

A small fin followed them, gliding through pulsing waves. It couldn't keep pace with the boat and eventually slipped under.

Before Reggie could mention it, Dad screamed out "Shit!" and began cutting the wheel to the right.

On the immediate horizon, the large ship was etched in shadow beneath the grey sky. *Eve's* radio crackled as soon as they spotted it.

"This is *Octagon* to unidentified vessel. Stand down at once or you will be considered hostile."

"I don't think so," Dad said, punching the throttle. The boat zipped along, suddenly running horizontal to the larger military vessel that had no trouble matching their speed.

"What is this thing?" Reggie shouted.

"*Eve,*" the radio squawked. "This is your last chance."

"Dad, please!" Reggie cried. This was suicidal. Dad knew it too. His face was folded in defeat. He killed the engine with a growl and left the boat floating in the darkness. The *Eve's* hull scraped the *Octagon's*. A chainsaw on metal.

Reggie craned his neck upward and saw nothing but the endless stretch of black gunwale that blended seamlessly with the night. If there were men up there, they belonged to the shadows.

"I'm sorry," Dad said as the woman, Barbara, began to whimper. She looked back toward Crystal Key with the realization of error stamped across her face. Wherever Manuel had gone, he was better off.

"None of this is your fault," Reggie said.

"I'm not letting them put their hands on you," Dad said. "Give me the gun. Mine's below deck."

Reggie was reluctant to hand it over, but Dad was short on patience. He tore the piece from Reggie's fingers and ejected the magazine to check his shots.

"Who are you people?" Dad screamed as he unbuckled his seat belt and marched across the deck. "You've terrorized us for two days... We are fleeing Crystal Key. I'm bringing my son to safety."

"Do not take another step." The voice hollered from somewhere far above. A deck light snapped on and a half dozen bodies were suddenly backlit against it. "Stay right where you are."

Dad crossed *Eve's* bridge to reach the bow. He waved his arms back and forth like he was signaling a plane. "We are not part of what's happening on that island. We spent the night in hiding, then made a break for my boat. Help us out, all right? Please, man, I got my son with me."

"Told you not to move!" the voice screamed down, amplified and agitated. Dad's face shifted in response to the hostility because this was starting to look like a different kind of problem.

"Man, where am I going to go?"

The *Eve's* hull vibrated beneath Reggie's feet, up through his bones. The boat rose, then fell with enough force to detonate an astonishing splash, water flooding up and breaking across them.

Barbara yelped and staggered back, slamming against the starboard bow, head smashing the railing. Her face slick with blood.

"Do. Not. Move!" the voice screamed from above, oblivious to their peril. Or unconcerned with it.

The boat rocked again. Barbara shouted something that was completely lost in the howling wind. Dad raced toward her as a cone of light enveloped them both.

"Gun!"

Dad had thrown his piece down. It skittered across the deck as he raced toward Barbara in slow motion, hand outstretched because the old sea dog could see what was about to happen.

Another crash struck the hull. The boat lifted. Reggie barely felt this one, more attuned to the desperate sight of Barbara struggling against the rail, screaming. Dad nearly there as her balance gave out.

The ship rose on a hurricane swell and Barbara's screech was louder than nature's outburst. She tumbled over the slick rail, but Dad reached down, shouting desperately for her to hang on because he'd been fast enough to catch Barbara's wrist.

The storm dropped the boat back down into rapturous water. Reggie started to cross toward the starboard side to help Dad when a patch of blinding light ignited against his face, making him squint and look aft. A range of barking, unintelligible voices manifested on the *Eve's* deck, coming from large shadows that were seemingly everywhere.

One of them appeared behind Dad, an armored trooper with a green stripe down the center of his helmet. Gun drawn, watching the scene unfold without the slightest urgency.

The men from the *Octagon* had bordered and Reggie barely registered the rappel lines dangling against the larger ship's black wall. They resembled oversized shriekers stretched out in an attempt to storm that ship. In this moment, Reggie wished that they would.

Barbara screamed again, Reggie catching a few hysterical words about her son, and Dad's face was twisted into a deadlift scrunch, using every bit of power to hoist her body up.

"Help them, man!" Reggie said, pleading with the shadows and gesturing to the obvious struggle.

"Told you to hold it!" that same voice growled back, menace cutting through the storm's constant fervor.

Another bump from below, the *Eve* rocking hard, tipping. Dad, bent over the slippery rail, all of his strength dedicated to preventing Barbara's fall, did a header right overboard.

Reggie somehow heard one splash for the two of them. No screams or struggles. Dad and Barbara, just gone.

Commotion echoed across the dark sky.

Reggie wandered to the rail, ignoring every command to stay put. His eyes pooled. This wasn't real. Dad was here a second ago, promising they would get through this. Now, his absence was as though he never existed.

Hands fell on Reggie's shoulders. "Let's go" were the only words said.

Reggie peered over the railing. The spotlight's edge

revealed a little bit of the ocean. The blood atop it was darker than oil.

As the arms wrapped around Reggie's waist and pulled him back, he saw that pointed dorsal fin jetting off toward Crystal Key.

And then he was being hoisted off the deck, through the air, up toward the vessel above.

THE OPERATIVE

Hannah Preston placed the revolver on top of her desk and thought, *Bloody hell.*

This was the last thing she needed.

"Private Norton is on his way," the intercom said. She felt no need to acknowledge it.

A deep breath helped steady the rage. This was the struggle. Always. Failure bothered her because there was never an excuse for it, and any voice to the contrary was more interested in ego at the expense of results.

She hadn't come this far by accepting that. The problem was that others could, in fact, fail.

And they often did.

For Hannah, the challenge lay in understanding the difference between failure and incompetence. Weren't they one and the same? As a cadet, she had exemplary grades in all areas, though her HR assessment reported that certain soft skills were lacking. Specifically, her interpersonal abilities and people management.

Recognizing her viability as a long-term investment, her mentors implored her to try and see things differently. Even that felt like a sign of weakness on behalf of the entire organization. When it turned out that Osiris leadership believed stupidity was acceptable, her world was thrown into upheaval.

It wasn't something Hannah wished to concede, debating the subject and arguing that the acceptance of failure lowered the bar and helped the incompetent sleep at night. Osiris could do better. But these arguments were refuted unanimously, at least publicly, and she'd been forced to disavow them before proceeding in their employ.

On the record, Hannah Preston no longer harbored those views. Off the record, however, was a different story.

On a day like today, when one of her soldiers got two civilians killed because he could not properly assess a situation, she felt validated. Because she'd been right.

The door to her quarters slid open, and Norton appeared in the frame. All 6' 6" of him, his beady eyes and receding buzz cut screamed state cop. He barked, body thrusting at attention, ignoring the fact that this was not a military operation, despite Osiris' similar rank structure.

"Come in," she said and returned her attention to the dim glow of the laptop screen.

Norton stood in front of her desk in silence, his eyes leveled straight over the top of her head. He scowled as if this was nothing but an inconvenience.

Hannah went about her work, allowing his shallow breathing to score her keystrokes. She imagined his nerves shredding inside as he inevitably noticed the fully loaded weapon an inch from her wrist. All of this was very good for him—a way to build character.

Somehow, though, Hannah doubted any of this was a learning experience in his mind. The scowl on his face seemed to be his natural mode as indicated by the rivulets around his mouth.

Did he regret what happened out there? She was tempted to ask, but wasn't in favor of the school marm approach. He refused eye contact, which might've been a side effect of his military upbringing, though Hannah read it as disrespectful. As she combed his dossier, she began to think it was his forthcoming discipline that had him stewing.

He didn't think he deserved any.

This was another thing that bothered her about failure. Osiris' insistence on being understanding was a way to skirt responsibility. He was guaranteed to blame her for any reprimand. It was already unfair in his mind because he was just being a good company man.

Never mind that he should've been smart. Never mind that Osiris doesn't stand by and allow civilians to perish through indecision. Not the point. Because, in his mind, Hannah Preston was already being The Bitch.

That bothered her, too.

Norton looked Cro-Magnon. Tiny features surrounded by lots of blank face. There wasn't enough of it to hide any emotion behind. On one hand, Osiris needed more people like him, ones who could act in the company's best interest without concern for the absurd humanist component that had stifled every other major institution in the twenty-first century. On the other hand, Norton was sloppy in a way that could hurt them.

Under her command, that was not going to happen.

"Private Norton," she said in a way that ensured her voice was professional and inviting. Easy to do with her Australian accent, which she used to full advantage. "I have been fully briefed on the situation by the away team commander. Explain to me, in your own words, what went wrong down there."

"The insurgent had a gun," he said. "Seemed to me the entire deck might've been hostile and I—"

"Insurgent? I didn't realize we had decided to classify the residents of Crystal Key as rebels."

"Protocol says that we must do everything within our power to mitigate risk."

"His weapon was a caliber so low it couldn't cut butter, let alone your body armor."

"I made a judgment call."

"You let a man die in front of his son."

Norton's gaze wandered back to the top of her head, cheeks puffing. Obvious he had no interest in addressing this further.

Hannah wondered if she'd ever been this type of burden on her superiors. Was her credo of personal responsibility as worthless to them as Norton's murderous instincts were to her?

No, they promoted me.

With a few taps on the keyboard, she was deep into his file. Kicked out of police academy at twenty-two because of volatile temperament and a disdain for authority. The Marine Corps had been eager to receive him since the United States government continued to force its agenda on desert countries that didn't want them there. Norton enjoyed it all so much he did five tours in the Middle East, but his jacket was anything but honorable. Lots of confirmed kills, just as much disciplinary action.

An American Asshole.

Hannah wondered how he wormed his way into Osiris. Having gone through recruitment herself, she could confirm their rigorous screening process. Her issues with the organization aside, they vetted you so deeply they checked your drawers for streaks.

It had to be that way because Osiris did not officially exist. That's why they were decentralized. That's why Drew Norton was her problem.

"What else do you have to say for yourself, private?"

"Our men are alive right now because I acted," he said. "I will not apologize for that. I saw a gun, the man began to flee and—"

"You disobeyed an order to assist him."

"There was no time assess the situation, and I thought we needed to clear the ship before offering any assistance to those who may or may not be infected. Ma'am."

This rhetoric carried a rehearsed quality, and Hannah wondered how many times he'd given the same spiel to his commanding officers in the military.

Osiris didn't fire people. It was in your best interest to stay employed. You did that, and you did very well in life. If not, you were a loose canon. A free agent and a liability.

"I have to talk to the boy now," Hannah said. "I have to explain to him why we stood there and watched his father die. I have to apologize for the girl we allowed to fall overboard in the confusion."

"Ma'am, this is war," Norton said unrepentantly, and as though Hannah simply needed to have it explained.

She picked up the semi-auto revolver and shot Norton through the forehead. His skull split down the center with sledgehammer force, coughing brain matter as he was lifted off his feet and thrown backward. He crashed to the floor in a crumpled husk while spilt blood pooled around him.

Hannah watched his twitching body. Murder brought no pleasure, but its simplicity as a solution was perfect. She placed the gun down and hit the communicator button beside it.

"Going to need clean-up."

Her office was unseemly now. The sliding door to the right allowed her to escape into her personal quarters. She typed the code for no entry into the keypad so the barrier would lock and nobody could bother her. The communicator screen was on the far wall, and Mister Wyatt was already on it, waiting.

"Operative Preston," he said.

Wyatt had a way of making Hannah feel as though she was speaking to a shadow. He was so obscure on screen that even his desk was a faint outline. She didn't know what he looked like despite having been in a room with him more than once. He wore a loose suit and styled his hair to be deliberately unkempt. Once, during a face-to-shadow meeting, she'd noticed a streak of grey in the light. "I trust the recovery is proceeding as planned."

"We've had some setbacks," she said. "Nothing that puts us off course, though. I had to remove one of our own for going rogue."

"An essential?"

"Most definitely un-essential," she said.

"Good. What other setbacks are there?"

"The package was opened, and I'm afraid Crystal Key is compromised as a result."

"To be expected," he said. "That was the projected outcome in your initial assessment."

Hannah bit the inside of her lip to prevent a show of pride from spreading across her mouth. "There were enough similarities to the New York incident for me to suspect the events were connected," she said. "And they are. I try and be prepared for every contingency, but this is the worst case."

"It's because of your diligence, Operative Preston, that we're here at all," he said. "A word of caution, however. Once the storm passes, it is going to be harder to function."

"My hope is that we won't have to. Once we remove the obstruction, we can proceed with recovery and clean-up."

"I have the utmost confidence in you."

"That's nice to hear, sir."

The line went dead, and Hannah was quick to power down the communicator to avoid further interruption. She dropped into bed and stared at the cabin's ceiling while the rocking ship tempted her to nod off. She closed her eyes and was back on her parents' waterbed, remembering for a second what it was like to be a kid. But there were too many pressures to indulge in needless nostalgia. A complete disaster just a few miles away. Mass casualties. Her responsibility.

All she wanted was to take a few more heavy breaths in silence.

Through the ship's thin walls, she heard rustling in the next room. The cleaning crew's arrival. She wasn't excited about the lingering chemical smell that she'd be working in from here on out, but it was the cost of doing business. There was no punishment severe enough for Norton to remain in her employ.

Peace of mind was short-lived as Hannah considered her plate. What was she supposed to say to the boy? *Sorry kid, this kind of thing happens?* It would, of course, be easier if she could simply kill him, too, but that cruelty was beyond her measure.

Then there was the obstacle. Osiris had succeeded, barely, in severing all communication to and from Crystal Key. They had jamming equipment that could send everything within a twenty-mile radius back to the Stone Age. Keeping the residents in the dark was a bleak necessity. No one could have known what had gotten loose there, although Hannah had suspected it right off.

It wasn't the first time she'd seen the alien.

Mister Wyatt had given her unlimited funds as long as the package was secured.

And the shark was preventing them from accomplishing that.

The shark dove with the female in his mouth, drowning her before his falling jaws could wrangle the last bits of life out of the meat. She squirmed so much he thought he'd captured an entire school of eels in his teeth. She came apart in pieces, indiscriminate chunks sliding down his throat.

His brain, what had become his thoughts, resented that his body was trying to retreat into the deep.

Deep waters were safer. He knew this. His passenger, however, felt it would be best to attack the danger head-on. Destroy the ship that so eagerly hunted them. They both recognized that it would come directly for him soon, though his passenger was against the dive. Against retreating.

Fight, it told him.

The shark ignored his passenger's request. He had no desire for death and its suggestions were against his best interests. He'd taken enough human prey and would be satisfied with the bounty given by more hospitable fathoms. His diet of cephalopods had served him well for a quarter century and would again. All that mattered was food, and there was plenty of that at lower depths.

He had gorged over the last twenty-four hours, feasting on swimmers as well as local flavor: Snapper, tuna, and part of a fishing boat for good measure.

The passenger's ever-increasing mass also alarmed him. He felt the creature stirring on his basihyal, but could no longer feel the actual muscle that had once been his tongue. He only felt the rider in its place. It wiggled around and picked tiny shards of shredded meat out of his teeth, growing after every feeding in strength as well as size, its instincts becoming the dominant ones, contradicting millions of years of evolution.

Earlier today, it had forced him to follow a smaller boat out of the harbor. It considered devouring the human body that had fallen into the Atlantic and floated out to sea, blood drizzling from a hole in the center of his face. The shark watched as the parasites inside that body abandoned their host, wiggling like seaweed, then withering immediately in the salt water. His passenger outraged by the sight.

The passenger had been determined to take the smaller boat down, instigated by its obnoxious vibrations. This brought them into the path of the larger vessel for a second time. The shark recalled the flurry of spears that had pierced his hardened brown skin and did not wish to experience that again.

Only his passenger did.

It was safer for the shark the further down he swam, but the passenger's grip on his mind tightened in a way that refused this motion.

The living tongue crawled up his throat to remind him that it was in charge, and in that moment, demanded he return to the surface to deliver even more prey.

The passenger wanted to keep growing.

Hannah stepped onto the deck in her Osiris field command uniform: navy blue pants that teetered on black. The fabric consisted of taclite TDU, with 7.5 ounces of poly/cotton ripstop fabric that reduced the likelihood of embarrassing tears while in the field. The Teflon finish further enhanced durability, and since Hannah was hands-on, that peace of mind was essential.

Her top was a matching long-sleeve navy shirt that could house a thick tactical vest. She had no intention of lugging that around while aboard the *Octagon*, however.

Her boots were ripstop nylon, roughened suede, and Helcor leather that stomped large and delivered comfortable mobility at all times. The hidden knife pocket housed an 8 AUS stainless steel blade that she carried everywhere—even into her meetings with Mister Wyatt.

Her gloves were dual-layer cowhide leather palm with molded hard-shell knuckles and fingers for when you absolutely had to punch someone.

The pistol that killed Drew Norton hung in the holster off her right thigh.

She wanted to show the troops that see she was ready for battle.

Everyone tensed as she passed, even Executive Officer Chris Bradley. His shoulders clipped back, and his occasional hunch straightened toward the sky as she took a spot beside him. The windows of Command & Control looked down at the thin bow, where everything appeared to be progressing nicely.

Osiris men were spaced out on the deck, dropping gallons of chum into the waters around them. This was the beginning of their endgame—seduce the shark to the surface, then annihilate it.

She folded her arms across her chest while XO Bradley delivered a status report. As advanced as Osiris was, there was no magic bullet for catching sharks. They might've been standing on the bridge of a billion-dollar, private sector version of the U.S. Navy's littoral combat ship, but they could've been in a rubber dinghy and their trapping technique would've been the same.

An away team had motored to Miami to retrieve large sections of cow carcass they now used as bait. Each piece was outfitted with a custom forged steel hook and attached to floating orange buoys. XO Bradley explained their options once they had the shark ensnared. Capture or kill.

Hannah was leaning toward kill.

It was just a shark, but that shark had killed several of her men, divers, as well as the observation team she'd ordered onto Crystal Key as the hurricane hit. They were to observe and return a sample of the organism. Instead, they went dark as soon as they got ashore.

She had no tolerance for failure, but payback was necessary to absolve her of the guilt.

"We'll get that thing," Bradley said.

"Of course," Hannah said. None of this was surprising. The team hadn't failed her yet. This would be no different. Her thoughts were too fractured to oversee the capture of this fish. Instead, she was thinking about the young boy they'd brought aboard. Witness to his father's untimely death and prisoner on a black site ship.

Dammit.

She should've gone to see him first, but getting a quick status check was the less challenging of her two tasks.

"How's the kid?"

"Hasn't said a word," Bradley said. "Completely shut down."

Hannah knew she had to go see him, though sadly she was the least equipped to handle it. Osiris' best operative, sure, but as comforting as a drowning scream.

Throughout her command, she'd heard the chatter. Caught little snippets of it here and there. *Ice Princess.* The least creative of all honorifics, but the one her people most commonly used. She was fairly certain it was Bradley who had coined it, as it appeared in rotation shortly after he'd made a drunken pass at her while on a weekend of shore leave.

He'd shown up at her room with a bottle of whiskey and a stumble in his step, professing his love as if he was Lloyd Dobler without the charm of Peter Gabriel on boombox. Single malt sweated from every pore in his body and he could barely speak, tongue dripping with gibberish.

The whole gesture had been unseemly and unmoving, and Hannah wouldn't pretend otherwise. Hence, she suspected, her nickname.

She'd been tempted to remove Bradley from command after that. But having promised her superiors that she would try and relax her stance on staff failure, she'd written it off as a lapse in judgment and told Mister Wyatt she was evolving just as he'd encouraged.

Hannah had to find solace elsewhere, and that was in catching little bouts of shame paddling across Bradley's face every now and again. Flashes of his failed pass flickered each time they spoke—scars in his eyes. Weaker minds might've begun to feel bad about that constant torture, not Hannah.

She liked it because she never wanted XO Bradley to forget his mistake. That was how she prevented him from making another.

"Keep me appraised," Hannah said and started off.

"Good luck," Bradley said in a *better you than me* tone.

"Just worry about the shark," she said. "We're almost out of time." Hurricane Margot was supposed to finish her rampage before midnight, and their anonymity was over as soon as the storm passed. Osiris had enough top-level connections that the right wheels could be greased and the worst problems could be made to go away, but Hannah considered that a last resort and not a perk of the job.

"We'll get it," he said.

She left Command & Control, and an Osiris Trooper in similar dress—only combat ready with full Kevlar, FN SCAR rifle in hand, and battle helmet on head—offered a nod of acknowledgment. His eyes traveled to the holstered pistol on her thigh as he said, "Ma'am."

By now, word had traveled to all decks that Norton was a goner.

Hannah didn't want her men thinking that Draconian rule was now the order of the day. She'd have to address them soon and let it be known that the consequence of Drew Norton's failure was unique. Many on the ship had served under her for so long she hoped they already knew that.

"Bradley," she called from the stairwell.

Her XO spun right around.

"Move the Recovery Team into position," she said. "I don't want them in the water until we've got the big boy in sight, but they need to be ready to go at a second's notice."

"Understood," he said.

Hannah headed two decks down to the crew quarters and habitability area. This was where their ship's design offered dramatic improvement over the Navy's messy *moving day* aesthetic of nomadic workstations and overgrowth of extension cord wires.

The *Octagon* had a fully realized living space that consisted of a mess hall with a made-to-order menu, an observation deck/recreation space with plasma screens, PS5s, and foosball tables, along with a medical bay. It was important that the crew had creature comforts and the play space necessary to blow off steam at the end of a shift.

The young boy was in medical under the care of Dr. Ellen Medford. The grey sliding door glided open on silent runners and Hannah stepped through.

Dr. Medford looked up from her computer terminal. "He could probably stand a face friendlier than mine," she said.

"Then he's out of luck," Hannah said.

Dr. Medford shrugged. "At least you're prettier." She sipped from her steaming coffee mug. "Should keep a nanny on staff for things like this."

"How's he doing?"

"He's in shock," the doctor said.

"So I hear."

"To be expected. Exhibiting every last symptom of it, too. Clammy skin, quick pulse, quicker breathing, nausea, the occasional spike in hysterics."

"Can I see him?"

"Of course, but—"

"I know," Hannah said. "I'm not exactly mother material. I get it."

"I was just going to suggest taking it slow. If he doesn't want to talk, don't force him. He may not remember what happened. If that's the case, don't remind him. Not yet. If he does and he's agitated because of it—"

"I get it. Really."

"He's back there. One last thing... try dropping the Wicked

British Nanny thing. Remember *The Omen?*"

"I'm from Australia."

"Even so…"

"This is how I talk."

"As soothing as a rape whistle." The doctor took another sip of coffee and winked as the mug covered her grin.

Hannah sighed. She wasn't in the habit of apologizing for anything, let alone the failure of a rogue agent. Still, this was her command. That son of bitch Norton had been her responsibility.

She stopped short of the med room's sensor that would slide open the next door. Her heart pounded.

This was pressure she hadn't felt in years.

She resented it.

The shark cut north, having found what he thought was a safe distance from surface predators. He slithered down to twelve fathoms where the water was darker and anonymous. He floated there, conserving his energy, shifting his wounded fin only when he needed to circle back.

The hull's constant deposits of ripe, bloody meat into the ocean interested him. He thought about knifing up and taking a taste. Not because he was especially hungry, but because the passenger inside of him demanded it.

The shark didn't accept this. He questioned the urge. The female human was fresh in his belly, and that would keep him sated for a while. The passenger tried to make the prospect of bloody chum appealing, but the shark was content to hold his position in the gloom.

He was used to outwitting creatures of the sea—larger

predators that stalked deeper fathoms, and lesser ones imbued with faster speed. But this was the first time something had been striking at him from inside.

The passenger wanted more than to merely *exist*, and it grew desperate. That rage seemed to make it stronger.

An explosion rocked the surface. Vibrations rippled well beyond twelve fathoms. The smaller hull that the shark had followed from the island came sinking toward him—frayed aluminum and metal drifting into oblivion.

This could've been another part of their trap, but the shark was willing to circle the wreckage from a curious distance. There was no sign of life. He lost interest as it fell toward the hundreds of other wreckages lost to time.

As a creature of habit, whose habit was to eat and eat often, the shark had no use for the chum that bobbed on the raucous surface. He did wonder about the dark hull from where it was coming, the ship seemingly so determined to capture him.

It housed plenty of carrion, of that he was sure. The good stuff. The stuff that was more difficult to resist.

The passenger wiggled in excitement and drove the shark up to four fathoms... three... two. His dorsal fin would be a dead giveaway if he were to go all the way and break the surface.

He was close enough now to sense humans moving across the ship's deck, the hull sending their vibrations rippling down. Were he to swim all the way up, there would be many eyes with a single goal. Destroy him. The shark had no understanding of fear, just preservation. And the longer the ship remained, the longer his life was at risk.

He swam on, eager to destroy it.

Reggie was numb. Walking to school in a Boston February numb. He was aware of the door opening but didn't care enough to look.

"Reginald Bradshaw?" The woman's voice was slathered in Vegemite. He didn't want whatever it was she was selling because, in his mind, Dad kept slipping overboard around a platoon of witnesses. He tried thinking of Becky St. George, desperate to focus on anything else, but whatever imagery he put up in defense was torn through like wet tissue. And then Dad was dying all over again. "Mind if I sit?"

She edged into his peripheral. His heart thundered. He feared her and everyone else onboard. They'd stolen him off the deck of Dad's boat with a bear hug, and the last thing he'd seen as he was rappelled up was an aerial view of blood-strewn water.

These people weren't military. They had no uniform. No flag. And he'd heard at least four different languages since his capture. They would never have to answer for what happened.

The woman said something else, but to Reggie's ears she was Charlie Brown's teacher. He tuned her out, searching for a wormhole into anything other than death. Memories reached up out of memories. They were black and white and quickly cut down by a splash of water. Only Dad's blood was in color.

He was determined to hold onto one of them. Just one. He thought maybe the trick was to focus on something singular instead of allowing every damn life moment to cycle through. There was Dad from years back... still bald, but before the accident had taken his eye. This memory was from when they would drive over to Cambridge every Saturday to hit the local comic shops.

First stop was always New England Comics, a little door in the wall in Harvard Square that Dad preferred because of its back issues. He didn't like the new stuff much. Reggie liked ComicaZi more thanks to their action figure selection—sprawling walls and endless choices. He wondered if that was an accurate reflection, or if everything just seemed bigger when you were a kid.

Dad let him get a few books each week, and when it was time to celebrate something, a good report card or an 'A' paper, he could pick out an action figure. The prices of those things were always going up, up, up, though, so that happened less and less. When you had to plunk down twenty-five bucks to get the really good ones, it was over.

Those Saturdays were a ritual. Dunks on the drive home, always, where their orders were unwavering. Dad ordered a large hot while Reggie got a Pepsi and a dozen jelly munchkins. Then it was time to go home, get comfortable in the living room, and dive into their hauls while Mom eventually brought out tuna fish sandwiches buried beneath BBQ Lays.

On the last of those days, right before Dad left for good, he sat staring at the issue of Superman #1 from the DC "New 52." And Reggie could tell that something was on his mind because he only stared at it. The pages never flipped.

"It's going to kill me to let this go," he said.

Reggie was always asking Dad what he meant.

"My father was never the most pleasant man to be around when I was kid. And this," he held the Superman book out for emphasis, "this was my only escape. I don't know where my interest came from, 'cause no one else in our complex had it, that's for damn sure, but I went in big for this stuff. Used to redeem bottles to buy a stack each week. And when I saw *Superman* on the big screen, forget it. Magic."

"Kinda boring, though... I think the new one will be better."

"Blasphemy." Dad started to argue before he collected

himself and remembered why he was having this conversation in the first place. "But I got to pass my love of this stuff on to you. In the process, I got to finally rise above my old man, that bastard, and say, '*I won.*' That means the world to me. I love you, man."

Dad didn't read any of his books that day and spent the afternoon packing his things instead.

That was the first time Dad had walked out of his life.

Today was the second.

Reggie turned toward the voice that was still blabbing, anger igniting at the sight of her. All he could think was, *Of course.*

He dug his fingernails into his palms. Hadn't heard a word she'd said and didn't want to start now. She would try and explain this as a terrible mistake, how there's usually protocols and procedures, and how the man who stood nearby and allowed Dad to slip away was a really good trooper in a bad situation.

There was no making this right.

The woman finished speaking, then sat there looking at him. Wavy black hair dropped just past her shoulders, and her eyebrows matched that color, though were angled in a way that made her look permanently sinister. Her blue eyes were chips of ice. He felt cold just looking at her.

"I want off this ship," he said.

"I know... as soon as the storm passes..."

"You're not listening to me. I want off this ship *now.*"

"Reginald..."

"Don't call me that. Ain't earned the right to say my name."

"Where will you go? You going to swim to Miami? You'll drown in one-hundred-foot waves if the shark doesn't get you first. Or should we take you back to Crystal Key... the place you were trying to escape from. Is that where you want to go?"

Reggie could've punched her. She *was* close enough to take a fist to the nose. He would enjoy it, even, but these monsters weren't above murder. If he socked her one, he'd never leave here alive. He had his doubts about that anyway.

"You're a bunch of killers," he said. "I'll take my chances with A, B, or C. As long as I'm away from you."

The woman studied his face, watching his eyes for a long time. "I don't blame you," she said. "And I'm not going to patronize you. Tell you that I understand. Of course I don't. What I will say to you is that the man who disobeyed orders and allowed your father to fall has been dealt with."

The door behind her opened and a second, older woman in a white coat entered. The doctor who had checked Reggie over before throwing him into this cell. "That's enough, Hannah."

"No," Hannah said. "The boy is exactly right."

"You can't do this," the doctor said.

Hannah whipped her head so fast Reggie thought he heard a growl go with it. The doctor stepped back and raised her arms in defense. She wasn't happy about this, her expression said, though her body promised not to contradict Hannah's wishes.

"What do you mean, *'dealt with?'*" Reggie said.

Hannah's glare stayed on the doctor until she retreated through the door. When she turned back toward Reggie, her lips were stretched into a thin, victorious smile. "What happened to your father is... not who we are... certainly not who I am."

"Right."

"Look," Hannah said, taking the next part carefully. "*Reginald.*" When Reggie didn't protest, she continued. "This is not customer service. I cannot apologize for what happened. We're not talking about a bad experience during your stay at the Ramada. Someone on my team made a mistake, no question. A careless, cruel mistake. And the soldier who did it has paid dearly."

Reggie wanted to find that guy and put bullets through his heart. He thought back to the infected islander on the docks. The ease with which he'd shot him. The greater ease with which he could shoot the man who had refused help to his father.

Dad wouldn't want that, of course, but Reggie did.

"I killed him," Hannah said, then sat back with a matter-of-factness that was almost comical in its unexpectedness. "He put this operation at risk. It's unforgivable, and I don't allow men like that to remain in my employ."

Reggie stared. It was unforgivable. And knowing that he had been dealt with... well, it brought no additional comfort. In some ways, it was even more depressing because he knew now there was nothing that could be done to make the pain go away.

"I can show him to you," Hannah said.

The doctor attempted to intervene once more via the two-way glass and intercom speaker across the room, but Hannah raised a single finger to the air, prompting her silence.

Reggie cleared his throat. "Show me his body, you mean?"

Hannah nodded. "I can show you video of him returning to the boat. You can see him take his helmet off. You'll see his face. And once you've seen his face, I'll take you to see his body. Reginald, if you see all that, we won't be even, but you'll know that I am trying to do right by you."

It was the strangest offer he'd ever had. Maybe Reggie would feel better once he saw the body on a slab and knew that he could never hurt anyone else.

Doubtful.

"What do you say, Reginald? Want to see the body?"

He didn't have to think long about it. "Sure."

The shark rocketed up and snatched a bit of chum. Not because he wanted it, but because he wanted to see what sort of trap was lying in wait for him.

For the brief second he broke the surface, he heard excited shouts and scrambles overhead. None of this concerned him because he could dive and be gone before they had a chance to attack. Gunfire was so loud that bullets zipped past and lost inertia in the choppy water.

He dropped several fathoms before looping back around. The glossy dark hull taunted him and he went right for it, barreling in a death charge, determined to prove these waters were his.

Human screams came to his ear canals as distant commotion. The predator dipped back beneath the waves as the water above him splashed to signal the arrival of additional bait: large hunks of meat he knew better than to take.

This was the trap.

He'd shown them he was there. That would make them eager. That meant they'd come in after him. He glided further into darkness thinking that he would be ready when they came, and for once, the passenger agreed.

Reggie followed Hannah out of medical as she speed-walked the *Octagon's* halls. They went down a flight of industrial stairs made from welded aluminum, and the comfortable *Star Trek-ish* interior of the ship fell away, the rest of it looking like a warehouse.

"This is our mission bay," Hannah said as they stopped on

a platform that overlooked the floor. A series of shipping containers were strewn beneath them, double stacked and with doors opened on each end. Temporary offices. Each container was a workspace populated by three or four people hammering away at work desks and futuristic consoles. "The morgue is back here."

The dead man was inside the furthest container. Unlike the others, it was single stacked and hermetically sealed. Hannah wrapped gloved fingers around the handle and gave it a powerful tug. The door decompressed with a sweeping *woosh,* cold air striking them as it opened.

Hannah walked in first and stopped in front of the single gurney. She had a tablet in her hand. Tapped it a few times and handed it to Reggie.

"Push play," she said. "It may be... difficult for you to watch."

Reggie took it without hesitation. His thumb gave the play button a violent push, eyes clocking up to meet Hannah's, giving her a *this better be good* glare before it started.

The footage was grainy. A couple of armored bodies standing at a row of equipment lockers. The man closest to the camera took his helmet off and tossed it down, dropping to the bench. He put his head between his legs, hands on his thighs, and vomited all over the girdled floor.

Behind him, the other troops seemed equally troubled by the way things had gone in the field.

"That is my team," Hannah said. "A few hours ago." The time stamp in the corner of the screen confirmed her story. "Do you recognize him? The one in front?"

Reggie did. It would've been difficult to tell for sure except for the green stripe up the center of his helmet. He'd seen it on the man as they rappelled upward, being *rescued.* Some of the men voicing their displeasure over his apparently rogue decision to let the situation play out without intervention. "Yeah," Reggie said.

Hannah didn't wait for Reggie to be ready. She gave the gurney sheet a violent tug and flung it aside. "His name's Drew Norton," she said. "I don't know how he got assigned to me with his history, but that's no excuse. I shot him dead."

Drew Norton's pale face matched the one in the video, except for the cratered hole in the middle of his forehead.

Hannah stood with her arms folded and watched Reggie, gauging his satisfaction.

Reggie didn't know how to feel. Truth of it was... he was glad Drew Norton was dead and maybe a little disappointed that he couldn't have done it himself. Glad the cold-blooded fuck had grown a red third eye. But somehow, Reggie felt worse than he had before.

And Hannah was suddenly terrifying, because this was some James Bond SPECTRE stuff.

"This organization does not tolerate failure."

Before Reggie's worry had a chance to become a full-blown freak out, he reminded himself that Hannah had shown him this to prove the bad guy was gone. It should've made him feel better, but as he looked her over, he saw that she didn't have a comforting bone in her body. She projected impatience as she stood there, not so much interested in his catharsis, but instead waiting for the appropriate cue to return to work.

"Okay," he said and gave the tablet back.

She took it, and Reggie followed her out into the mission bay where Hannah signaled the first able body in sight, ordering him to re-seal the morgue.

The ship rumbled as, beneath them, gong-like reverberations shook through everything, including Reggie's fillings. Nervous chatter stirred among the personnel as the intercom summoned Hannah to the bridge. She and Reggie rushed up to the catwalk, climbing a second flight of stairs, then taking a long corridor to the bridge: A hectic mass of people, all tuned to their stations.

Hannah led Reggie to the front.

"You'll see we're on the same team," she said in a way that wasn't particularly reassuring. "What have you got, XO Bradley?"

"Shark, starboard side."

The word made Reggie tense.

Hannah lifted on her heels and glanced below where a flurry of men were flinging buckets of meat into the ocean.

"He's getting more confident," XO Bradley said. "Came up and grabbed a mouthful of chum. We're ready to take him now that we've got visual. If he dives, we've got depth charges ready to disperse."

Time passed in slow motion. Reggie stared at the waves like his life depended on their mercy, and Hannah's attention was every bit as focused. Cold blue eyes assessing the shifting battlefield visible through each of the bridge's tempered windows.

The rest of the room chatter, from those maneuvering the ship to the ones monitoring radar and sonar, lowered into whispers while Hurricane Margo's violent sways tipped them left and right, reminding them they weren't welcome anywhere on the ocean.

Steep waves appeared as shadows on the edges of darkness and rushed the ship, breaking over the exterior, flooding away everything that wasn't bolted down. That should've been reason enough to force a retreat, but Reggie knew this ship wasn't going anywhere. Not while Hannah was in command.

"Anyone got eyes on the fish?" XO Bradley asked, getting nothing in response.

"It knows," Hannah said, her smile forged in admiration. "The bloody bastard knows we're hunting it."

"Maybe it's just full," XO Bradley said.

"These things are never full," she said. "They swim, shit, eat... and eat. We're rolling out a buffet and it wants nothing to do with us. What does that tell you?"

"That it's full."

Hannah pushed the comm button. "Have the body of Sergeant Norton retrieved from the morgue. Outfit him with a transmitter, bait him, and bring him to the bow."

"He has a family," Bradley said.

"He *had* one," she corrected. "His lifeless body isn't going to make a difference in their lives. As of right now, my report is that Norton was lost at sea. Let's make it official."

Bradley stared at the swirling storm through the glass, saying nothing. Hannah turned on her heels, glaring through the side of his face, seemingly trying to melt the flesh off his bones. Pronounced silence from each of the surrounding workstations. Reggie had to turn to make sure they were all still there.

"Get Norton up here," Hannah said, speaking loud and slow so there could be no misunderstanding her order. "Tie him to those barrels. If the shark wants people, not cows, we'll give him one."

Two men hurried off the bridge to carry out her directive.

Bradley leaned in and touched her elbow. "Jesus, Hannah—"

She flinched. "Operative Preston, XO. There *is* a chain of command here."

"Yes," Bradley said. "Operative. Preston. Some of the men are already on edge because of what happened with Norton. What you did—"

"They should be worried about what *he* did." Hannah glanced down at Reggie. "Norton isn't a fallen comrade in arms, XO. He was a liability to all of us. If he can still be of use, it's the least he can do to redeem himself."

"But—"

"Argue with me again, Bradley, and I will strip you of command."

Bradley's silence gave Reggie the confidence to pipe in. "That thing's a monster," he said. "Grabbed a girl right off her surfboard and seemed to enjoy squeezing the life out of her. If you all can kill it, please do."

Until a few hours ago, that incident under the pier had been the most horrific sight Reggie had ever seen. Then Dad's silent fall flashed through his head and he hated everyone on this ship all over again.

"We're going to," Hannah told him.

Roughly ten minutes passed and the men carrying Norton's naked body appeared through the window, heading toward the tip of the bow, moving cautiously while nature threw everything she could at them. Gigantic buoys dragged behind Norton's corpse, tied from wire knots around his ankles and torso.

One of the men down there looked up at the bridge and tried speaking into his mouthpiece communicator, but the furious wind and lashing water dominated the channel and denied his voice.

"Get a patrol boat out there," Hannah ordered. "I want them ready to go as soon as the shark takes this bait. The transmitter will lead us right to it... wherever it goes. We'll hit the bastard with everything we've got."

Reggie went to the starboard side windows where part of the ship's rear exterior lifted open, a hatch that extended out over the thrashing water.

On the bow, the men flung Norton's body into the Atlantic, the floatation attachments following him down into the dark and stirring waves.

At the rear, four troopers in an inflatable PVC boat dropped through the newly opened hatch, bobbing around on riled water.

The troopers on the bow were hunched over the rail, pointing to the ocean below. A gigantic swell broke, spraying roaring water across the deck, sending them sliding in all directions.

Hannah folded her arms and her already expressionless face twisted into a hardened mask. "What?" she said once she noticed Reggie staring.

"Who the hell are you people?"

"The Discovery Channel."

The intercom buzzed, delivering a wave of chaotic screams from down in mission bay.

Hannah touched her leg holster and then started for the exit.

"Look!" Reggie cried, stopping Hannah in her tracks. He pointed at the open hatch at the ship's rear. A massive wiggling shape had somehow appeared atop the horizontal platform, its weight beginning to force the plank down, bending against the ship's hull.

"Shit," Hannah said and took off running.

Reggie struggled to process the sight at first. It was the shark. Somehow, it had leapt from the water and was now perched on the jutting lip. The lightning crashed, giving him a glimpse of the fish, twisting around on the plank while beneath it, the small rubber boat rocked on harried waves. The crew brought its motor to life and went zipping out across open water.

Reggie went to follow Hannah out the door but XO

Bradley grabbed his shoulders. "Stay here, bud. Where it's safest."

He broke free and took off running. Maybe she was covering her ass, but Hannah had been straight with him, and that was all he could cling to. He ran to find her, trying to remember the way to mission bay.

Reggie sprinted down two decks and rushed through the open door frame, bumping into Hannah's back, knocking her against the metal scaffolding that overlooked the modular floor plan.

She leapt in shock and then pushed Reggie back through the door with her free hand. "No closer!" she screamed. She held her weapon in her other fist and was taking aim at the shark, its monstrous face, those blazing eyes and delighted grin, visible through the opened hatch, storm water rushing in around its demonic head, flooding across the floor.

The shark's head flopped one way, and then the other, attempting to wiggle through the frame. Such an unnatural sight that Reggie screamed. The platform that held it in place slipped toward the ocean on groaning hinges. The fish looked from person-to-person, the bodies scrambling across the mission bay floor, assessing who was to be eaten first, its monstrous mouth becoming a yawning cavern. The pink tongue visible behind the rows of its forked teeth made Reggie's eyes pop.

It wasn't a tongue.

It was the biggest shrieker he'd ever seen. It slipped from the shark's mouth in a graceless escape, lumbering, too engorged to properly move, floundering across the slick and collapsing deck, unable to locate the necessary traction to propel itself forward. Men and women closed in around it, opening fire, shots sinking uselessly into its glistening, slime-crusted flesh, never so much as slowing it.

From outside, the boat crew did the same, opening fire at a safe distance. Their shots were inconsistent on spastic waves.

The platform snapped off the ship, dropping the shark's body down into the water, an imperceptible splash in the raging storm.

The tip of slug bent over the interior wall and gravity did the rest, tugging its body along in one slow and inevitable slither as it absorbed gunfire like sunlight.

The shrieker was the *Octagon's* problem now. The size of a damn mountain lion. It lifted its head to the air, charcoal eyes narrowing into hateful little slits. A wiggling mass detached itself from the shrieker's body, becoming a much smaller version of the creature. It darted along the ship's wall, careful to avoid the floor that was now filled with salt water from the permanently open hatch.

Another slug separated from the shrieker, and then another, each one reducing the size of the central parasite until they were all roughly the same, an infestation that went scattering in every direction, along the walls and ceilings, some leaping onto the shipping containers, too many to keep track of.

"Shit," Hannah growled and took a step back so that she was with Reggie in the ship's hallway. Her fist smashed the console and the door slid closed. "Abandon the mission deck," she barked into the intercom. "Now!"

Her order created a mad rush for the stairs.

"How's anyone supposed to get out when you just sealed them in?" Reggie asked.

The screams from beyond the barrier answered his question.

Two troopers stormed down the hallway behind them. Their bodies were so armored they looked only vaguely human, more like walking fortresses. They had oversized rifles in their hands with propulsion tanks screwed into the bottoms instead of magazines, and eager blue flames flickered at the tips of the barrels.

"Whoever isn't up here in ten seconds is compromised," Hannah said. "The package has been opened... seal it off. Burn the room."

The men took position at the door and Hannah opened it. The screams had already subsided, becoming a series of terrible choking sounds as the slugs found their way into new hosts.

The men entered and Hannah locked the door behind them. Sporadic gunfire trailed off into silence that was almost immediately replaced by the excited rush of cleansing fire.

Hannah took a deep breath and then nudged Reggie along. They went up one deck as she thrust her weapon back into its holster. "Those things have taken the entire island, right?"

Reggie nodded.

Around them, insect chitters rattled through the ventilation system, skitters passing overhead in the ceiling, inside the walls. In the span of ten minutes, the *Octagon* had become a ghost ship. That's what shriekers did.

"They're a plague," Hannah said, shaking her head in frustration. For one quick, fleeting second, her face was vulnerable.

"You need to drown those things," Reggie said. "I have no idea how it managed to survive inside the shark, but they can't handle saltwater on its own."

She looked at him and her chilly eyes sparkled with uncharacteristic warmth.

"I have an idea," she said.

GRANITE TRUTHS

Manuel made it back to Anne's apartment where the door remained ajar, the entry hall soaking in stormwater. He moved a storage shelf across the foyer, barricading the entrance to keep visitors out.

Navigating the island hadn't been as difficult as expected. Most of the shriekers were preoccupied, gathering along the shore, trying to figure out how to escape the island.

Manuel had seen Luther's boat putter off through the chop and heard Luther's former friends and neighbors groan their disapproval. The things inside their bodies so badly wanted to leave, but Margot ensured they remained in place.

For now.

Anne's laptop was where he left it. Manuel pulled Reggie's instructions from his pocket, praying the girl had never thought to encrypt her files.

She hadn't.

The videos that Luther had mentioned were simple to find, in a folder grimly labeled BOYFRIENDS.

She had a record of twenty-three lovers. Young—one boy looking a lot closer to sixteen—and old. Black, white, Asian. Man and woman.

Manuel felt impossibly sick as he sampled them because Anne looked the same in every video. Numb. Bored. Scared. Screwing her way through the island, not because it was fun, but because she needed to feel something. *Anything.*

Luther's video was last. They were fucking on the floor in the middle of the living room, the camera watching from somewhere atop the couch. Anne on all fours, Luther behind her, hands gripped around her hips, pounding. He leaned down across her back to kiss her mouth, and their tongues danced while she encouraged him to go much, much harder.

In the video, Luther's good eye swung up and leered at the audience while fingers curled around her throat, squeezing off her moans. He ordered her to look at the camera and tell everyone what a little whore she was.

Anne was glad to oblige.

Luther had told Manuel that she'd taped them without *his* knowledge, but this… It was performative. Consensual.

"What else did you lie about, Luther?"

Manuel clicked out of the BOYFRIENDS folder and felt incredible nausea coursing through his stomach. There was another folder below it called CUCKS, and he almost didn't want to click it.

How much worse can it get?

Lighting flashed through the window, giving Manuel a glimpse of island hell. A fallen tree embedded inside a crushed Jeep Cherokee. An oak the size of a rocket ship was horizontal inside the living room of the home across the way. Another building was nothing more than a shattered matchstick house. At the far end of the street, three shriekers stopped at the divergence in the road to consider their path.

Then the lightning was gone and everything was pitch black again. Manuel may have been trapped inside an apocalyptic nightmare, though he still thought Anne's life was worse. He could escape this island, put the shriekers behind him. Anne was stuck with herself wherever she went. She'd come to this hideaway only to discover that fucked up was forever.

The second folder had two videos. In the first, Lawman Frank was on his knees in the bedroom. Anne shot it handheld, lording over him from the center of her bed. Frank followed the lens with a desperate gaze, hands clasped together in prayer.

"No," she giggled. "You cannot fuck me." Her voice was heavier now, in the early stages of smoker's rasp. But even in that, Manuel heard the innocent little girl who once spent summer afternoons dancing through sprinklers on his lawn.

Frank pleaded in a way that might've made Manuel laugh under different circumstances. Anne zoomed in on Frank's bulging manhood, which was covered behind a thin pair of boxers.

"You know what to do," she said.

"I won't," he whimpered. "I love you too much."

"Let's go, sissy," she hissed.

"It's always the same," he cried. "Give me a chance. You wouldn't ask me here if you weren't thinking about it."

Her laugher was hopelessly cruel.

The camera glanced down at the bed and a hand reached out to grab the mace can.

"How much do you love me?"

"I'm in love with you."

"I keep thinking I'll find the one thing you won't let me do." She sprayed his face.

His grunts took a second to pass. Then he smoothed the anguish out of his expression and looked straight at the camera. His cheeks were streaked with tears, and his eyes were so bloodshot his pupils were crimson. "I love you," he said.

She sprayed him again and laughed as he shielded his face and screamed out.

Abrupt cut to black. The end.

The last video opened on the familiar face of Breyer, the rifle man who accosted he and Barbara on the beach before meeting his end below the deck of Luther's ship. The shot was an unflattering close up that showed his crooked teeth and miserable skin. The camera panned back to place him on her couch. He was nude, fully erect, and an object of ridicule for the laughing camerawoman.

"Show me how bad you want me, you fucking weirdo. Get yourself off by looking at me and maybe... *maybe*... I'll actually give you something one of these days."

Manuel slammed the laptop screen down and tossed it on the couch, grateful to be out of that world once and for all.

He crossed himself and mouthed a silent prayer to St. Jude. "As the patron of hopeless cases... of things almost despaired of... Pray for us, we are so helpless and alone..."

The irony of the Miami's biggest lost cause reaching out on behalf of another was not lost on him, but prayer was Manuel's oldest habit. The only thing that gave him comfort most nights.

The only thing I do that makes mí madre smile up there.

He pushed the barricade away from the front door and took an old, rusted hammer off the dryer, figuring he needed something for close combat if he encountered any resistance on the way to his next stop. Fire a gun and those things were bound to come running.

Lawman Frank's street was less than fifteen minutes away, a small ranch boxed in by a white picket fence. Beth had been right: the old sports car on cinder blocks made it easy to find.

The grill cover flapped wildly against the wind. The grill itself had been knocked against the house, the propane tank beneath it exposed.

Manuel jogged across soggy grass and shielded his face from random debris as he reached the porch. The front door didn't budge. ADT probably had a terrible response time out here, so he smashed the glass with the hammer and reached through, unlocking it from the inside.

Frank's place was like any other beach house—cramped, but inexplicably made to house six people in rooms the size of closets. He swept them all, listening for signs he wasn't alone: creaking floorboards, desperate breathing, or shuffling bodies.

There was none of that, and Manuel was confident in his conclusion this place was abandoned. He cased it with a greater sense of freedom, keeping his rifle at the ready. One of the rooms was stuffed with boxes, what appeared to be remnants from Frank's mainland life.

His bedroom was worse. It smelled the way any single man's bedroom did—like musk. The queen-sized bed was almost too big for the space, and the décor was sparse and random. A canvas photograph blown up to poster size hung over the bed and resembled the lighthouse that the ferry had passed on the way over. The place where Beth told Manuel they had partied.

A cheap Ikea dresser wobbled when touched. Mirror glass sat behind a layer of dust, but the photographs over it seemed recently placed. Creep shots of girls in string bikinis, printed on photo paper.

The picture tucked into the mirror's bottom corner was Anne. She was topless and pushing her breasts together with her upper arms. The smile on her face was wide but empty. Was this the first time she'd teased him by offering a glimpse of what she wasn't willing to give?

Manuel plucked it off Frank's wall of shame and frowned.

The living room was even more claustrophobic. The LED television was at least three sizes too large for this space, and the couch was wedged against both walls. The laptop on the cushions was encrusted, and two gun racks, fully stocked, save for a few weapons that were likely out with their owner, decorated the wall.

The house on the whole was a complete picture, and Manuel decided he didn't need to waste another second in here.

He was at the kitchen door looking out on the back yard when there came a knock from out front.

Manuel hugged the wall, sliding along it until he could peer through the jamb, across the hall, and through the living room beyond. A shadow moved against the window. A hand slapping the wood over and over.

The shriekers knew where he was.

He pulled the rear door open and slipped into the howling night as that awful chirring found his ears.

Figures swarmed the yard from every direction, converging with purpose.

Manuel ran for an opening between two bodies, going back the way he came. He cleared them and turned back to squeeze off a shot just as the wind kicked up. His bullet wasn't intended for any of the islanders, but for the propane tank tilted against the house.

The shot rang out, the boom lost in the immediate explosion. Four bodies flew outward, scattered limbs raining down.

Manuel took off running for the trees as screeching cries shook the night.

This was good. Now there was a burning house at the center of the island. A pyre for all to notice. They would come investigate.

And when they got here, Manuel would be long gone.

Because there was only one place left to go.

Reggie leaned against the ship's wall, suddenly seasick. They were through Margot's eye and crossing the angriest band of weather that followed—higher waves, rolling thunder, and rampaging lightning. If he moved at all, he'd puke.

Hannah's office had no windows, no horizon to stare at. "Do you know if the kitchen has any ginger?"

Hannah sat at her desk, chilly eyes glaring from just over the laptop.

"It's my stomach," he said.

She chose not to acknowledge him, returning to whatever interested her on screen.

The room was pearl white and nearly empty, minimalist by design and something out of a futuristic movie. The desk and chair were modular in style. Big square blocks. The desk blended with the room, save for the leg space at its center.

Hannah didn't seem the type to surround herself with personal belongings.

Her gloved hands flew across the keyboard with fury, and her eyes dotted back and forth like a machine. She mumbled curses beneath her breath.

"You're part of a company?" Reggie said, trying to keep his mind off his stomach. "Osiris? I heard somebody mention it while on the bridge."

"Sure." Hannah sounded more dismissive than ever. Her nose fell against the screen, completely attuned to its contents.

The mission bay section of the ship was quarantined. Reggie knew that much. Hannah wasn't happy about it. Many under her command had gone the way of Crystal Key's residents. Dead at best. Something else at worst.

Every door in and out of that sector was sealed. Protocol was that she and XO Bradley were to remain on different decks of the ship, so if something happened to one, the chain of command would hold.

The men on the bow continued their shark hunt while the weather gave them a constant beating. The shark had damaged the *Octagon's* bay door, which no longer functioned.

In the time it had taken to activate the airtight security shutter, the ship had accrued more water than the drainage system could effectively filter—which, in a stroke of blind luck, had solved much of their infestation problem.

"How come they die in ocean water, but not the rain?" Reggie said.

"Their bodies can't take the salinity of ocean water," she said. "Too salty. It's their dumb luck they were sent to infect an island like Crystal Key."

"Sent?"

Hannah's face was harsh for a moment, the way Reggie imagined she might glare down an enemy. Maybe the face she'd given Private Norton before putting one between his eyes. The side of her that Reggie didn't wish to explore.

"Something up there doesn't like us," she said. "These, what do you call them? *Shriekers*? They're a means to an end."

"A weapon?"

"A weapon that's being wasted," she said. "They know they're going to have to find a way to reach the mainland. That can't happen."

"If they can't hack saltwater, how'd that big fucker survive inside a shark?"

"They mimic their host's biology," Hannah said. "As long as the parasite was attached to the shark, it could use the shark to stay alive."

"Freaky."

"The salinity of salt water is only fatal if they're without a host."

"So the slug unhooks itself and—"

"It is also fatal if they're no longer able to draw sustaining nutrients from said host. For example, if it's inside a person who falls into the water, the water doesn't kill the parasite immediately. The person has to drown first, during which the parasite will attempt to flee the body like a sinking ship."

"How do you know so much about them?"

"It's what I do."

"Discovery Channel?"

"Right." Hannah grinned, and Reggie suspected this was as close as she ever got to laughing.

"But in the mission bay, that thing was... like... shedding itself to make smaller versions of it."

"Do you know what a tapeworm is?"

"Science sort of hates me."

Hannah sighed. "The slug doesn't have to live inside an intermediate host for it to develop, much like a tapeworm. Only this parasite is far nastier. It searches out an opening to the body, any opening, and begins to incubate once inside. When they've built enough strength, they crawl into the throat and latch themselves to the host's tongue, syphoning blood from the muscle as a source of nutrition. They bleed it dry until it withers and falls off. Once that happens, they literally become the tongue."

Reggie touched his tongue, requiring immediate assurance that it was, in fact, *his* tongue. "Why are you telling me all this?"

"You're asking."

"I mean... *should* you be telling me?"

Hannah looked at him with a blank and unreadable expression. "Obviously not," she said. "But, Reginald, I am sorry about your father."

"Noted."

Hannah nodded, the slightest mark of discomfort on her face. She took a second to find her thoughts again. "A body is their ideal home. Once they've rooted themselves, they control their host's thoughts and actions while replicating themselves in order to spread to other bodies."

"Like worms?" Reggie said. "Because I do remember that from class. You cut 'em in half and they grow another head."

"Sort of... these parasites share the quality of our planarian worm, except they're a hundred times bigger and, naturally, deadlier. They possess cells similar to cNeoblasts that can transform into any body cell type so when they've amassed enough strength through nutrients, they clone and spread."

"You've encountered them before?"

"Once," Hannah said. "A few years back in New York City. It killed a hundred people in a hotel and very nearly escaped.

Since then, I've been waiting for the next volley and, well, here we are." She frowned. "At last."

A voice Reggie didn't recognize came over the intercom to deliver a status report. Every deck was secure, straggler worms in the ventilation shafts caught and destroyed, while the monitoring system had eyes on one gigantic creature amassing itself inside mission bay.

Hannah clicked a few buttons on her laptop and Reggie peered over her shoulder. They were looking down at the area where Sergeant Norton's body had once been stored. A live feed showing the shrieker hanging on the ceiling, its nub head glaring down at the flooded floor. A man's body was sprawled on top of the morgue container, one arm bitten clean off and a deep crimson gash on his neck.

The camera showed what Reggie thought was a nightmare, certainly not a scene from two decks below.

The slug slithered until it was hovering over the body and dangled down. Slow, rhythmic chirring as its throbbing pink form began to swing like a pendulum. Hannah brought the electronic eye closer with a single mouse click, and they were right up against it.

Reggie was so repulsed he felt his flesh crawling and checked himself for slugs.

The tip of the slug reached out for the dead body. Its pink head peeled back to flash a layer of curved teeth.

"Bastard," Hannah mumbled.

Its mouth dripped with phlegm-yellow jelly, approaching the corpse's lips and tearing a flap of skin away like chicken. It released itself from the ceiling, plopping down atop the corpse, slithering up to greet the frozen face.

It was still a big shrieker, though much smaller than it had been, having shed copies of itself in its attempt to divide and conquer.

Prickly pincers pried open the cadaver's lower mouth so the bulbous head could wiggle past raking teeth, coating them with its sickening lubricant. The body's cheeks ballooned like a chipmunk in winter as the slithering pink obstruction forced itself inside. Soon, the host's throat stretched and expanded, muffling the shrieker's excited sounds.

Hannah clicked closer. The host's face dripped with slime. Dazed eyes lifted with indifference.

Neither Hannah nor Reggie had been expecting to see him blink so soon. They leapt back, startled, as the body sat up and coughed, hopping into waist-high water, then wading out of the shot.

"It's using the body to maneuver through the flood," Reggie said, his voice flushed with panic.

Hannah clicked around, but the cameras had lost him.

"Bradley," she said. "Tell me you've got another angle."

"Negative," he said. "We need to burn the room."

"Do it."

Before she could finish that sentence, the mission bay was engulfed from above, the laptop screen becoming a mash of indiscriminate orange and red flickers.

"Shit," Bradley growled from the speaker.

"What have you got?"

"Feed five."

Hannah clicked over to the camera that offered the widest shot. The reanimated body lumbered up metal steps, completely engulfed in flame as he ascended toward the catwalk. Another gust of sterilizing fire shot out, wrapping the walking body like a blazing towel. The corpse continued his forward march, undaunted.

"What's it carrying?" Reggie said.

"A cutting torch."

The cadaver activated it, and sizzling blue flame engulfed the door. He wobbled on fire-eaten legs, falling to the metal floor, muscles singed into extinction. The torch continued cutting through the door as his skull burst apart, a tangle of worms wiggling free from the splatter, and fleeing the dancing fire.

"Shit," Hannah said and grabbed Reggie by the arm. "Let's go." She tapped her earpiece as they ran. "Bradley... I'm coming to you. Tell the crew to prepare the helicopter."

Reggie wanted to ask why, but he knew the answer and was terrified. The decks shook beneath them as armed men converged on the stairwell, troopers marching down toward mission bay while Reggie and Hannah went up.

On the bridge, the storm had gotten even worse. The bow looked like it was permanently underwater because of the endless procession of breaking swells. Two of the men who hunted the shark were swept up and tossed overboard, vanishing in an indiscriminate instant. Others were fastened to the dock by harnesses, their gestures exaggerated in palpable confusion.

This was utter madness.

"Casualty report," Hannah ordered as she marched toward the controls. XO Bradley seemed to materialize out of the chaos, answering her in a way that was too quiet for Reggie to hear. The *Octagon's* interior alarm sounded, a violent grinding wail everyone was shouting over.

Reggie dropped to his knees and puked. Nobody noticed. His second retch was timed perfectly with another tremor along the ship's walls. This one a prelude to an explosion. The gunfire rocketed up through the vents, indicating that the hall outside mission bay had become a warzone.

"Seal the bridge as soon as we leave," Hannah ordered.

"Where are you going?" Bradley asked.

"Kill the contaminates by whatever means necessary," she said. "That thing has breached the mission bay doors and I don't know that our men will hold it off. We're falling back to Crystal Key."

"What?" Bradley said.

"The Firewalker must be recovered at all costs… I'm going to find it."

"Literally jumping ship," Bradley said in a way that sounded a lot like, *"You bitch."*

"I have a job to do," Hannah said and turned away. "Make sure you do yours." She hurried toward the door, unfazed by Reggie's weakened condition, calling for him to follow as she passed.

They hurried up to the flight deck where a wall of water broke against the ship as soon as Hannah opened the door. She went sliding across the deck as gushing water shoved Reggie back through the stairwell.

The sound of gunfire was somehow closer out here. Out on the waves and all around. Reggie tried to scramble, but the metal was slick, like trying to cross a patch of ice on whittled soles. Every motion brought him crashing to his knees. He gave up and pulled himself forward with his hands.

Hannah appeared in the doorway, hair slicked down against her scalp, shouting something Reggie couldn't hear. The howling wind seemed personally determined to thwart their escape. He crawled on, was almost to the jamb and Hannah bent down, thrusting her hand forward.

Another swell of water crashed down. Hannah sputtered forward face-first. Her head smashed Reggie's and they tumbled back together, his skull cracking on something hard, stubbing out his eyesight. Water flooded into his mouth and down his throat.

Hands slid beneath his armpits and hoisted him with a surprising display of strength. Hannah's hair was plastered to her face, though beneath it, her eyes blazed, never livelier. Her determination gave Reggie the slightest assurance, bordering on comfort, as she dragged him toward the exit one step at a time, into the howling hell storm raging across the open flight deck.

She threw her weight against his and wrapped her arms around the railing, pinning their bodies as another wave rose and broke across their backs.

Their feet threatened to slide out, Hannah screaming in defiance of nature's insurmountable strength. Her arms hooked around the rail, keeping them rooted against all odds. Once the wave was gone and all that remained of it was a thin layer of dripping water pouring through the grates to the lower decks, they went on the move again.

The helicopter dangled off the helipad, blades whirring, ready for takeoff. The Osiris pilot waved them on.

Hannah tapped Reggie's shoulder and they broke into a run.

"We don't have time to spare," the pilot said as they climbed inside the fuselage. Reggie pulled the sliding door shut. They weren't even strapped in when the chopper lifted off.

Reggie and Hannah scrambled to their seats, fumbling for the seatbelt buckles in a race to see who could be less coordinated.

"This is a terrible idea," the pilot screamed.

"It's the only chance we've got," Hannah fired back. "Get us to that island."

"Visibility is shot," the pilot said. "We'll be lucky if we can find it in this mess."

"I trust you," she shouted over the chaos, her face becoming animated as she glanced out the window, spotting the massive wave rushing toward them.

It lifted out of the darkness, so high that neither of them could see the top of it.

The pilot shouted something about bracing for impact, but it was too late to even brace. The water smashed them so hard the chopper went spinning.

Reggie was the only one screaming, the world spiraling around him. The helicopter tipped to its side, then went plummeting toward the ocean below.

Hurricane Margot continued to spit down on Crystal Key with such force that the grill fire Manuel had provoked had already extinguished, save for a couple of scattered embers glowing in a crater.

Manuel watched the scene from his stomach, beneath a shrub bush that was itself nestled between two palm trees. He planned to be further away, but the shriekers had swarmed the site like a pack of wolves, limping and crawling from every shadow, their movements buoyed by desperation as they searched for another host to infect.

Mouths dropped, heads fell back, pink worms slithered up into open air. Those little malicious faces twisted with discomfort and annoyance as the rain pelted them. Their unified insect chirp was constant, had become part of the island ambiance.

One long cicada song.

The shriekers paced the fiery crater with restlessness, each worm's slithered motions becoming increasingly erratic. They were beginning to realize they'd been duped.

One worm retreated inside its host as the body lifted an axe into the sky, swinging down, chopping dirt. His head flew back, and in a crash of lightning, the insect's bellow was at its loudest and most frustrated.

Others quickly joined in, externalizing their irritation.

Manuel waited until the creatures were distracted by their own tantrums before crawling from the assembly area on his elbows, his own clumsy slither. Once he was far enough away, he rose into a crouch, moving down the hill through tickling grass. The beach was close by, and he was grateful to Reggie for telling him how to catch the last train out of town.

A piercing whistle carved through the storm and an explosion ignited the hillside—a sound louder than every grill on the island going up at once. Manuel turned back, startled, as a second blast went off against his face, propelling him through the air in a volley of debris. He crashed down and rolled toward pavement.

Eyelids parted and he glimpsed undefined fireballs in the distance, blurry and edgeless tufts of flame. Docked ships exploded one by one, transforming Crystal Key's harbor into rubble.

They'd gotten smart. The shriekers couldn't be allowed to leave the island. Finally, the mysterious ship was taking action to prevent that from happening. Manuel would've smiled if he wasn't trapped among them.

He thought for a second about staying put, annihilation in the next round of artillery. A merciful end, through no fault of his own. Only he couldn't quit here. Quitting meant that Anne remained lost forever. Maybe she was just a stranger to him, but that hardly mattered. She deserved an angel, and Manuel was the only one she was going to get. He'd failed her in life, and his final purpose had to be bringing peace to her soul.

By finding the truth.

There was still time if he hurried, and Manuel knew he didn't wish to be among the tallied dead, so he shook off the daze and ran, sprinting gracelessly through beach sand, determined to resolve this and then find Barbara again on the far side of this catastrophe.

Artillery shells dropped from the sky so fast it was as though Margot had somehow added explosions to her repertoire. Shops and homes were obliterated, trees burned in gale force winds, and the inland was now severed from the coast by a crescent-shaped wall of flame.

Manuel couldn't turn back if he wanted to.

The inflatable boat was where Reggie said it would be, stuffed behind some beachfront crab shack. Manuel dragged it down to the water and climbed in. Visibility was garbage in the lashing rain, but the lighthouse was... somewhere straight ahead. He'd seen it from the ferry, but it was going to be like finding sobriety in a crack house this way.

One tug on the boat's ignition cord got the motor humming, and Manuel steered straight for the climbing swell before him. The boat skimmed along like a flat rock, skipping across the surface, stuttering, then lifting high on the storming wave. Manuel had never been much for heights and his stomach tightened as the boat dipped, then plummeted back toward the rippling ocean.

Crystal Key was no longer visible behind him, raging fires already tamped by Margot's all-encompassing rage.

Manuel stayed low through the breaking waves, the motor beginning to exhibit more give. He kept the rudder steady, buzzing through darkness that was the same in every direction.

He gnashed his teeth and mouthed a prayer as the boat's constant buzz became a confused sputter, coughing and then lapsing into sudden death throes. Then he was dead in the water, bouncing around in storm winds that were determined to capsize him.

Except, there was a sliver of sodium light that glowed in the distance, a window in outer space.

It was difficult to gauge how far Manuel had come from the island, but the rising waves were ebbing the stalled boat backward, threatening to recede whatever progress he'd made.

Manuel squinted through the night to make sure the light hadn't been a figment of a desperate imagination, and once he found it again through the swirling horizontal rain, he took a deep breath and dove headfirst into the raucous drink.

His mind shoved the monstrous shark to the forefront of his imagination, but logic refuted his primal fears. It was a big ocean, right? What were the chances?

Pretty good when God doesn't believe you worthy of redemption.

The water resisted Manuel's every advance, each paddle gently nudging him back the way he came, igniting his determination.

A rush of saltwater poured past his lips…

His ability to breathe was taken…

Manuel fought the choking spasms, just kept kicking and thrashing through the water—an animal clawing toward its prey. The heavens would allow him to complete his task, or God had resigned His benevolence and nature would smite him.

Smite Anne.

He pushed through, believing.

The sliver of light was close, its warmth revealing the lighthouse base and the granite earth surrounding it. Manuel could almost touch the rocking boat hull that slammed against the dock just a few feet ahead—if only he could stop coughing long enough to reach up and take hold.

Instead, the surging water pushed him under, waves dragging him along, bashing him against island rock as his hands clawed for purchase, fingers scraping into granite crevices for leverage. Manuel pulled his exhausted body up out of the ocean, collapsing across a bed of pointed rocks, gasping for breath. His muscles were noodles as he tried to sit.

This patch of land in the middle of oblivion would be his salvation. This lighthouse, the gateway to confronting his failure. He could've nurtured Anne instead of allowing her to become a lost girl, a child shaped by negligence into an emotional vampire who devoured misery to survive.

There was no making this right. There was only making sure it was over.

Manuel wobbled toward the door, unsurprised to find it unlocked. He'd lost his gun during the marathon swim, couldn't recall the moment it had slipped from his hand, but knew he needed a weapon against whoever had piloted that boat out here.

The lighthouse interior was a chamber of echoes. The creaking door hinge made Manuel feel as though he'd swam straight into a Vincent Price movie. He glanced up toward dancing fire light atop the twisting stairwell as the front door roared shut, slamming out the wind that continued to howl through tiny spaces in the jamb.

The tower creaked with each gust of hurricane wind, suggesting it could give way at any moment and send Manuel tumbling back into the Atlantic. The entry space was dark, the torch light high above never finding its way down. The electric white beacon that was visible from the ocean must've been in a separate chamber, housed somewhere over the living space. Useless now that Manuel was inside.

The flickering orange light above him produced shadows that looked as though they were flapping around in the wind and were accompanied by the harsh sound of scraping metal.

No sense in stealth, Manuel thought. Whoever was up there knew they had a visitor.

Manuel's lungs were raw, his body reacting to the long-nested mold in here, as well as from being overexerted on the swim. He steadied a shoulder against the wall to steal a couple more breaths and the smell that hit him was everything bad rolled into one putrid wave—spoiled garbage on a sweltering day.

There were no weapons to use. Whoever was up there would almost certainly get the drop on him, one way or another.

Manuel took the coiled wood stairs one step at a time, feeling his way toward the light with an opened palm that raked along the curved wall, bracing for a bullet that never came.

Maybe this *was* some poor bastard trying to take shelter in a storm, but that would mean Manuel had lost Anne's trail somewhere and that wasn't like *El Rastreador* at all. Every sign pointed him here, and the smell of death growing in his nostrils confirmed for him a grim truth.

Something he'd known since Garcia had forced that envelope into his hand and told him to get packing: It was always going to end this way.

Howling wind was louder up top, rattling the lighthouse's reinforced windowpanes as if there was no enclosure at all. Manuel lifted his head past the open floorboards at the top of the stairs, realizing that you couldn't hear anything up here except Margot's wails.

The floor in front of him was furnished. A patterned throw rug housed dust older than the Carter Administration. An old dresser that must've been hell getting up the stairs, and a flickering lantern on top of it, revealing a metal-framed bed in the center of the room. Two people on it.

A naked man, thrusting violently between a pair of spread

legs. Bed hinges groaned louder than his ecstatic grunts. His partner accommodated his rhythm in silence.

Manuel reached for the shredded jean shorts on the floor, denim caked with long-dried blood. He rifled through the pockets, sliding a can of mace into his palm. It provided the confidence to ascend fully into the room, moving toward the bed where the naked bodies paid him no mind.

Until the lantern caught his silent approach, broadcasting his shadow as a hulking silhouette.

The man leapt off his partner with a startled yelp, rolling off the mattress. Manuel maced him, keeping his thumb on the button until half the bottle was depleted and even his own eyes watered.

The man cupped his hands to his face as he writhed across the floor, screaming.

The woman on the mattress was stained with violence, her neck every color of the battered rainbow. Her lower stomach resembled chewed hamburger and the sheet beneath her body was darker than tar. So much damage that it was impossible to say what had killed her, and her corpse was bound to the bed by thick rope binds against her shoulders and hips.

"Anne." The word was nearly silent as it passed from Manuel's mouth. This tableau, a cruel manifestation of his life's failure.

Her body stirred, head lolling, consciousness returning.

Manuel leapt back in surprise, spotting an overturned mason jar on the far side of the floor. A fresh splotch of neon slime circled the rim. He looked from it to the writhing body knotted to the bed and knew what happened.

Anne lifted her head to regard Manuel, eyes lacking even the slightest recognition. Her unbound legs flopped and kicked as she opened her mouth, an inhuman growl for the unwanted intruder.

"She wouldn't have you in life," Manuel said, crossing the room, lifting the groaning man to his feet. "You used those things to force a second chance."

Lawman Frank stared back, those same bloodshot eyes from Anne's video shimmering in the lantern light. The *Bleeding-Eyes Man*, at long last. A revelation that absolved Luther of any suspicion.

"I am having her," Frank said, his face tinged with unrepentant madness. The kind that was always present in the deepest recesses of even the most enlightened soul. The immoral sovereignty we pretended to be above, but inevitably surfaced once the barriers of civilization came crumbling down.

Manuel's knuckles crashed into Frank's jaw, dropping him back to the ground with a smack. He stomped down on the naked man, ribs cracking beneath his heel. He grabbed the lawman's rifle off the floor beside the bed, racking it, finger falling gently against the trigger.

On the mattress, the shrieker worm pushed from Anne's mouth, suddenly interested in the unencumbered bodies moving freely around the room, chirping with excitement, forcing Anne's forearms into a struggle with the rope across her waist.

Manuel retreated to the stairs and drew a bead on Frank, but that lawman had given up, just a pile of sobbing mush on the floor. Whatever fight might've existed inside of him had been extinguished.

A rabid dog to be put down.

Manuel's finger curled around the trigger with *El Rastreador's* willingness. The blast shattered Frank's cheek, collapsing his face like a piece of hollow chocolate. The body tumbled back into the shadows, lying motionless as gun smoke rose off his face.

Anne roared, but it was the insect's displeasure that protested Frank's broken skull.

Manuel watched her.

A person's eyes never changed, never aged. Only the face around them. Manuel told himself this wasn't the little girl he'd taken for Cuban sandwiches every Tuesday, when it was his turn to pick Sanson and her up from school. But the lie couldn't hold, because when he looked at her eyes, he saw the truth.

Anne had been conscripted by the creature hiding inside of her, but Manuel recalled the same exact gaze when her thoughts had been her own. And yet, any apologies he might've offered would be lost on this writhing abomination.

So for Anne, it ended in much the same way as it had for both of her parents: thanklessly. Butchered by an entitled stalker who couldn't stomach her refusal to love him, never understanding that it wasn't rejection at all, but inability.

"I'm here," Manuel said, more for his sake and without any purpose beyond assuaging his ever-burning guilt. "Here is the peace that I could not give you in life."

The old lantern sloshed with kerosene as Manuel lifted it. Anne became more agitated as he moved. The constraints around her hips loosened with every thrash and were slack enough for her to thrust her hips upward and kick her legs out. The bed frame wobbled and threatened to break apart beneath her weight.

Manuel opened the lantern's funnel and flicked it forward, dousing her with a small stream of oil. She growled like a demon taking holy water, her body's pain receptors screaming out beneath the flecks of stinging gas.

A few more flicks of Manuel's wrist and the jar was empty. He took Frank's Zippo off the dresser and flicked it.

The worm reappeared between Anne's lips, wearing a distinct look of offense, narrow eyes and a snarled, disbelieving mouth.

Any reluctance Manuel might've had to see this through was gone at the reminder of what now occupied her.

He threw the lighter and Anne's body ignited. The fire engulfed the mattress and burned away the last vestiges of her miserable life. Manuel watched, wincing beneath the high-piercing insect shriek, feeling a sense of closure at last.

He crossed himself and mouthed a silent healing prayer, then collected Anne's strewn belongings, placing each on the dresser, sorting through them. Three yellow pad pages were folded and stuffed deep inside one of her jean pockets. He took them out and placed them aside while holding her bloody shirt in his hand. It was soaked through and impossible to tell what color it had once been.

He threw it on the fire and then unfolded the pages, finding part of a manuscript, ink scribbles, most of which were crossed out.

On the smoldering bed, the parasite's chirps diminished into a sporadic, dying cry. And then there was only the raging storm outside, the crashing waves below, forces of nature continuing their assault.

Manuel sat at the foot of the stairs with the pages in his lap, thinking it best to read them now, rather than risk losing them once he went back out into those elements, used Lawman Frank's boat to escape.

He shivered, the dying fire throwing off precious little warmth for his soaked bones.

A large shadow glided across the wall beside him like *Nosferatu*. Manuel didn't have to turn to know.

Frank had risen.

Manuel struggled to his feet, but it was too late. The lawman's arms shot forward and took Manuel by the neck, squeezing him against the wall, lifting his feet off the floor. The bloody, recessed cavern that had once been Frank's face shifted and stirred and was suddenly filled with thumping, pink color.

Hannah lifted her head. It was heavy, her cheek crusted with golden sand. She rubbed her face with the back of her bloody hand and took stock of her surroundings.

A few feet off, Reggie lay on his back with his eyes closed. Blood daubed his forehead, and she watched for a minute until she saw his stomach rising.

A rubber raiding craft sat deflated on wet sand and was splattered with crimson stains. It ignited the memory of a killing mouth striking at them from on rampaging water.

She should've been dead.

They should've been dead.

If Hannah believed in God, this was where she would've thanked Him.

Getting to her knees was easy, but her body resisted further mobility. Her torso swayed and her temples pounded like a jackhammer—a five-alarm hangover without the fun.

With the *Octagon* compromised, Hannah had decided in a moment of desperation that reaching Crystal Key was of tactical importance. They would waste too much time engaging the parasite in deck-by-deck combat, and time was the one thing they were running out of.

Well, that and luck.

The objective, Firewalker, was her responsibility. Whatever the cost, she had to accomplish it. The troops she'd ordered into the water for a shark hunt had managed to track the chopper crash and pulled them from the sinking fuselage just as the shark descended upon them. It had been too late for the pilot, and Hannah shivered at the memory of him fading into the black depths, his scream no longer verbalized, signaled instead by a nest of rising bubbles.

Two of her men had gone overboard during that battle— one swallowed whole by the fish as it returned a second time, and another lost at sea when the wild waves tossed him overboard.

The rest of them had made it to shore, but where was—

Hannah turned and found one of the troopers face down on the beach, unmoving. She flipped him over, found his side torn away, a hunk of stomach entrails spilled across the sand.

"When the waves flooded the motor, Hautanen hopped out and dragged us in the rest of the way." Another Osiris solder had come over the dune, rifle in hand. Hannah didn't immediately recognize him. This embarrassed her in the moment. The only man to survive, and she couldn't thank him by name.

"XO Bradley shelled the island before we landed," he said. "A safety precaution he believed might help with the success of our mission."

"You've been in communication with the *Octagon?*" Hannah said.

"Just before we saw your bird take a header," he said. "They were suffering heavy casualties, went offline right after that..."

"Shit," Hannah said. "Where's your radio?" She reached for her belt clip and rubbed the rough nylon where it should've been. Hers was where she'd left it—on the equipment stand in her quarters. Everything at the end had been about getting off the ship.

"Out there," the solider said and lifted a finger toward the ocean.

"And him?" She lifted her chin in gesture to Hautanen's shark-eaten body. Directly above, seagulls were circling.

The soldier shook his head.

"Okay," Hannah said. "Nothing's changed. We recover the Firewalker and head to International Waters for extraction."

"Yes ma'am." The trooper wore a puzzled look. It took Hannah a second, but she realized why and gave an exasperated sigh.

"Except... how do we recover it without contacting the *Octagon*."

"Right... Ma'am."

"Shit."

If the *Octagon's* LAN was down, they were incommunicado. If they were incommunicado, they were unable to raise Osiris HQ. And if they couldn't reach HQ, there was no way to plan extraction.

Hannah wasn't ready to accept a Critical Mission Failure check in her jacket, not when Mister Wyatt thought so highly of her. There was no doubt in his mind that she'd succeed. Her heart pounded as she considered losing his trust. Everything... every moment of her adult life had been spent earning that, and she wasn't going to give it away.

Not for anything.

The sky overhead looked like ash. The air carried a chill. Over the dune, Crystal Key had been leveled. Decimated buildings. Scorched forest. Shriveled bodies. Imagery from a third world genocide brought to the Florida coast.

"You've scouted the island," Hannah said. "What's out there?"

"It's quiet. Nothing on the road. Was inching my way inland when I heard you stirring. Thing is, ma'am, I could *feel* eyes on me. Eyes that I never saw."

"We need to reach the south side of the island," Hannah said. The Firewalker, their code name for the meteor, had smashed into the water just off the coast by the Shifting Tides resort. It would be easy enough to find. Now they only needed to get through to HQ.

"I'm not sure I follow, ma'am."

"The organism can't handle saltwater," she said. "Bradley knows that. In an infestation scenario, protocol is to blow the *Octagon* and evacuate to the nearest friendly shore. Crystal Key might not be friendly, but it's our job to convince him that we're alive. If he hasn't started the purge yet, he's about to."

"If he puts lifeboats in the water, that shark will chew them to pieces."

"Not if we kill it." Hannah grinned as soon as she suggested it.

The trooper looked to his fallen brother-in-arms beside them as if to ask, *"Oh, is that all?"*

"I'm sorry," Hannah said. "Everything seemed so clear last night... trap the shark, eviscerate it..."

"Not even you could've predicted what happened out there, ma'am."

It's my job to predict. No one else on this mission had been in that New York hotel. The limited knowledge that Osiris had of the parasite was because Hannah had lived to talk about it. Those things get the upper hand at the drop of a dime. As careful as this operation had been, isolate, assess, recover... it wasn't careful enough.

That was on her. Failure Hannah would have to own.

"I'm sorry, soldier," Hannah said. "Your name is—"

"Danny Taylor, ma'am."

"Right. Taylor. We've got a second chance to do this because of you." It was the closest Hannah could get to *thanks*.

"It's the job."

"Even on days like this."

Reggie stirred, had been watching them in silence.

"You okay?" Hannah said.

He barely mustered a thumbs up.

"How well do you know the island?"

"If we're going to the resort, we want to go that way," he said, pointing. "Better to stay on the beach, though. Shriekers can't glide on sand."

Taylor handed Hannah his sidearm and stood guard atop the dune while she helped Reggie up and checked him over.

"Shriekers," she said. "I like that."

"Picked it up from a friend."

"You're intact," she said, giving him a reassuring tap on the arm.

"Do I get a gun?"

"Sorry, we're fresh out."

Taylor took point as they headed down shore, walking single file at his insistence. They passed through soggy reeds with a broken wood structure on their right.

"This is where it fell," Reggie said. "Dad was at this old fishing house the night it dropped."

Hannah nodded but said nothing. She and Taylor's ears were tuned to their surroundings, eager to avoid any unnecessary confrontations.

The resort was a mess when they got there. Its bar and restaurants reduced to rubble. The pier was gone, just a pile of jagged wood and chunks of concrete with jutting rebar. The central lobby's window front was busted out, and a glass mulch bed littered the ground around it. The rear wall, which would've led to the pier, had been pulled apart when the dock collapsed, taking the back half of the lobby floor with it. A significant drop into the now placid Atlantic below.

"This can't be the same place," Reggie said.

"It's not," Hannah said. "Not anymore." Some of that was Osiris' fault, but the second those parasites got loose on the island, Crystal Key was gone. What had to be done now was for the good of everyone on the mainland.

For the good of humanity.

They moved up the dune to pass into the lobby and stepped over large splotches of red-stained sand. Only the front part of the floor remained intact, countless corpses strewn across it and along the stairwell that was still connected to the second floor.

Hannah's boot gave a light kick to one of those bodies, expecting the parasite to come rushing into her gun barrel. The corpse's head rolled to the other side and continued to stare lifelessly across open water.

Taylor knelt to examine some of the other bodies, prodding each of them with his gun barrel. He shook his head when there was no response. "If they're not infected... what killed them?"

"They didn't die from fright," Hannah said. There were no fatal wounds on them.

Taylor lifted his rifle and performed an awkward hot step over the cadaver, as if simply touching it could infect him.

Hannah glanced at Reggie. "You okay?"

"Just get us out of this," he said, about to come unglued.

"That's the plan."

The carpeted steps oozed blood like they were stepping on dish sponges. At the top of the stairs, Taylor recruited Reggie with a tap on his shoulder, and they went to work on barricading the staircase with scattered lounge furniture.

Hannah lifted the pistol toward the narrow hallway and moved for the door at the end marked OFFICE, the ground creaking beneath her boots.

A fire axe was embedded in the wood there in such a way that the blade looked like the "I" on the sign, while the "O" had a bullet hole the size of a quarter blown straight through it.

On the ground was a body, its head split open like a melon.

Hannah's finger leaned against the trigger as she shuffled the corpse aside with her boot. There was a curious lack of pink residue on the skull fragments, indicating to Hannah that someone else had done this.

A kick to the office door sent it swinging inward, where she immediately found her culprit.

A small fat man was huddled in the corner, knees to his chest like a battered child. He winced as she filled the jamb, drawing on him.

"Drop it!" she shouted.

"Hey, take it easy," he said, and tossed his pistol into the center of the room. "It's empty anyway."

"Who are you?"

"Hamilton," Reggie said, suddenly right behind her. "Manager." Hannah pointed Reggie to the axe, having him pry it from the door as she strode into the room, gun trained on Hamilton.

"The manager," she said. "Just the person I wanted to see."

"I'm ruined," he said, eyes distant.

"You're alive." She had no time or interest to coddle him. "So start thinking about how you can be of use to me."

That got his attention, though his scowl suggested that he did not enjoy taking orders. His knees popped as he got up, leaning against the wall, grumbling something about arthritis.

"I need some way to signal my ship," Hannah said. "What have you got?"

"You're from that ship? You're the people who cut our throats?"

"We didn't bring those things to your island," she said. "I'm trying to stop them. I need to get word to my people to make for Crystal Key. If I don't get a signal to them, they're going to evac to the mainland instead."

Hamilton hobbled to his desk, collapsing into the memory foam chair. "Let me think for a second."

"You do that." Hannah left the office and headed one floor up to the observation deck. The *Octagon* was in the distance, dead in the water. Getting them here was everything. Their mobile comms would be able to reach HQ and request immediate extraction.

The weather had cleared, meaning Osiris wouldn't have anonymity much longer. Soon people would be out surveying storm damage. People might even come looking for loved ones they hadn't heard from in a couple of days.

Shit...

Hannah hurried back down to the office where Hamilton was giving Reggie and Taylor the lowdown on what had happened here. You didn't have to be CSI to piece it together, but she hovered on the fringes of the conversation anyway.

The guests had gathered at the hotel after the shark had pulled part of the pier down. For a long stretch of night, it seemed like they were going to make it. Then the natives began to gather on the beach, more of them arriving by the minute until the whole of Crystal Key was out there trying to get in.

The doors were barricaded, but the islanders had overwhelming force. It wasn't the door that gave, but the large glass windows surrounding it. The islanders shattered them with makeshift weapons and rocks, commencing mass slaughter.

"I hate to admit it," Hamilton said. "But those fuckin' barbarians folded as soon as your people opened up on us. Bombs were a great call. Felt like the Pacific theater of war here, but it sent those things scurrying."

"Okay," Hannah said. "Enough with the history lesson."

"You're a real benevolent bitch, aren't you?" Hamilton said.

"And you've been useless to me so far..."

"That's because I've been thinking about your problem. You want to get a signal to your boys. How about a fire?"

"How big a fire?"

"Grease fire?" Hamilton said. "This place is a memory now. I'm thinking we use the kitchen equipment to stoke some major flames. Might as well go all the way and burn it down. I never liked half measures."

"How do we do that when there's no power?" Hannah said.

"Got a generator at my place... just around the bend. It stalled out. Someone goes for the genny, refires it, and suddenly we're cooking with gas."

"What about your sprinklers?" Taylor said.

"Our irrigation system has a shut off valve. I can kill that while I wait for you to juice this place."

"That would take care of the signal fire," Hannah said. "We've still got a shark to kill." She looked at Hamilton. "My men took out the main dock to prevent those things from fleeing the island. Tell me there's another boat close by."

Hamilton laughed. "Lady, you're luckier than a double-dicked tomcat."

Hannah made an exasperated *this guy…* face in response.

"You'll find everything you need in my boathouse," Hamilton said. "Provided it's still standing." He reached into his pocket and tossed her a ring of keys. "We figured you people would try and blow us to hell if we tried escaping…"

Hannah gave Reggie a sideways glance, that deduction a little too close to home, as she headed for the door, freezing at the onset of trembling walls—a freight train rocketing over some nonexistent railroad crossing nearby.

The familiar cicada chirr grew out of that vibration, and Hannah ran across the second floor balcony to glance down into the lobby below.

Pink slugs crawled from the sea of bodies there, wiggling around in eye sockets, squeezing from stretching eardrums, gliding out from between the legs of men and women, a hundred of them, beginning to converge on fresh hosts who'd willingly trapped themselves above.

"Did those motherfuckers set us up?" Reggie asked with incredulity. He was beside her and Hannah shoved him back toward the office.

The kid was right, though. The shriekers wanted them to come up here and let their defenses down.

The slugs glided on globs of neon slime, slicking a path for those to follow, an army moving along the metal window frames. Their unified chirr was the cadence of soldiers on a death charge. The dripping slime became a curve that resembled an upside-down U as they slithered along the upper wall, the trajectory enabling them to drop onto the second floor with endless plops, completely circumventing the makeshift barricade at the top of the stairs.

Hannah stared at this invasion in disbelief. How could she have fallen into such an obvious trap?

You're desperate, she thought. *And desperation breeds stupidity. Which is failure.*

"Come on, Hannah!" Reggie screamed, his voice shaking her free from the doldrums. She spun and sprinted for the office, pink slugs nipping at her boot heels as she raced for cover. Reggie slammed the door as she passed it.

Hamilton moved quickly. He stuffed torn window blind fabric inside the bottle of Wild Turkey 101 on his desk. Once the fabric was appropriately soaked, he flipped his BIC and lit it up, screaming, "Open that fucking door!"

Reggie did, and the bottle twirled through the air in slow motion. Hannah's eyes followed it on its downward slope into the hallway that had suddenly been redecorated with a pink, squiggling floor.

The sound of shattered glass signaled an immediate roar of flame. A pulse of heat that pushed in on them as the worms shrieked their way into extinction, their pitch so fevered, Hannah's eardrums threatened to burst.

A few slugs had been ahead of the pack of wilting, burning lemmings. They came slithering into the room, rolling out a slimy pink carpet for themselves. Hannah and Reggie stomped at them, her heel catching one dead on, its body buckling in an explosion of day-glow.

"Can you make another Molotov?" Hannah said as they caught their breaths.

Hamilton pulled an unopened bottle of vodka from the bottom drawer. "This is it," he said. "Has to be an insurance policy because if we're going to cook the whole resort, those things will move on us again."

"He's right," Taylor said, edging into the hall, checking their exit path.

"Just get to my place, okay?" Hamilton said. "Follow the shore past here and you can't miss it."

"You're not coming?" Reggie asked.

"Told you, someone's gotta disable the sprinklers." Hamilton spread a slice of duct tape across his mouth, then wrapped another piece of fabric around his hand in a makeshift headband to cover his ears.

Hannah might've told him he was wasting his time, that those things would chomp through his eyes or burrow through his stomach if they wanted to get in bad enough, but there was no harm in precaution.

So she held her tongue and they headed out, stepping again over now-vacated host bodies that were slathered in radiant slime. Hamilton saw them off and then disappeared through a side door into a part of the building that remained intact.

"Nice guy," Taylor said dryly as they continued down beach toward their new destination.

Hannah eyed the *Octagon* as they hurried. Everything about her ship seemed peaceful from here, though the pessimist in her was certain they were down to their last hour. Bradley wouldn't abandon ship until absolutely necessary, but he wouldn't be able to hold out forever.

And there had to be at least a couple concerned relatives en route to Crystal Key right now to check the radio silence.

The light blue water was deceptively calm. It housed a terrible obstacle, one that wouldn't be swayed by conventional bait. Its tastes, more refined now.

Hannah's heart rumbled as Hamilton's house came into view down the shore. There was only one thing the shark responded to. One thing they were going to have to give it.

Live bait.

The shark thought about heading for different waters.

He possessed more instincts than he was ever consciously aware of having, and some of those receptors attempted to force the move on.

Against all odds, he had rid himself of the passenger, and all of the mounting pressure that had come along with it. His basilhyal was gone, but it served no function to his species, and so he barely noticed the absent cartilage.

At twenty fathoms, water rushed through his nostrils, carrying the scent of a large octopus hiding beneath him. Its bulbous head and latching tentacles were restless along a sprawling notch of coral reef, but the shark passed the prey with little interest, guided toward the only discernable motion that stirred above ground.

Mainland life had gone quiet, replaced by the kind of crushing silence that was often reserved for life at the deepest fathoms.

Marine life had long since vacated these waters, too. That made more sense, as they possessed the type of instincts and sensors that gave them a natural defense against predators. There was no choice but for the shark to focus on those who remained on the island.

He allowed himself to float to the surface, searching them out. He found them in almost no time. Rough vibrations pulsed through the water, summoning him right to their spot.

Whether they were baiting him was irrelevant. He would take his time, and would have them.

Within seconds of fiddling at the generator's interface, Taylor restored power to the carcass of Shifting Tides.

An electric hum followed Reggie and Hannah as they moved around the house, hardware and appliances starting back up, all of them heard easily through the shattered windows and busted doors.

The boathouse had survived both the storm and the *Octagon's* artillery assault. The Hamilton key allowed them to access it without having to break in. The various noises from inside Hamilton's home probably already arousing slithering neighbors to their whereabouts.

"We have to hurry," Hannah said, grabbing a wetsuit off the wall and then hopping the gunwale to the large boat that ebbed against the small storage structure. She disappeared below deck, leaving Reggie to scrounge supplies.

The boathouse smelled half like saltwater, half like the inside of a sporting goods store—everything in here with that "off the shelf" smell. Dad had always said the better the brand the less it was used.

"The rich got the bread to buy the best, no time to use it."

Hannah crawled back above deck and hopped the rail to the dock, collecting the equipment that Reggie had scavenged. Her wetsuit was like a second layer of skin, squeaking as she lifted her thigh to strap a spear gun holster to it. Her large feet slipped inside blue, full footed fins, and she fastened a knife sheath around her ankle.

"You look like you're going snorkeling," Reggie said.

"Hamilton did promise he had everything we could need," she said.

"You're really going down there to face that thing?" Reggie considered all the times he'd seen that monster and couldn't imagine somebody willingly seeking it out.

Hannah didn't respond. She wasn't particularly enthused by the idea. Just out of options. She reached for the diving tank and loaded it over the stern, then hopped back aboard the boat and climbed the five-wrung ladder to the flying bridge where she started the motor.

Reggie lifted a second tank over the rail, shrugging when he realized Hannah was looking. "You never know," he said as he hopped the boat and went below deck to check things out. His only interest was in Hannah's pistol, sitting on the table atop her discarded clothing. "Hey," he called out. "Can I have this gun?"

Overhead, footsteps pounded. Taylor shouting, "Permission to come aboard?"

Reggie took the pistol and climbed back above deck as Taylor hopped the rail and the anchor ascended from the ocean with a slow, mechanized whirr. The boat bucked, then started moving out of its aquatic parking space toward open water.

As they cleared Hamilton's dock, Reggie saw what Taylor had been running from. A dozen shriekers shambling across the yard, stumbling toward the shore like they were prepared to give chase, stopping as the Atlantic climbed to their ankles.

Taylor lifted his rifle and squeezed off a shot. A shrieker's head exploded like a watermelon. The floundering slug that rose out of its neck tried to maintain its host's balance without dropping into the water, succumbing to its battle with gravity almost instantly. It splashed down and Taylor had another shrieker in his sights. He took that shot and immediately replicated it again, then again.

"Damn," Reggie said, looking at the gun in his own hand, wishing Dad could've taught him to shoot like that. Only now realizing the full scope of things that had been stolen from him.

The remaining shriekers turned tail and retreated to dry land, scattering aimlessly across the grass with an insect's indifference. Taylor lowered his rifle and turned to survey the starboard side as Hannah steered the ship along the bending shoreline toward Shifting Tides.

"Why can't we just zip out there and rescue Bradley?" Reggie said while Taylor searched the open water for that familiar fin.

"We're leading the fish away from our men," he said. "So they have a fighting chance."

The crumbled resort looked even more like kindling from here. It was disheartening to see that Hamilton hadn't yet transformed it into a bonfire, though the power had only been on for about ten minutes.

Hannah hopped down off the flying bridge and took a deep breath, staring at the placid water. She slipped one of the diving tanks against her back and fastened the straps. "Here goes nothing," she said and gave a hard swallow.

The *Octagon* was the size of a model replica at this distance, floating on the horizon. Reggie's time aboard that ship felt like a lifetime ago. Now, the gun in his hand gave him a confidence that hadn't existed last night. Dad's parting gift had unlocked something inside of him, the ability to not only take care of himself, but others. "You should let me go with you."

"Out of the question," Hannah said.

"Know how hard it is to watch your own back down there?"

Taylor climbed to the boat's controls and dropped anchor. "Gonna need you on shark watch with me, bud."

Hannah nudged Reggie on the shoulder, pointing to the beach off the port side. "We're right in front of that old fishing shack... this is where your father saw the meteor crash?"

"That's what he told me."

Behind them, the *Octagon* rumbled, the deck's length

igniting in a tuft of white-hot flame, followed by explosions against the gunwale and lower hulls. Controlled detonations designed to cripple its structural integrity and send it down to the depths.

"There they are," Taylor said, nodding to the raiding rafts that were suddenly visible. Little hummingbirds zipping along the water, fleeing the wreckage.

Hannah smiled for a second, and the relief on her face made Reggie feel the slightest bit better.

Maybe they still had a shot.

The *Octagon* was sinking fast. Its stern side dipped beneath the waves and elevated the bow above the water.

Reggie glimpsed the dorsal fin in the distance. A little brown hook speeding toward the *Octagon's* crew. He grabbed Hannah's arm and pointed.

"Shit," she said and hopped the rail onto the boat's swimming platform, her flippered feet hovering right above water.

"It's not stupid," Reggie said. "It knows you're trying to trap it."

She pulled the diving mask down over her eyes. "But I'm hard to resist."

From the shore, a plume of black smoke appeared over the resort.

"He did it," Taylor said. "They must've spotted the fire."

"Then I've got to hurry." Hannah adjusted the diving tank straps, then pulled the knife from its sheath. She dragged the fresh blade up her arm from the top of her wrist to the ball of her shoulder until the scuba sleeve was soaked with blood. Through the mask, her eyes were pained squints.

That didn't stop her from leaping into the blue without another word. She was gone in a second, leaving only a patch of blood to dissipate across the surface.

The shark felt the sudden tremor of someone paddling downward. By the time he smelt her in the current, the blood dripping from her body was all the incentive he needed to circle back.

She was maybe one hundred feet away and knifing toward deeper waters.

He descended to meet her, slowing at the realization that she was headed toward *it*.

The thing that had given him his passenger.

But the blood was an irresistible lure and he glided on in confident search.

Hannah glimpsed the Firewalker at approximately ten fathoms. On first impression, it resembled a coconut the size of a Prius, resting on the ledge of an ocean plain.

The slightest earthquake would be enough to send it tumbling into darkness, forever lost. Her heart drummed as she kicked toward it, navigating a haze of seaweed.

Her hands caressed its rough and rippled surface as she circled it. There was a deep recession on one side—the gap the parasites had likely escaped from. She guessed the shark had been in the wrong place at the wrong time. A shame, since the shriekers would've perished almost instantly had nothing come to their aide.

The ocean was permanently murky, a field of alternating shades. Deep blues and sickly greens.

Hannah swam above the Firewalker's hovel and peered inside. It was too dark to see anything, but the safest conclusion was that everything in there was long dead. She wondered if there was any danger in being so close to this alien. Normally, she wouldn't be playing so fast and loose with protocols, but this was beyond desperate. One last chance to save what remained of her command.

The shark was a no show, and her runny arm continued to drizzle her surroundings with blood, crimson tendrils littering the gloom around her. *C'mon, you bastard.*

It was a cunning creature, but still an animal. It would swim to her on instinct because, to a predator, she was an easy meal.

Hannah unholstered the spear gun.

Everything had been worth this moment, provided Osiris could successfully retrieve this rock. It was the only chance of getting answers to the questions she'd been asking since New York.

Where did these things come from?

Who sent them?

Why did they send them again?

This was the second attack. Their second failure. The law of averages suggested they would not screw it up a third time.

Hannah needed every answer the Firewalker could provide.

Her trigger finger itched as she looped around the meteor again, peering inside the hole with a little more confidence.

A piece of the darkness inside the rock took on a wiggling shape, and then leapt from the fold, darting toward her face. Hannah's reflexes were spry enough to push her neck back as the slug connected with her cheek, peeling a flap of her wetsuit hood away and drawing another sprinkle of clouded blood.

She kicked off the rock's surface with her spear gun ready, drawing a bead on the pink bastard that had somehow survived down here.

This changed things. *All* her data. Everything she knew

about the shriekers. Panic took hold, and she couldn't keep her nervous wrist steady enough to find a clear shot.

But the slug wasn't pink. It was black, and it dangled off the side of the Firewalker with seven identical brothers, each of them lifting in synchronicity, revealing endless rows of suckers across their undersides. Hannah saw the creature's mantle rising out of the recession. Squinted eyes regarded her with suspicion, but not malice, as it passed.

The octopus skittered off for deeper waters. Its tentacles lazed behind its head like a flapping cape.

The side of Hannah's head was numb from the creature's sting and she took deep, hollow breaths through her face breather, struggling to suppress the all-encompassing panic that spread through her body. She'd never been more terrified.

Something slammed her from behind and she rocketed toward the Firewalker, crashing against the riveted surface. A crack so loud she thought her ribs had broken clean off inside her.

Some clearly had, because breathing was more painful than the deep gash across her arm.

With a crane of her neck, the shark's checkmate grin and predatory green eyes glided past.

Hannah's arms pushed through the water, but maneuverability was difficult for as much crushing pain as she felt in her chest. Each breath was like touching a raw nerve and she floated as if in stasis.

Through the haze, the shark swam away and then slithered back around wearing a wide enough grin to fill the entire ocean.

Hannah whimpered at the demonic sight that was locked onto her, then reminded herself this wasn't a monster. It was nature, a living fossil that was eager to purge an intruder from its waters.

Pins and needles rolled through her hands and feet. Or maybe that was her broken ribs crying out. Her eyes welled as she braced for the attack. Counter maneuvers were a pipedream. The shark was faster, and if she tried to reach the boat, she'd be chewed up before she could climb two feet.

Her fingers closed instead around the edges of the Firewalker's opening, and once her grip was firm, she pulled herself inside at the same moment the shark's mouth charged past, snatching one of the flippers off her feet. Hannah turned back and the creature's smile was agitated as her bare toes rubbed against the hardened skin of its jawline.

She let loose a soggy shriek, and oxygen bubbles filled the water as she adjusted her position to face the entrance. The diving tank clanked against the interior wall. This wasn't enough distance from the shark, but she couldn't get any more. The spear gun trembled in her hand as it looked toward the opening.

You get one shot. One.

Otherwise, this rock was going to become her tomb.

The shark paced the entrance to the Firewalker in a frenzy detonated by Hannah's drizzling lifeblood, moving back and forth as if to remind her that it wasn't going anywhere. That it had all the time in the world.

The *Octagon* refugees were closer now, boats nodding up and down on approach to Crystal Key while, on the beach, Shifting Tides had become one massive signal fire.

"We've got to get their attention," Reggie said.

"Yeah," Taylor agreed. "Need a few of those boats to come to us. Hannah's going to need help."

"So what do we do?"

"I grabbed some flare guns out of the boathouse," Taylor said, rushing aft to the duffel bags he'd carried aboard. "Let me——"

The tackle box beside the bags burst open and a pink slug attached itself to Taylor's face with a smear of neon goop swabbed across his chin.

Reggie shouted in feeble protest as he lifted Hannah's pistol, clicking the safety off with his thumb, exactly as Dad had shown. Yeah, maybe Dad had wanted to teach Reggie how to fish instead, but Reggie's ass would've been twice dead on this vacation had that been the case.

It was shocking to see how fast Taylor slipped away, gagging on the shrieker as it glided beyond his lips. His eyes dissolved into milky white orbs as the alien assumed direct control, gliding down his throat and forcing his body to perform spastic motions that no longer resembled human grace.

Reggie steadied his shot. "I'm sorry, man."

Taylor lunged forward, arms stretched out, fingers wiggling. The insect chirp in his throat, anticipatory.

Reggie fired twice without hesitation. Both shots sunk through Taylor's skull, blowing what remained of his thoughts out the back of his head. His second kill in as many days, and so much easier this time.

The body wobbled in place at the back of the boat. Reggie didn't wait to see which way it would fall. He charged it, screaming, knocking it over the gunwale, Taylor spilling overboard, his occupying slug vanishing into the saltwater with a splash.

More slugs lifted from the tackle box, and suddenly there was another on the stairs leading below deck. Cold, instinctive chirrs in the air around Reggie, their only purpose to invade, possess, destroy.

On the ocean, the approaching boats sped toward the resort fire, on the verge of passing the boat entirely.

Reggie backed into the corner, gun drawn on the closest slug as he reached for the spare diving tank with his free hand. *You never know*, he thought, lifting it, slipping it around his shoulders, pressing the breather into his mouth.

The shriekers intuited what was about to happen and were converging on Reggie, a half dozen of them, wiggling out from undiscovered hiding places. No time to grab one of Taylor's flare guns.

Reggie turned toward the boats as he climbed over the gunwale, firing the pistol into the air until the gun clicked empty. There wasn't a second to spare, so he flung himself overboard, kicking down into the Atlantic without knowing whether he'd gotten their attention.

All he could do was dive.

It was the only place the shriekers couldn't follow.

Hannah chewed on the rubber breathing apparatus in her mouth, trying to calm herself, enraged that even in this moment of life or death, her brain thought to chide her for this display of weakness. As though she weren't allowed to feel such things as fear.

The shark's jaws lunged against the Firewalker, chomping through water with mounting frustration. Rows of killing teeth pushed against the rock—an inescapable nightmare that hovered inches from her face just beyond the hovel.

Hannah squeezed the speargun trigger, not because the shot was right, but because she had been startled into taking it.

The bolt whizzed forward and tore through the shark's gum line. Drizzling blood formed a red beard around its mouth.

That didn't prevent it from looping around and charging again.

Hannah braced and the creature darted forward like a bolt, colliding with the meteor, wedging itself inside the Firewalker's opening where the tip of its nose caught Hannah in the belly like someone had jammed a fist into her stomach.

Her screams became bubbles and her hands clawed at the intrusive brown face, desperate to avoid its almost mechanized chomping mouth.

The shark's head banked left and then right as it attempted to reposition itself, only its wide body was lodged at the entry point, preventing it from advancing any further. The fury in its eyes grew, dark orbs darting around with the resentment of any trapped animal.

It blamed her for its misfortune.

Hannah's back was against the meteor's interior wall. If she moved forward an inch, she'd be within the shark's striking distance. She bent to one side and her ribs screamed out on fire as she stretched her bloody arm down so that her fingers could close around the knife's handle, unsheathing it.

She jammed the blade inside the shark's gills. The front of its body shifted to expose them further. She flexed her arm and dragged the knife across the fish's length, forging a long horizontal slash in its side, blood spilling out, blotting the world inside the meteor so that it was just Hannah and her nightmare, a monstrous grinning face waving mindlessly around in the crimson gloom.

The shark's eyes somehow widened in reaction and its head swung toward her like an anvil moving through water.

Her free hand worked to loosen the tank on her back. It

slid down her spine and she caught it by the straps, ensuring that it remained attached to her breather.

The shark's mouth dropped wide and Hannah hoisted the tank, swinging for its teeth, mouth closing around the aluminum, puncturing it.

It took small bites, attempting to break the tank down, get it out of its mouth. Hannah used this time to wind her arm back and plunged the blade straight through its godforsaken eye, demolishing it in a single stab. She wrestled the knife free and raised it high, slamming down on the shark's dome, using the last of her pained breath to bury it to the hilt, stainless steel pierced all the way through its head.

The shark's body slumped through the interior of the Firewalker until it crashed against the lower wall.

Hannah drifted toward the floor, her face falling against wilted shrieker egg sacs that were like shriveled raisins.

The breathing apparatus no longer had a tank to draw from. She spit it out as her lungs burned. Her chest begged for relief. Her eyes shifted toward the entrance and saw only the shark's corpse plugging it up.

Time to let the water in.

She told herself that Bradley and the men had made it, and that they wouldn't leave her body down here. They would know exactly where to find her.

Her eyelids were heavy, nearly ready to close. Overhead, the shark twitched. She glanced up and saw its red mouth opening again.

Hannah's hand ran along the floor in search of the blade and realized it was still sticking out of the creature's head.

Its body disappeared in an avalanche of bubbling blood, and then its front half dislodged and nosedived to the Firewalker's floor. Suddenly, there was a tiny semblance of light through the fast-dissolving cloud of blood.

A human apparition appeared at the opening and another joined, cutting torch in hand. They reached through for her.

Hannah wanted to laugh, but that would hurt too much. Reggie was beside her again, mumbling something as he slid a new breather into her mouth. It had a mini oxygen tank attached. Her ribs hurt so much she was sure they were poking through her chest, but she stole a few pained breaths anyway.

Reggie and one of her men from the *Octagon* lifted Hannah and eased her gently through the Firewalker's mouth.

All Hannah could think was how she was going to have that shark's jaws mounted and displayed in her office.

She'd earned that much.

CLEANSED BY FIRE

Hannah sat on a makeshift field stretcher on the beach. A host of bandages around her stomach, ribs, and head. Reggie sat beside her and couldn't seem to find anything to say, so they simply stared out across the calm water in silence.

The survivors of the *Octagon* had noticed Reggie's gunshots and XO Bradley ordered them make for the boat instead of the shore, thinking it was a more easily secured destination. He'd sent three men beneath the surface, and they'd spotted Reggie right off, swimming clumsily toward the rock that Osiris regarded as Firewalker.

Somehow, Hannah had killed the shark with a damn knife—very Lara Croft like. A God-tier achievement, as far as

Reggie was concerned, though now that it was over, the fight had left her entirely. Her blue eyes were so tired they were almost grey, and there were lines on her face that he hadn't noticed before.

Bradley wandered over to check in, asking if Reggie wouldn't mind giving them a moment of privacy. That was fine with him. As Reggie started off, Bradley called after him. "How's it feel to be a hero?"

"Excuse me?" Reggie said.

"This might've ended differently if not for you."

Reggie thought about that, decided there were no heroes here and didn't answer. He ambled down beach and watched a small platoon of Osiris soldiers march inland with flamethrower rifles and he heard those whooshes even after they were out of sight, the crackle of sterilizing fires signaling where they'd gone.

Hamilton sat nearby on a fallen tree, watching the smoldering remains of his resort. Bradley visited him next, giving assurances that Osiris would compensate him for the abrupt foreclosure of his dream.

"Don't worry about buying my silence, son," Hamilton said. "I ran operations in the desert you wouldn't believe. I know a thing or two about secrets, and I'm not about to betray this one."

"We're not worried," Bradley said.

Hannah hobbled toward Reggie, wincing with every step and brushing off Reggie's efforts to assist her. Her expression was weak and the smile at the corners of her mouth, insincere—an android trying to replicate human emotion without a soul to spark it.

"Bradley might be an asshole," Hannah said. "But he's right, you know."

"About what?"

"You are a hero. Mine."

Dad had shown him that sometimes life requires you to do

what needs doing, whether you want to or not. "We're not even," Reggie said.

"I know."

"*You're* welcome, Hannah."

"I'm taking you home now," she said.

"Mind if we swing past Dad's house?"

"That's not a good idea."

"With you as my escort, what can happen?"

Hannah thought that over, then nodded. Bradley glanced up from his mission tablet, appalled by her decision. "Hannah," he said. "You can't—"

"Operative Preston," she told him.

"I don't need to be reminded of the chain of command, but—"

Her grin widened as she talked over her XO. "Ready to go?"

Reggie was.

They followed the path cleared by the flamethrower men, what Hannah called their "sweep team" and the grim sights along their walk reminded Reggie of the atrocity photos that people posted online when they thought they were being good humanitarians. Shriveled, burnt bodies were face down, still sizzling from dying fire.

Reggie wondered if Osiris had even bothered to sort the infected from the survivors—if any existed.

He nearly asked Hannah but decided he didn't want to know. Or maybe he already did.

Silence carried them into town where the sweep team was conducting a door-to-door search of the remaining buildings. Every once in a while, there came an excited hiss as a prelude to shrieking slugs. And every time Reggie heard that, he felt a little better.

Maybe the worst really was behind him.

Dad's house was still standing, though a lot of the hurricane boarding had been stripped off in the storm. They walked out back to get in through the porch, but Reggie stopped as soon as he rounded the corner. Hannah attempted to pull him back once she spotted what he was looking at.

A body slumped on the beach. Behind it, a motorboat with the words *White Knife* stenciled on the hull had run aground.

Pink residue was splattered across a familiar cheek.

Manuel.

Hannah took a fresh sidearm from her holster and brushed Reggie aside, grunting in pain as she did it. Her movements were too sudden, and her body buckled from the damage. She slumped against Reggie, and he had to use his weight to keep her standing.

"It's okay," he said and pointed to the sandy lump beside Manuel's body. "The shrieker's right there."

Once Hannah regained her balance, Reggie darted out from underneath her arm and stomped the shriveled creature into the sand. Its broken body spat glowing ooze all over his shoe.

Reggie looked Manuel over, making sure there weren't any more wiggling surprises waiting for him. How he wished he hadn't seen this. How he wanted to believe that his strangest friend had found everything he was looking for, and then escaped.

Manuel had a loose grip on some sheets of yellow notepad paper. Reggie fished the pages from his fingers and hurried to the patio as Hannah hobbled over, looking like she was ready to collapse as she struggled to holster her gun.

He unfolded the pages while Crystal Key got cleansed by fire, flamethrower whooshes all around them as he began to read:

The Bleeding Eyes Man follows me like a puppy. He's at the grocery store when I go. He's getting take out at the same time I am. And last night, he happened into the laundromat ten seconds after I did… without any fucking laundry. Sometimes I feel like I'm being watched, violated by eyes I cannot see, and the next time we meet he acts like my biographer, and then I know why I have those feelings. He knows all kinds of shit I didn't tell him because he's always watching me.

"Oh, Sharon, I heard you spent the night at so-and-so's place…" He's a dog with a bone, only he's just begging to stick that bone between my legs.

Roxy thinks I should just fuck him and get it over with. "What's the difference?" she asks this like I'm choosing between black nail polish and black nail polish. The difference is, I think he's a fucking sissy every time he tells me that he loves me and wants to take care of me, and I spray his ass and he looks at me with those stupid weepy eyes. He's so weak it's laughable, and I laugh because people treat him like he's unbridled masculinity and only I know the truth. "Don't mess with him, 'cause he's the man," they say. Yeah, right. I think about his cock cage, him wearing my panties when I allow it, and I just laugh. I'm tempted to tell everyone what he's really like… make him regret thinking he can have me.

I'm so fucked up…

Wesley, on the other hand, is my salvation. He promises love but that's just words and 'love' honestly makes my skin crawl anyway. The devil's in the doing, baby, and Wesley does it all.

At first it was just hot sex. A hand around my neck, a violent tug of hair. Yeah, he does what I want, but he doesn't exactly have a problem with it, either. Unlike the Bleeding Eyes Man, he knows it's pain I need. Pain's what I like. Domination, baby.

But then I got the diagnosis. And when you're looking at the end of your life, everything else seems trivial. I already live in paradise, so I know that you can't get peace of mind anywhere once you find out you've only got six months to live. Your disease is advanced and inoperable. And pretty soon, it's going to be hell on Earth before you die and go to hell.

So... I asked Wesley to do it... Oh, he did not want to. Nor did he believe me. Had to get a note from my doctor before he'd even hear me out. But you know what? He's come around, knows it's a mercy killing. Take me out to that lighthouse and give me one last night of peace beneath the stars. And then, when I'm dead and gone, without any more suffering, he'll drop me in the ocean and my body will float away while the spirit goes... God knows where...

Wesley is a good man. The world won't understand that I needed him to do it. I'm not supposed to get a say in how I go out, which is just one fucked up part of the world we're living in. So it's going to be our little secret, and he's such a man that he says he'll take it to the grave and I believe him. I guess it's the best I could hope for since I was never all that good to him in the first place.

Sometimes, I think it will feel good to sleep. Be at peace for the first time in my life. I don't even know what that will feel like...

The paper slid from Reggie's fists and breaking waves rushed up the shore and drenched Manuel's ankles. Manuel must've gotten one of those things inside of him, had somehow fought off the control long enough to make it here. To deliver these pages.

Reggie isn't exactly sure what the information means, though he intuits the purpose behind it. It was the last thing Manuel had done with his life. Letting Reggie know what he found. The messy truth.

Hannah's hand closed around Reggie's shoulder, giving him a soft jostle. "We should go."

"Yeah," he said. "I think I'm ready." Reggie stuffed the papers into his pocket and wiped his eyes.

"You don't want to go inside?"

"No. I already have everything I need."

The sweep team was nearly finished downtown when a fleet of helicopters swept through the skies, landing just beyond a line of surviving trees. Dad's place was the last on the strip to burn.

"Make sure to get the body on the beach back there," Hannah told the men as they headed down the perimeter road to catch a ride. "No loose ends."

On that, a gunshot rang out across the distant sky. Reggie jumped at the sound, wishing they could move faster. Hannah's pace was strictly *limped stagger* and she grunted with every footstep.

The choppers had touched down on the beach near Hamilton's house. Black, heavily armored, and with military weapons attached to the wings that held enough firepower to blast the moon out of orbit.

Soldiers disembarked and were fanning out to secure the area.

Hannah limped past them, taking Reggie's hand in her palm as she weaved between the dark suits of armor.

An Osiris agent hopped down from the chopper's fuselage, fingers hammering against the tablet device in his hand. "Operative Preston," he said. "Mister Wyatt would like you to conclude your business and get back to headquarters for debriefing."

"Arrange for a jet to take us from Miami International to Logan," Hannah said. "From there, we'll need a car."

The agent started to say something, but Hannah lifted her hand and killed the conversation. "I'm taking our survivor home," she said.

"Are you sure you don't want to hold off on that?"

"He's going home," she said. "Home. Understand?"

"That directive comes from the top?"

"It comes from *me*."

On the radio, Bradley announced that Firewalker had been secured by the retrieval team.

Hannah grabbed the receiver. "Have the shark's jaws brought back to HQ for me," she said. "Everyone says my office has no personality."

They boarded the chopper with no further resistance. It lifted off to reveal little pockets of orange blaze all over the island.

"There's not going to be anything left when you're done, is there?" Reggie said.

"Depends on how bad it is," Hannah said, killing herself to stretch out on the bench across from him. Teeth gnashed, neck thrown back, eyes closed.

"It's bad," Reggie said.

"You should try and get some sleep."

"Yeah right," he said and searched for something in his thoughts that might calm him before deciding on Becky St. George. "I'm not sure how I'm supposed to get back to normal after this."

"You don't," Hannah said. "All of that back there is a part of you now. You take it with you and adapt to it. That's the thing about life nobody tells you."

"Sucks," he said.

"I agree."

From this height, Crystal Key was a collection of glowing embers adrift in a sea of calm blue swells. The sight should've been depressing, but Reggie felt alive as they flew toward Miami.

"What are you going to do when you get back?" Hannah asked.

"I'm going to ask a girl on a date."

"There you go. Will she say yes?"

"No idea," Reggie said. "But it's time I found out."

BONUS STORY:

A SOUL TO CLING TO

The Lookout moves across a stretch of land that's darker than charcoal, his boots grinding burnt flora into ash.

Heavy breaths filter through the oxygen tank that's clipped to his belt because nobody knows for certain whether the air here is safe. He hates the way this device fogs the eyeholes of his mask.

But this is a big assignment. And it was given to him. That pride has carried him far, through three years of repetition and loneliness that isn't supposed to eat away him but does.

The July sun traps scorching heat inside the golden beaches that encircle the island. He stays somewhat cool inside the radiation-resistant suit that sheathes his body. This place, once called Crystal Key, according to records, is contaminated, if not by Alpha and Beta particles, then by the lingering parasites he's here to find.

Encounters with them are further between now. He barely leaves camp anymore. He's lost count of how long it's been since the last sighting and he greets each morning with a heavy sigh. One recurring thought getting heavier all the time:

I'm still on this island.

This slab of floating earth is his responsibility, but in the furthest reaches of his mind, pride only stretches so far and is beginning to wear. He once thanked the gods for helping to land this gig. Now he's not so sure they had anything to do with it.

He's following a growl through what's left of the forest. Naked palm trees jut from the ground like matchsticks, branches long gone, foliage singed all the way down to scuffed palmetto bark.

Animal snarls vanish into an abrupt wall of silence and the only sound is ocean waves breaking in the distance. Even those are muted beneath his hooded head and gas masked face.

"Krite," he calls. His voice is deep and synthesized behind the apparatus that connects the facemask to his breather. It's the only way the animal has ever heard him speak.

The bobcat has been at camp every day for as far back as he remembers. That lovely orange mane dotted with black spots, tolerant eyes that regard him with a kind of casual relief, blinking in immediate and loving acceptance, because whoever the Lookout is, in the animal's mind, he's preferable to those creatures.

Repetition made the animal happy. The Lookout supplied an order to the chaos on Crystal Key. The two of them crisscrossing the island in unending pursuit of the assignment: Destroy all worms.

Night was always a crackling fire, chowing together on the

Lookout's rations. The emaciated creature did not seem to like the food at first but learned in time to love it, purring as it ate, grateful for sustenance and companionship.

Krite repaid the Lookout's generosity with a nightly patrol of camp, protecting the Lookout's entry hatch against unwelcome intruders.

Which is how he knew today was going to be bad, emerging from his shelter to find that Krite was nowhere to be found. For a year, the animal had always greeted him from his bed of fronds beneath the nearby coconut tree.

Today, his sickly yowl was a distant warble from an inland corridor.

Now it's the end of the hunt and the Lookout hears the bobcat's growl, once an instrument in his search for the parasites, now a threat against him.

It's what the creatures do. Pervert normalcy, use it against you.

"Krite," he says again.

The animal's head appears from around the base of a tree, crimson-caked fur around his mouth. His eyes regard the Lookout with a kind of desperate hunger, though there seems to be a tiny bit of the old Krite still in there, warning him of what's to come, as if he doesn't know.

Anything but this, the Lookout thinks, lifting the flame thrower, a fresh cannister of propane slotted like a magazine. He sights his buddy down barrel and says, "It always ends," then squeezes the trigger.

A whoosh engulfs the animal, taking the tree with it, a screech rising from the bobcat's throat. The animal's roasting head on a swivel, erratic motion giving way to that familiar insect chittering.

The Lookout presses the trigger again, holding it down, drowning the worm's protests beneath the stream of fire. The bobcat slumps over, gnarled and smoking, belly rising and falling—not with breath, but with worms. Parasites gliding through his innards, searching for a way to vacate their dying host.

Worst part of infection is that nobody gets a peaceful death.

The Lookout unsheathes the blade clipped to his belt. One slash along Krite's roasted underbelly and the bobcat's guts plop to the ground. His gloved hand sifts through wet organs until he finds a slithering worm.

A slack, cylindrical body folds down over his gloved fingers, a tiny head sways lifelessly, its microscopic mouth propped open in performative defeat. A human gesture that's deeply unsettling. The Lookout makes a fist and turns the parasite into a jelly stain, pink splatter in his palm. Then he's back at the guts, rummaging, searching out another worm, then one more.

Three of them inside a single host. Desperate times.

Once they're all reduced to pink paste, he incinerates the ground again just to be sure. Then he slings his rifle over his shoulder and starts back, habitually checking his side for Krite, who's always trotting alongside him.

Oh, but those days are over now and it's getting harder to coast on pride alone.

This is his fault. The Lookout became lazy once the worms grew more infrequent and Krite, he now understands, had grown to miss their walks, disappearing today to take one himself.

And paying the price.

Exterminating a friend is traumatic. The only way to get over that kind of thing is to leave. He's not supposed to want that, not according to his training, but this assignment has taken its toll.

You sign up because you need to distinguish yourself and there's only so many ways to do that.

Pay your dues. Get ahead. But at what cost?

He accesses his bunk through a hatch in the ground where a former resident once stored casks of fermenting wine. The building that used to cover it is long gone, save for broken and scattered debris that he now uses for firewood. But the basement trapdoor makes for perfect, impenetrable cover.

He wrestles the latch open and starts down the ladder, locking up behind him before descending. Electric torches line the shaft and ignite all the way down. Once he's at the bottom, he removes his protective layers, straightening out his cabana clothes underneath—a pink button down and bone white linen shorts.

Threads he salvaged from the remnants of a decimated storefront once he could no longer stand the thought of wearing standard issue fatigues for another day.

The comms console at the far end of the shelter rests on top of an old barrel that's still flush with wine. He tried to drink some once and spent the night vomiting out his nose.

The Lookout sends an encrypted message to command notifying them that three more parasites have been exterminated. He's smiling, can almost taste the hero's salute that's coming in response.

Long-range communication is delayed as it moves through all necessary channels, but the Lookout is so eager that he sits riveted to the screen until the console beeps in reply:

CONTINUE PROTOCOLS.

That's the message. It doesn't sink in at first. He watches the screen like there has to be more, but his hope is bleeding out and his shoulders slouch while his eyes begin to water.

"I don't want to be alone anymore," he says. His voice is wobbly and without confidence.

He's been alone so long the sound of himself is startling. Suddenly, he's sick of his dwindling rations. Maybe he'll stop eating them and die.

He checks the logs. It's been two hundred days since the last encounter. Flipping back even further paints a picture of how infrequent parasite sightings have become. There is no more life on Crystal Key, and there cannot be anymore worms. They simply do not last outside of living hosts for very long. And yet…

Continue protocols.

That's exactly what he does. Because he's got to be close to the end. He's back to rising at dawn. Walking the island. Torturing himself because if he'd just done this the whole time, Krite wouldn't have become restless and tried to make the trek on his own.

Your fault.

He crisscrosses the island back and forth, day after day. There isn't so much as a squawking bird or a chittering crab—he'd give anything to hear those noises. Everything has learned to avoid this place.

The ocean makes noise, sure, but he's come to regard those crashing waves as a taunt. He begins to doubt there's anything beyond them. No such thing as a mainland. In all his time here, there hasn't been so much as a boat on the horizon.

Days become weeks. It's all the same. He pokes the bear by telling command daily that signs of life are negative. His scanners haven't detected anything in so long he performs a manual check on each device and finds that they're all functioning. Good as new.

When he does receive another reply, the words are predictable: CONTINUE PROTOCOLS.

He stays out all night in defiance of that order, sitting atop an old hill in a ruined neighborhood at the highest peak on Crystal Key as a tropical storm throws debris around.

To the Lookout's ears, this chaos sounds like ghosts. The memory of people going about their lives. He shuts his eyes and pictures the world here before the worms, the paradise it must've been.

He falls asleep in the lashing rain and awakens to grey dawn, a glint of sunlight poking through a black cloud. He staggers home unrested.

Routine. Month after month. The weather grows colder. Daylight becomes shorter. He only wants to leave this place. Pride be dammed. He swallowed his, then spat it out.

The Lookout is passing the remnants of a collapsed boathouse when a gunshot tears through the southeastern sky. He's running before he realizes he's moving.

There is nobody else on the island. And with the sensors still working, he knows there's only one patch of unguarded land because the devices kept getting swept up in the tide.

A second shot like thunder and the Lookout realizes it's not urgency that's pushing him forward, but excitement.

Somebody's here.

What took you?

He comes up over the dune and the beach is a golden band that separates burnt land from placid water. A speedboat is wedged into the mud on the shoreline and, twenty feet in front of that, is a woman in a string bikini groaning because her leg is caught inside a bear trap.

The Lookout plows down the embankment without thinking about the gun in her fist, eyes blazing behind his mask.

English is not his second, or even third, language. The way he speaks it is fragmented and perhaps even more difficult to understand beneath the layers and filters of his protective material.

In contrast, the woman in the trap is nearly naked, tattoos

scrawled across every inch of her body. The Lookout cocks his head at the unlikely sight and is ashamed of the manifesting urges.

"Hold it, motherfucker," she says through a clenched jaw.

He's too far for his rifle's throw to catch her, should it come to that. Burning her alive is the last thing he wants so he lets the weapon fall from his grip and swing down against his side.

A ripple passes through her forehead and then her gun dips toward the sand.

His gloved hands go high as he approaches. A chance he's willing to take. Should she kill him… he no longer cares.

"You got me." His words are overly annunciated to the point where all playfulness is lost.

"Not from where I stand," she says, eyes clocking the sprung trap on her ankle, metal jaws punched straight through her tanned skin. Gobs of jelly blood doting the sand around her.

"Do not move."

"Have I got a choice?"

Her face shifts as he crosses the beach, reservations taking hold. It's clear to her there's something off about him, but the Lookout might suggest the same. A young woman, no older than twenty-five, in a sparking diamond bikini and a handgun holster strapped to her waist.

"Could you—?"

Her question jars him back to the task at hand, and he's bent down before he knows it, prying those steel jaws apart. She lifts her leg with a sharp gasp then tumbles into the sand.

"Goddammit," she says with her knee all the way to her face, keeping her wound high. "Fucking hurts."

"Can you walk?"

"Get my bag out of the boat."

He pulls himself up and over the gunwale where a

speargun rests against the seatback and there's a wetsuit lying in a tangle across the floor, freshly peeled from her body. Beside it is the bag she's requesting. He carries it back, unzipping and tossing it to her side.

"Great," she says. Her panting suggests the pain is getting worse. She digs through the supplies and says, "Maybe I shouldn't thank you at all."

"I do not follow."

Her attention slides back to the bloodstained trap. "Got something against visitors?"

"Not my trap."

"Uh-huh." She sizes him up while dousing her wound with bottled water. She uses a strip of gauze to pat it dry and then sprinkles Hydrogen Peroxide on the fresh blood beginning to seep. "Guess I don't have to shoot you, then."

The Lookout is distracted by her tattoos. The word DIAMOND in cursive around one side of her face, eye to eyebrow. A lightning bolt on her cheek. A cross on her throat flanked by roses and the words CHOKE ME in cursive on the bottom of her jaw.

Every angle reveals more: a face peering out between fronds on the left cheek of her ass, a pirate ship sailing the high seas across her thigh, the numbers 1 9 9 7 on her knuckles. Men with horns on her forearms, women with vacant eyes, mountains of skulls beneath a sky of fire.

He's never seen anyone like this.

Life is interesting again.

She wraps a bandage tight around her ankle, wincing as she clips it into place. "What's with the getup?" she says, after a few calming breaths. "There's no radiation out here."

"We do not know what is out here."

"Okay, but there's no radiation."

"How do you know?"

"A friend in the Florida State Department says they did all sorts of tests on the soil and air. They circulate the rumor 'cause they don't want visitors."

"Then why are you visiting?"

She gets to her feet, wincing at the pressure on her injured leg. "This is going to slow me down."

"I do not understand…"

She looks him over. "That makes two of us." Without another word, she starts toward the east, holstering her gun and limping along.

"Wait."

She whirls back with arms outstretched. "If we're not enemies, then I don't want to know."

"There are traps like this all over the island."

"I thought the teeth weren't yours?"

"The people who lived here were desperate. I have seen others like them."

She gives a drawn-out sigh as she stands with her back to him. The Lookout hurries to catch up. The rifle swings against his body, reminding him of the protocol. What he's supposed to do with trespassers.

What he cannot.

They walk an inland path, side-stepping uprooted trees and other obstacles on what was once a main road and she's grunting with every step because her ankle is chewed to hell.

"You are not sightseeing," he says.

"No shit." She stops and looks him over and there's a challenge in her eyes. This weirdo in a gas mask. Equipment hanging off his belt, her eyes sticking to the flamethrower. "And you're ready for what? Some kind of outbreak?"

He doesn't answer and she's back to limping, the Lookout following as the road bends and brings them to what's left of town. Burnt out buildings, annihilated structures.

"Recon," she says, slack-jawed at all this destruction.

"For?"

"Why do you think I'm showing off," she says, snapping her bikini string. "Anyone stops me and it's *'whoops, I'm on my way to the Bahamas and accidentally ran aground on this rock, can you point me in the right direction?'*"

"Why?"

She stops in front of a house that has collapsed and it takes her a minute to bend down with a damaged leg. She sifts through the detritus as a tiny trickle of blood dribbles along her foot, eventually pulling back a golden locket. "All the lives here," she says. "All the stuff that went along with them…"

"You are a thief?"

She grabs the Lookout's waist and uses him to stand. Her touch sends a current of electricity through his body and he steps back because it's more than he can handle. She smirks at this confirmation of power. "Thief? I like to think of myself as a… resource distributor."

"Disappointing."

"Well, shit, I don't want to disappoint you."

"A looter."

"Beats having a job."

The Lookout nods. This he can understand since his job feels more like death every day.

"I know you pulled me out of that trap back there, but… Are you going to let me leave when the time comes?"

He studies her eyes. Warm and shimmering jade that's slightly diffused with a greyness. She's beautiful and interesting and he does not wish for her to go anywhere, no matter what. Loneliness is darkness and no worm is scarier than that. "You are no prisoner."

Her face softens. A sincere smile follows. She tells him her name is Caitlin. She's from Miami. Grew up in a family of marine biologists and lived on a boat called the *Nautica*. Came to crave a seafaring lifestyle, "Without having to get an academic degree."

According to her, the mainland dismisses what happened here as "bad luck." Crystal Key was in a nasty storm corridor and the residents perished because they had gathered in a large resort building when an electrical fire broke out, trapping and then killing them all.

"I mean, that's the official story," Caitlin says. "But there are many more unofficial ones. All of them more interesting."

They're moving along the downtown tract, surveying. The Lookout usually avoids this route because there are days when the wind is right and you can still smell the propellant in the air from when soldiers shelled this island into oblivion.

Caitlin stops to study the rubble of a fishing shop. "It could take years to excavate all this." She's got her index finger on her chin, thinking it over. She throws a careful glance over her shoulder, eyes alive with possibility. "You wouldn't want to be my partner, would you?"

Best he can manage is a stutter and she giggles as she goes limping across the street, drawn toward a slab basement. The building around it, long gone. "Here's what I'm talking about," she says.

The Lookout moves to Caitlin's side. She's watching an old dresser drawer drift through muddy water, a haze of insects buzzing around it. The coiled jewelry inside looks like a nest of sparkling vipers.

"That right there is enough to fund a dozen return expeditions."

She climbs down, her body dangling vertical against the slab, dropping into knee-high soup, a sharp intake of pain as she lands on her injured ankle. She recovers quickly, muck rippling around her calves as she wades toward her treasure.

From above, the Lookout follows her around the perimeter, watching and plotting. It's too good to be true, meeting someone so lively. All he can think is how to keep her here?

"That's what I want," she purrs and for a moment the Lookout thinks she's reading his thoughts but it's really the pearls clacking in her fists. Her triumph is short-lived because a hand springs from the muck, closing around her damaged ankle.

Caitlin screams, her face overly animated as the pearls slide down her forearm like oversized bracelets. She's stumbles, trying to get free from the grip as another hand breaks the surface, skeletal fingers clasping her other foot. Then she's horizontal, falling face-first into the water.

The bone hands disappear and before she can scramble away they break the surface again, closing on her throat, her CHOKE ME tattoo becoming an instructional guide as her cries turn to scrapes.

The skeleton sits up and congealed muck plops off its bones, little splashes hitting the water. Its flesh is long gone, save for errant patches on its forearm and thigh, one tiny hunk of stubborn muscle around the rib cage too.

In each of those rotted mounds of stinking meat are worms, pale things rising from their hiding places, squawking with desperation, somehow mushing the skeleton forward, eager to raid new flesh.

The Lookout hops down into the chop but the flamethrower is too inaccurate to risk firing at this distance. He'll ignite Caitlin.

Instead, he swings it like a club, breaking the skeleton's body apart and igniting a cloud of bone dust that clogs his filtration unit and makes him gag. Caitlin crabwalks in retreat, cheering as the Lookout swings the rifle again, reducing its skull to powder, revealing another worm that dives for the anonymity of the mud.

These things wilt and die upon contact with salt water, but Caitlin had the bad fortune to go diving into collected rainwater and now there's four little ripples knifing toward her.

"Up, get up!" the Lookout screams, and Caitlin is scrambling toward the cement foundation. He boosts her feet in his palms, helping her to reach the road. Around his legs, the worms are scurrying to catch their host, slithering up the slab wall, ascending toward her wiggling toes.

The Lookout grabs the closest creature and crushes it in his fist, repeating the process again, then once more. They're too slow, too weak to put up any resistance. But the last one strays wide, is nearly to the top—

—where Caitlin stomps her good foot down, snuffing the creature with a splat, pink ooze bubbling up between her toes. "Ew," she says, then reaches down to help the Lookout get clear. "What the hell?"

"Forget it," he tells her, slumped over, catching his breath. He's thinking about how there's more worms to report. About how that's the worst news of the day because he can't stand to see those two words again:

CONTINUE PROTOCOLS.

It's never going to end.

He's never leaving this place. And he doesn't think he can stand to be alone here ever again.

"Second time you saved me," she says, hands on her thighs. "What now?"

"I have shelter. We can gather more loot tomorrow… if that's what you need to come back."

"Oh, it is." A smile at the corners of her mouth and then she's leaning on him as they cross the island, her arm around his shoulder, using his body to take the sting off her busted leg.

He's never felt better, protocols be damned. All this connectivity. His mind runs wild with limitless possibilities as he assures her that she'll be safe here.

He opens the hatch and allows Caitlin to enter first. She goes without question, wincing each time her bad leg touches down on a ladder rung.

The Lookout follows and he's so happy about where this is all going that it doesn't hit him until he begins to descend:

Never once has she asked about the worms.

Her hand closes around his ankle and then her other hand is pulling too.

Caitlin isn't clinging to the ladder anymore. She's clinging to the Lookout, her weight unmooring his hand from the rung while his other is locking the hatch. His fingers heave, and they're plummeting through the darkness, her legs smashing on concrete, bending and buckling behind her back.

She breaks the Lookout's fall as he crashes onto her with enough force to shatter every bone in her ribcage.

She just laughs, her voice morphing into familiar, unfortunate trilling. A pink worm bleeds out of the darkness that is her mouth, gliding along her panting tongue, eyes bulging with madness as the creature charges straight for the Lookout's mask.

His eye, which blinks from left to right, goes dark in the shattering glass. It's the least of his problems, because the worm is inside his head now, burrowing into his thoughts.

Caitlin pushes him away, rolling onto her side, grunting as her legs flip back into position, her lower body re-inflating, flesh rising and falling as parasites slither through her busted limbs to reinforce them.

Then she's up on wobbly footing, thighs shifting and sliding like varicose veins, worms doing the heavy lifting as her hands close on the Lookout's mask, tearing it off his face, throwing it aside and then bending down to get a good look.

The human side of the young woman is sentient enough for her face to register as shock.

She can't believe what she's seeing.

"In the years we've lived on this terrible planet," she says, "we have learned to coexist inside of our hosts."

The Lookout isn't listening. He's ceasing to exist. The parasite glazes his brain, a software update that is fundamentally altering his functionality.

He sees a swirling nebula at the center of an expansive starfield, vacuous space crying out around it. The howl is a pit of voices filtered through broken wavelengths, the disruptive sound of metal warping itself.

The Lookout comes from another world, but the one he's remembering now is foreign to him.

He's an abstraction now.

"I only," he starts to say, but words are difficult to find. Caitlin cocks an eyebrow, amused to see that he's attempting to fight off control. He lifts his rifle and sights her down barrel.

"Oh no," she says, and plucks the gun from his grip. "You mustn't. Our survival depends on my success."

The Lookout falls to his knees because that's what the worm inside him wants.

"You sent us here," she says. "So you could observe. You wanted to watch us infect the humans. We did. You wanted to study the outbreak. You did. And now that you know, you want to know more."

The Lookout shakes his head but he no longer understands what he's denying.

"We are going to show you," she says.

The Lookout is crawling toward the communicator and the worm is telling him to stop fighting. Surrender. If he'd been smarter, Caitlin would've been dead on the beach and he'd be closer to home. Maybe.

CONTINUE PROTOCOLS.

"This planet is a waste," Caitlin says. "Paranoid. Violent. Under attack from within. We could conquer, of course, but... we do not think it was an accident that you sent us to a planet that is mostly water and hot tempers. Our lives would be nothing here and for that reason alone, colonization is off the table."

She's crawling along the Lookout's back, pulling the hood away from his horned head, her hands caressing his jutting protuberances. One of his mouths snaps angrily at her nose once she gets too close and she whispers, "There are better worlds than this, you'll see."

His biology houses multiple sets of organs, and the parasite inside finds it difficult to control him all by itself. It makes this admission out of all the Lookout's mouths at once, his voice reduced to an insect's garble.

Caitlin understands, eyes rolling back, becoming egg whites, bulging, one of them bursting, a pink worm slithering through, making the leap to the Lookout's head, circling his dome as the parasite inside forces one of his mouths to open wide and take another tenant.

The rest follow, leaving Caitlin's body to collapse on itself, a broken husk now because her task has been completed.

The parasites have the Lookout under control, commanding him to climb into the console seat. Then he's making contact with home base through one simple admission:

I AM INFECTED.

The response takes forever. And once it appears, what's left of the Lookout's mind can only laugh at the cruelty of the situation.

WELCOME, SPECIMEN.

Another message follows soon after.

PREPARE FOR ARRIVAL.

The Lookout would laugh if he could. Instead, he waits. Reality sinking in. The worms were on the mainland this whole time.

He gets it now. This job was given to him because, back home, he was the lowest of the low and was never supposed to amount to anything more.

Dreams of a better life become a nightmare as the worms disperse through his body, acclimating, stripping away the last vestiges of his rebellious consciousness.

But before the Lookout goes, he understands: He job was to fail. They knew that he would.

But hey, he thinks, all his mouths smiling in unison, *that makes me a success*.

The worms force him to climb through the hatch into blinding light that's spreading across the sky. The trip is an exciting one to his new mind because it's only a matter of time before their arrogance is their demise. Containment protocols will fail.

They always do.

Conquering is a long game. One that's just getting started.

AFTERWORD

Island Red was originally released in July of 2016 and it was a surprise hit for my publisher, Severed Press. I did not originally want to write this book. Now, the novel you've just finished reading is something I am proud of, though the initial idea of doing a straightforward nautical horror story did not excite me in 2015 when I was searching for my next project.

Severed suggested I write about an angry fish killing a bunch of hapless people. No reason to overthink it, they said. That type of book was selling big in 2015, which is why I originally declined to participate. There was no shortage of excellent authors mining that territory.

But I was beginning to think about all these disparate elements, loose strands of characters I might like to follow through such a story: A soul sick gangster doing one last job. A teenager spending the summer with his estranged father. A missing girl with a troubled past. Shadowy operatives on the edge of it all. None of these threads alone felt like the path forward for my story, but once I combined them, I realized I had the cast I wanted. And they were going to face off against a creature that hadn't been overused in these novels—the frilled shark. That's how I was going to keep myself interested.

Oh, and I thought I'd make their lives even more miserable by way of an alien invasion because who doesn't love parasite worms?

It was surprising when Severed Press approved my pitch, but by then I was already high on the idea and *Island Red* was going to be born no matter what. I wanted two things from this book: It needed to be my homage to chaotic Italian horror films. Something like Franco Prosperi's *Wild Beasts*, in which PCP turns zoo animals into feral psychopaths. It should also remind readers of the wonderfully schlocky paperbacks my mother was always buying me from Bradlees discount bins. A kindred spirit to the madness of Guy N. Smith's killer crab fiction, for example.

More importantly, *Island Red* had to be the sort of novel you take on vacation with you. I think this book is best enjoyed when you can hear seagulls cawing down beach while your feet are buried in the sand and breaking waves score the distance. It's the only way to safely reach Crystal Key while ensuring you make it back alive.

If I'm being honest, I think some people in the summer of 2016 felt duped by the original printing of this book. It promised sharks and little else. My publisher did not wish to reveal the alien element for fear of spoiling the surprise. With the arrival of my expanded edition, I thought it best to be up front about the kind of story you're getting and the brilliant new cover by Justin Coons perfectly encapsulates this.

Island Red isn't Peter Benchley. However, Peter Benchley by way of Lucio Fulci is an apt comparison.

Island Red has been very good to me. It sold well and has been stocked on indie bookstore shelves across the country. It's also been in Barnes & Noble. It gave me bona fides in terrific publications such as Fangoria and Scream Magazine, and now it lives again in a more confident edition that fleshes out character arcs that were originally cut for pacing. This is my "preferred edition" and the restored material makes the book stronger and more satisfying without question.

If you enjoyed your stay on Crystal Key, please consider telling a few friends about *Island Red*. Put that worm in their brain, if you will. It's the best way to ensure this invasion lives on.

Matt
September 2022

ABOUT THE AUTHOR

Matt Serafini is a screenwriter and the author of *Rites of Extinction,
Under the Blade, Ocean Grave, Feral,* and *Devil's Row*. His non-fiction
has appeared in the pages of *Fangoria* and *HorrorHound*.

Matt lives in New England with his family, where he
spends way too much time tracking down obscure slasher movies.

Printed in Great Britain
by Amazon